SPECIAL KIND OF FALL

G.J. Quinn

PART ONE

CHAPTER ONE

He is twenty-two minutes late. I stare into my glass of prosecco and pretend to be distracted, busy, absorbed in the sipping. As if the dull, habitual act is helping to write some sort of thesis: 'the representation of fizz in popular fiction; the class, gender and social significance of the bubbles that rise, the ones that pop and the mischiefs at the bottom of the glass that never seem to go anywhere. Thesis conclusion: all will be absorbed and destroyed by either a digestive or capitalist system. Consumed. Devoured. Imbibed. Broken down.

My life is not enjoyable. Less so when people are late.

I'm in a bar - I can't remember its name. 'The (Something?) Lace' sounds familiar - the something is presumably a colour - yellow, turquoise, lilac - or perhaps an adjective: delicate, serene, dirty. It's a clean and pleasant cocktail-lounge-bar-in-town sort of place with a small circular dance floor and a disco ball overhead - which will be turned on later when people require 'fun.' There are cream comfy-looking faux leather couches and chairs against the walls. A large neon sign above the bar instructs that the toilets and function room are upstairs. The latter being so compact that it is easy to get the two confused. Uncle Fred slipped on a turd whilst eating a cocktail sausage and pratting about to Come on Eileen at Jackie's twenty-first. His ankle was fine, but his eye took badly to that cocktail stick.

There is a long and polished metal-looking bar on one side of the room. Pre-Covid it had held inviting and evenly distanced bowls of olives and nuts. Now it offers hygienic squirts from bottles of non-descript hand sanitizer. The place is dimly lit in a dark Egyptian blue, which is harsh and unflattering. Without realising it, you look very ugly. The Lavender Lace (?) is currently frequented with those wanting a few Friday night drinks after a hard week at work. In a few hours it will be filled with Sharon's and Pete's. The bar will become wet. Stools dragged to tables for that friend of a friend. Fake-tanned thighs imprint patterns on sticky cream leather seats. Stair stumbles. Dancing tumbles. Slurred grumbles. Drunken fumbles. Sloppiness. And all the while that faint lingering smell of cleaning fluid. Forever present in these sorts of places despite attempts to cloak with cheap air freshener. By the end of the night the smell will be replaced by sweat and travel-sized perfume spritzes.

Why is he late for our first date?

'Eight on the dot,' he had messaged earlier. Smiley face. Teeth bared. Red heart pierced with a gold cupid's bow. 'I can't wait,' he added. Five exclamation marks. Three kisses.

To distract from the sudden and devastating, potentially suicide inducing, notion that he may not show, I begin to concoct scenarios and explanations as to why he is late. He has been forced to stop at a dozen red lights. He has mislaid/lost his house key. There is an unexpected detour caused by an accident or road repair. Perhaps nature has intervened with a fallen tree or vicious little flood.

I've been brought up to believe that a person of value considers lateness a rude and generally avoidable act. That they should set off in good time, plan their journey accordingly and factor in any possible delays. That they should realise the effects of their tardiness and how this can upset others and spoil subsequent events. If you are going to be late, then an apologetic phone call or text is proper etiquette. Then the person who is waiting feels acknowledged and that you value them and their time. They then know that despite being late, you are indeed a person of value. If you deem someone important or are trying to impress them, for example - a first date, then you ensure you are on time. Time is the greatest gift you can give someone. By wasting my time, he is inadvertently subtracting from tonight. A reverse gift. A silent non-connective slap. First impressions count. He

3

should have been here on my arrival. Eagerly awaiting and ready to bestow an energetic welcome. Accompanied by a formal yet warm embrace and a verbal sprinkling of anxiety-reducing compliments.

Am I the kind of person that Holden felt he could be late for?

He said he lives in Redcar West. I have previously researched on route planner and discovered that his journey should take the following: seventeen minutes by car, fifteen minutes by train, two hours and forty-eight minutes by foot and forty-seven minutes by bicycle. Bus times range from twenty-nine minutes to one hour and eighteen minutes, depending on where he lives and which bus he uses. On Facebook there is a photo of his house with the caption, 'lived here since taddy met eggy.' However, a left-handed thumbs up, presumably his thumb as it matches his skin tone, obscures the front door and window, which despite a lengthy investigation and a small amount of house possibilities as viewed from sat-cam, I failed to acquire. Perhaps it is I who does not value time: the constant self-slap.

Holden arrives. He is wearing clothes that I wouldn't wear if I were a guy. A pale blue shirt and beige jeans that sag around the knees. I have never dressed in pastel, and it is always disappointing when it is worn by a potential love interest. Is he the kind of person whose happiness is dependent on the cleanliness and tidiness of their clothes? Napkin sensibly tucked in at mealtimes. The iron always ready to steam out that crease – oh you darn swine of gathered material, the cocky un-pressed villain. He looks good though in a clean and conventional sort of way. Not bar drinking attire, more like we were about to go on a summer's day picnic: the exciting possibility of an outdoor fuck sadly diminished as it could result in beige jean suicide. His Washy L89395W 12kg 1400 spin washing machine cannot perform miracles and by gum his trusty and lusty Russel Hobbs has already slithered meticulously over his cotton glories twice this week.

Holden looks around the room. Before another girl catches his eye, I raise my hand in the air. He notices me and smiles. He comes over fumbling for an apology.

'Sorry I'm late, it was my mum giving me the third degree like I was a child. When will I be back, blah blah blah and all that parental bullshit!'

I go to say something, nothing significant, but I don't, because he continues to speak. So really it was a good thing I kept quiet, or I would have cut in and he will say, 'you first' to be polite. Then I would utter my trivial comment and he would look blankly and say, 'what was I talking about?' But he will have forgotten because I had interrupted. He would then hate me a little because what he had to say was more important.

'...She's worse than ever since my brother died, which I suppose is understandable, but give me a god damn break.'

Death on a first date. Let's put on our slippers.

'My dog died yesterday,' I spit out the comment, my jaw snaps jaggedly.

This is a lie. I don't know why I said it. I don't have a dog. It did not die. However, in the great wide world many dogs did die yesterday and I'm empathetic about this. So, a half lie?

'That's awful,' he replies with a tut.

Silence ensues. Holden shakes his head and gazes at the chair next to me before deciding to sit. The interpreter in my head awaits nervously. I wish I had enjoyed more than two hefty lines of coke and a bottle of prosecco before my date. I couldn't cope with this reality. My words could not flow and when they did, they poured too fast - each word insignificant and vile, over-eager to leave. As if the full stop, that final pause, is the true ecstasy, the actual point of what I was always trying to say.

A pride of guys and cheerleader-type girls' parade past our table. The kind of gals who wear obscenely padded bras and consider lip gloss their life companion. The guys being the type who high-five a lot and are always chewing gum, their square jaws over-emphasising each movement like cocaine cowboys. They recognise my date and become excited.

'Hey look who it is. Someone's hoping to get laid tonight!' A loud, and presumably leader, guy shouts over mockingly.

They saunter by - a blur of rehearsed laughter, pricey designer jackets and over-styled hair. They try to destroy every sensitive emotion in the room - as if anyone who isn't like them must be consumed and destroyed by their nasty, over-confident, smug, little lives.

'Oh god I'm so sorry,' Holden apologises, 'they're just some stupid idiots I used to know from College.'

Holden is twenty-three, so College is a not-so-distant memory. I am thirty-four. He doesn't know my age and has never asked. If he does - I'll say I'm twenty-four. I look young – five foot three, dyed mahogany-red hair, no wrinkles unless I smile, size twelve to fourteen, wobbly upper arms, above-average sized tits, a little cellulite on the thighs, blue eyes, mostly straight teeth, ten fingers, ten toes, a pulse. I act quite young for my age sometimes – full of tuts and melodrama, still a bit angsty and awkward. Peter Pan Syndrome but more Pete Docherty. Arrested development you may call it, emotionally immature. Some may consider it pathetic, others cute. These traits however are a veneer, an almost positive façade, to the darkness that lurks beneath.

'What a bunch of phonies,' I reply, 'I bet they have put zero effort into their entire lives…that is except on the football field or the incredible brain tease it must be for them to undo a girl's bra.'

Holden laughs hysterically, almost violently, as if God Himself had pulled a gun to his head and instructed, 'laugh your last and make it good.' I hadn't even said anything particularly funny. His subtle frame jerked and contorted with a passion I could neither comprehend nor admire.

'You are a hoot,' he laughs. Impressed by me. 'Listen I'll go get a drink, do you want another one?'

'Oh yes please,' I reply. 'Scotch on the rocks. I take my drinks like my previous romantic relationships.'

'Ok, be back in five.' Holden walks away.

Self-hate stirs immediately. Why did I cuntly have to add… 'like my previous romantic relationships.' It wasn't funny. He didn't laugh or smile. Maybe he didn't get it. Didn't get me? It seemed like we are on the same wavelength – first on the dating site and then our daily messenger chats. Perhaps I am wrong. Again. My comment will be a warning sign to him. He will go to the bar and think it over, think me over, and realise that I am a mistake. That I am 'on the rocks.' After our first drink he will make an excuse to leave. I will be ruined.

Holden suddenly re-appears. 'I'm leaving, you're an absolute fuck up.' He touches my arm in a sympathetic manner and walks away.

I kill myself.

The end.

Holden suddenly re-appears: 'I just realised what you said, you're funny. I'm not very quick tonight, think it's the nerves.' He touches my arm in a playful manner and walks away.

I do not kill myself.

This is not the end.

I close my eyes.

I reach a sacred cave buried deep in the hillside of stored dreams. At the end of this dark echoey cave I discover a huge, brown, silky, cocoon.

'What do you hide?' I ask. My question reverberates around the walls far louder than it was spoken.

The cocoon cracks and hundreds of butterflies escape and flutter about in the fragile way that they do. Wanting to absorb this delicate beauty, I capture and then eat them one at a time. Whole and complete. Each little wing hitting the lining of my stomach as if pounding lightly on a drum. It feels like a moving mosaic: a living, breathing, quivering splendour that is all mine.

This is what true love feels like and the only way I can try to describe it.

I open my eyes.

Holden returns with our drinks, visibly irritated.

'What's wrong?' I ask.

'There's just a lot of real phonies in here tonight. I was getting served at the bar and this guy tapped me on the shoulder, that's right he made actual contact with my body, to tell me, "*hey bud*, (he adopts a gruff masculine accent, the type a woman may use when imitating a man) *I think you'll find that I was waiting here before you*." Sorry, I said, to which he replied, and wait for this, it absolutely kills me, "*I'm not waiting here for the next god damn train*." Like have you ever heard anything like that, I mean of course he wasn't waiting for a train, so I said, sorry bud, your turn next. To which he replied, "*are you trying to be a smart arse?*"

Holden bursts into laughter, so I do too.

'So, tell me about yourself?' he asks composing himself as he sits back down.

'There's nothing to tell,' I shrug my shoulders.

I love shrugging: it's vague, mysterious and useful. A crucial gesture that children should be taught at an early age – forget clapping and waving, shrugging is the real deal. If someone asks you a question which you don't want to answer because it has absolutely nothing to do with them and they don't care anyway and are just thinking of something to say, crack out the definitive reply - 'oh you know,' and then shrug. Shrugging is the answer to a long and happy life.

'I absolutely, positively, do not believe that' Holden says and shakes his head. He pauses and then chuckles into his scotch, 'you're a hoot.'

'What about you?' I ask.

'Well I am...' Holden sighs, 'I guess I'm ok now, I was filled with all this.....' he searches around as if the right word is going to fly in from the window and pop into his mouth, 'angst, you know ...people think it's a phase but I don't know maybe it's,' he sighs, louder this time, and sips his scotch melodramatically as if he is an actor playing the part of a depressed alcoholic .... 'More than that.' He pauses. '...I guess I just feel so much pressure right now...from my parents, society...even myself. It's as if everyone is trying to make me be someone who I'm not sure I can be...to be a phoney... and make small talk with people I'd rather spit at.

The kind of people who live for money and power are the most disgusting people to ever walk the earth and we're over-run with them like fat, dirty, rats.'

'I'm glad we aren't like them' I reassure. I begin to feel at ease. I recollect how much we have in common. Our daily messenger chats – similar views on politics, art, music, and our general dislike of humans. 'I'd be more worried if I came home from some mundane job and didn't want to crack my brain open. Wouldn't you?'

Holden sniggers and puts down his drink, 'I could have done with you being around when it all fell to pieces. But apparently, I'm 'fixed.'

On the word 'fixed' he lifts his hands to either side of his ears and wiggles his middle and index fingers like bunny ears - I'm guessing to imply quotation marks - otherwise what an inappropriate and peculiar gesture to complement his tale- but an entertaining choice nonetheless! Had he put down his drink just to perform this gesture? Is this some sort of self-pitying spiel he has practised to perfection?

'I've gone back to work,' Holden continues... 'which is good I suppose.' He pauses. 'What about you, what do you do?'

'An incredibly boring office job which I hate, but bills are made for paying, soooo...' I shrug and let my words trail off. Just like I had let my dreams and ambitions many moons ago.

'You seem too interesting to do a job like that. What do you really want to do?' Holden asks.

He gets me. He understands me. The alien me.

'I can't tell you, you'll laugh,' I reply.

'What?' he asks giggly.

'Don't laugh.'

'I won't.'

'Promise?'

'Promise.' It is my turn to pause for dramatic effect: 'I want to catch children in the rye. Like in the book by J.D. Salinger. I just want them to be safe and protect them from the horrible fall into adulthood.'

'That sounds… cool,' he replies.

The interpreter in my head goes to sign 'cool' but decides a grimace will suffice. She can't be bothered anymore. She's thinking about the BLT sandwich in her handbag that she's brought for supper.

Holden's 'cool' was the kind of 'cool' you respond with just to be polite. Like when people say the most random things:

'My hobby is to collect tiny glass jars with copper lids: the lids must be copper.'

Response: 'Cool.'

'I can say 'would you like a wedge of lemon with your fish' in over a hundred languages.'

Response: 'Cool.'

'I have such an extremely developed sense of smell that I can tell if someone is barbequing in another postcode, I can even tell you what meat is burning.'

Response: 'Cool.'

Then you never ask any whys or what's because you really don't care. The other person desperately wants you to, because that strange thing is the very essence of who they are. That is their 'thing.' Their proud little quirk baby. 'Cool' destroys.

'What's wrong?' Holden asks, his face scrunches to convey some unidentifiable emotion.

'Well, I…I know what happens to all catchers in the rye,' I reply.

'Oh, is that all, with the look on your face, I thought you had wind,' he laughs loudly and looks disappointed that I didn't have wind.

A lump forms in my throat. I gulp it down. My chin trembles. I reach for my drink and take long mouthfuls to try and regain control.

Field of rye. Field of rye. Field of rye.

Holden lightly grabs my knee under the table and is about to say something, possibly meaningful, when he looks over my shoulder and begins to squirm in his seat.

'Well, I'll be damned,' he says twinkly, 'It's Jane, my old friend, we used to hang out together all the time.'

Over my shoulder there is a tall vague girl standing by a table. A knockout bore, from her big brown eyes to her matching cubic zirconia accessories. Guys get smitten with girls like Jane: the kind of good-looking yawn-fest that acts all superior so guys think she's too good for them (which she's not) and to date her would be an absolute treat (which it wouldn't) as they'd be punching to be with her (oooh as if).

Years later Jane will marry the head statue of a law firm: a loveless marriage resulting in lots of sex with a muscular guy who distributes leaflets about the dangers of eating bacon. Jane has an affair too.

'Jane is the best, you'll love her, she's a real hoot, reads books and everything. I'll just go over and say hi, be two minutes,' Holden says and walks away.

Reads books! Well let's all go over and cop a feel of Wonder Woman. Excellent. Absolutely fucking tops.

'Ask her if she still keeps all her kings in the back row,' I mumble quietly as he loudly shrieks 'HELLO' to Jane.

Holden is in absolute awe of the hideous creature. His hands flay wildly, losing all sense of decorum. Obviously trying to impress her with his exciting tales of college woes and dead Brother.

I get another scotch on the rocks. It rattles like a snake. I ingeniously position my phone close to my face, so it appears that I'm struggling to text in the darkly lit room. But I couldn't care less about my phone. My ogling is north of this. I watch them intently.

Ten minutes later and Holden is still there. He looks in ecstasy. Jane's date looks like he wants to pull the energized stranger through a mangle.

I have another scotch. Then a glass of prosecco, chased by a few shots. I am drunk at this point and reaching a state of melodrama. The darkness begins to hug me like an estranged old Aunt. The crowd becomes a prison - each nudge and whisper cause an anxiety-ridden paralysis. The toilet is my only escape.

I stagger past them like a grandfather clock. Holden doesn't notice me. Then I carefully walk up the dicky dancers.

The ladies' room is filled with women nervously applying lipstick, eagerly applying lipstick and jadedly applying lipstick. The torture and delight that man can cast on us creatures is reflected in every mascara-opened eye, every trembling hand and wry smile.

I gingerly go into a toilet cubicle. Women always enter toilet cubicles in a tentative manner- lest we intrude on an embarrassed user and their blushing gushing privates. Or if someone is indeed waiting for the coveted seat and we have accidentally jumped our place in the queue – in both instances our cautious approach gives us the opportunity to apologise loudly and back away. There is always a queue for everything in England – we very much respect and oblige, perhaps even adore, a good queuing system. If there isn't a queue for something, even a toilet, one becomes suspicious and paranoid. The trip is ruined, you might as well go home. After all, you only came out to queue! The toilet is empty FYI.

As I urinate the butterflies begin to stir. They are bored and hungry. They do not like to be ignored. They have not escaped their cocoon to sit on stained chairs and haggle for BOGOF shots under unflattering lighting conditions whilst listening to generic-pop background music. The music is played at a low volume so people can talk, but when you have no one to speak to, the barely audible melodies became oh so very loud and oh so very dull. The butterflies weaken. I leave the toilet cubicle.

I use the bathroom mirror to rub away face powder that has snuck into laughter lines. Those sneaky lines around the eyes and mouth that have savagely cut into my face since turning thirty: deeper and multiplying by the day. Hair fluffed and makeup re-touched, I go downstairs.

On my way to the bar Holden notices/remembers me.

'Hey,' he waves me over. Perhaps he has forgotten my name. I smile falsely at them both.

'I wondered where you were, you naughty girl. I couldn't find you so had to dance with Jane, this is Jane by the way,' he says and nudges the chocolate fox. Her date has vanished.

'Hi,' I smile.

There is no real music to dance to. Oh, what a show! What a disgusting show I had inadvertently missed! A show of desire and torment. I can see them: their bodies dancing firmly together like death. Holden's hands are balmy and moist on her back. Jane's skin is wintry and fills him with lust. 'Oh, to topple this tower' he thinks, groin ready. They whisper and laugh and dance. She says nice things like a mother might say. He admires her because she makes him feel normal. She is a thousand pats on his back, beating again and again. She will nurse his dying father, who is also groin ready for her. She will be a sister to his sister, a brother to his brother, a friend to his friend. She will pop out beautiful children like nasty little pills.

At eighty Holden will look back at his life. They have never had a burning love. It was not the romance felt in dreams. No butterflies. He has never felt complete or safe. Never understood or challenged. Rarely happy. He does not want to see Jane ever again. To lay next to her body or hear her voice – both of which are croaky and flat with age. In complete misery he will throw his crinkly body down a concrete flight of stairs. His body will squeak and break like an accordion that no one can be bothered to listen to. Afterall, no one likes accordion music.

His last thoughts are of Jane: he hates her, because she has made his life too easy. Why didn't he stay with that cute and strange little redhead from years ago? He can't remember her name. He couldn't remember it then. That unique creature he had a date with at The Turquoise Towel – the night he began to court Jane. He should have gotten to know her. Given her a chance. He could have helped her become a catcher in the rye. Whatever that meant. Oh, that silly odd girl.

'Are you ok?' Holden asks.

I half-smile a response.

'Where have you been?' he asks.

'To the ladies,' I reply.

He looks at Jane; there is a non-verbal exchange between them which I cannot fully decipher. The general gist is 'oh god, I want to have sex with you, but I'm stuck with little crazy here.'

'Are you sure you're, ok?' he asks ever-so-barely concerned.

'Why wouldn't I be?' I reply curtly.

'What were you doing in the ladies all that time?' he asks.

'Waiting.'

'For what?'

'For life to hurry up and god damn end,' I reply.

Justified by intoxication, I use my right hand, the one that is loaded, as a faux gun to pretend to blow out my brains.

'Okaaaay,' says Jane in a sarcastic, fake-embarrassed kind of way. She juts out her collagen-plump bottom lip and gazes at Holden with flirtatious empathy – which is the very worst type of empathy.

'Jane, why don't you go and fuck yourself,' I say.

Jane gasps. Holden laughs nervously and looks at me in the same way parents do when kids say something rude or uncomfortable. 'Wait until I DON'T get you home,' screamed his eyes and fixed grin.

'I think you need to take your date home, she's clearly drunk and making a fool of herself,' says Jane matter-of-cuntly.

'Yeah…. erm,' he replies and fidgets, 'maybe we should go, don't know about you but I'm tired and it's late and all.' Holden supresses a fake yawn.

We'd only been there an hour. He looks relieved when I reply with a nod. I think he was expecting a fight, for me to say 'cunt' a few more times and to perhaps use my hands to mimic other suicide methods.

'Can I order you a taxi?' he asks.

Holden wants to get rid of me ASAP so he can seduce Jane until vaginal entry. Perhaps after this, like most men, he will lose interest in her. Doubtful as she is too homely yet seemingly unattainable to be forgotten or ditched. She is girlfriend leading to fiancée leading to marriage leading to motherhood material. Oh, if only he could get rid of me and then woo and win wonderful doe-eyed Jane! Why do I have to exist! Why can't I drop down dead right there on the spot. They could then use my body as a little footrest whilst they verbally and then physically foreplay-ed the night away. Then kick my gross lump of a body out of the way, to make their way to a taxi and then swiftly home. Who can even think of a late-night kebab when fornication is on the menu?

'I only live ten minutes away, I'll walk,' I reply, as taxi money is vice money.

'I'll get you it on the app,' Holden says.

'I want to walk,' I reply firmly.

I need some cold air to try and settle my emotions and sober up - my housemate doesn't deserve to see me in this state again.

'I wouldn't dream of letting a young lady walk alone at night' Holden looks at Jane as he says this, trying to impress her with his chivalry.

I turn to get my coat. Then to make the whole situation worse, much worse, as soon as my back is turned, he quietly says to Jane: 'I'm so sorry, this is the first time I've met her, I'll come straight back.'

I collect my coat and go outside. There is silence for about two minutes as we walk. The interpreter in my head finishes her flask of tea. It helps wash down those crusts. Juiceless bacon trapped in molars.

'Listen,' Holden says nervously, 'I'm sorry about in there, you must have thought I'd forgotten about you. But you know what it's like when you see an old friend, we were catching up that's all. I didn't mean to upset you or anything.'

'It's okay,' I reply.

He sighs, 'I wish you wouldn't say, 'it's okay' when it's clearly not.'

'But it is okay,' I reply.

'I've had a really good time tonight,' Holden says with conviction.

The good time he refers to, clearly wasn't with me. My experience has been dire – dire being a euphemism for what I feel. Add whatever word you think appropriate.

'Hmmm,' I reply.

'You're really funny,' he chuckles as if remembering a humorous quip.

However, in reality - reality being the true source of all our pain on Earth, I never had chance to showcase my wit and wonder because one scotch in, he fucked off with Princess fucking A-bore-a. 'Joyful now to his princess he will cum.' The song *'Hail to the Princess Aurora'* from *Sleeping Beauty* goes a little something like that right? What's interesting here please note, even though he has regarded me like a leper, like a piece of shit, no not shit, diarrhoea, the kind of messy excrement you would avoid even more than shit, please note, that he thinks by being nice to me now, he might get laid. It's exceptionally funny when you indeed think about it.

'Do apologise to Jane for me, I'm sure she's a good person,' I lie.

I sincerely hope the following little story comes to fruition:

Death of a Cunt by A.E. Grant

Jane makes her way to the ladies' room, to look at her disgustingly bland face in the mirror and relieve her ridiculously odorous quim. En route, she is brutally pushed from an open window situated at the top of the stairs. The windows were purposefully opened in accordance with 'Jane's Protocol.' A local document circulated to staff in all indoor establishments in Middlesbrough. It instructs to open all windows as soon as Jane enters a building, as it is common knowledge that her downstairs pongs something dreadful – both orifices constantly leaking and belching as if trying to gain attention from Satan Himself.

Mid-fall Jane's dreary cubic zirconia necklace becomes ensnared on a flagpole, which is perfectly situated for murderous times such as these and for when England plays any sort of sport.

Jane hangs there in absolute agony. The necklace tightens around her flowery fragranced throat. The blood rushes to her head like champagne. Her thoughts are that of a complete idiot: 'gosh I wish I hadn't worn this necklace; it doesn't even match my handbag.' The necklace snaps and Jane continues the journey towards the cold hard pavement below.

The fall is just far and hard enough to break her legs, the bones protrude out of her body at weirdly abnormal angles. No one notices her fall or calls an ambulance. She is such a bore that passers-by merely see a streak of beige plummeting from the window and assume it's a basin of mucky water thrown out by an overworked employee who cannot be bothered to carry the heavy load downstairs. Or perhaps it is an unwanted pallid joint of pork. It is awful when you go out for a few drinks and your friend surprises you with a joint of pork. What can one do with this hefty slab in a bar in Middlesbrough. Plenty. But that's another story for another time.

Jane lies on the street, the pain unbearable. A huge, rabid Dobermann Pinscher is rummaging in a nearby garbage skip and sniffs the blood of a fellow hound. It rushes eagerly to suck and tear at her bulging bloody bones. Looking at Jane's face he mis-identifies his long lost, much uglier sister and grabs her bone between its teeth to playfully pull her around. It is an absurdly long and torturous time before Jane faints with pain.

When Jane wakes, she finds the dog next to her, its throat slit like a peach. She screams before a sock is shoved in her mouth. Jane then meets the crazed eyes of a crazed serial killer, who bored with her, as she is possibly the most tiresome person who has ever lived, has cut off one of her manicured fingers, a memento from a successful day, and has shoved a wooden lollipop stick in its place, which he then begins to burn. He ('He' because roughly ninety-three percent of serial killers are male) cackles in his balaclava. The last thing Jane sees are the words: 'what do you get if you cross a cow with a pig.' She never gets to know the punch line.

'This is my house,' I say as we stop outside.
'Aww so soon,' Holden pulls a sad face, 'this has been really good

fun.'

'Yeah,' I lie.

There is a horrible tension. What does he expect to happen now? Surely not a smooch...or more. I begin to shake inside as I think about my expectations for tonight. How we would talk. How we would laugh. How we would dance. How we would kiss. He would ask me on another date, and I would say yes. We would do everything together. We would be so happy. I start to cry. Big loud sobs that I can't contain.

'What's wrong?' he asks.

'Nothing, I'm....' I can't find the right word.

'Tell me?' Holden asks not really bothered but playing his part.

'I...I....' 'Just tell me,' he says.

'We're alike you and I...why can't you see that?' the words explode out between sobs. 'We were going to run away together...and get a wooden cabin in Vermont or Massachusetts and be happy forever... I would have done anything for you...but no...you had to waltz off...with that fucking bitch... she hates you; she thinks she's too good for you, but you can't see it.... you have ruined everything.'

'What?' he scrunches his face.

'Oh, for fucks sakes Holden,' I shout, 'you think I couldn't hear what you said to that little whore, *"I'll come back for you"* - I put on a squeaky voice as if he spoke like Mickie Mouse – 'whilst you're still on a date with me. Do you think that's fair, that I can be walked all over like I don't exist? And now do you really expect to kiss me and then come in my house and paw me like a porn doll? I can't believe you've done this to me. I just...I really felt like we had a connection, that you were my Holden.'

'Holden?' he edges away, 'what are you on about, my name is Frank.'

'That's right walk away.'

'I'm walking away alright; you are acting like a crazy bitch.'

'Good, I wouldn't let you near me now.'

'You're crazy,' he says, 'I've just met you. I know your dog just died but this psycho behaviour is ridiculous.'

'I'm crazy, oh no help me, help me. I'm crazy, get me a doctor, I've lost my mind cos I don't want to sleep with you!'

'What are you on about? You need help,' he shouts.

'Piss off loser,' I scream, but he is already half-way down the street.

'Craaaaaaaazy bitch,' he yells as he turns the corner and disappears.

I'm on my street, in the open, sobbing like I'm at a funeral. I compose myself and go indoors. The front door is unlocked. The hall smells of coffee and washing powder – home. My housemate is watching TV – silver flashes jump through the bottom of the lounge door. She doesn't shout hello. She is with her boyfriend, so they are probably busy fondling and grunting as noiselessly as possible.

As I creep up the stairs not a creak is heard, as if I am already a ghost walking the earth.

I go into my bedroom and switch on the lamp next to my bed. I take off the shoes that have been fighting with my toes. I look at myself in the dressing table mirror. Has this really happened again? Why do I do it to myself? I take a make-up remover pad to my eye and begin to wipe. Aggressively smearing the grease into my skin. A buttery feast ready for consumption. An oil leak polluting the sea. I'm absolutely disgusting. A sight to behold. The enemy of enemies. The piggy in the pen. Queen Elizabeth I. I nip at my face. Tear at my hair. Rip my dress. Longing to see everything tattered and destroyed. Ugly. I violently scratch my flesh. Squeeze my fatty arms. Scoop and rub my juicy gut: an over-whipped scoop of vanilla ice-cream.

Then peace. So still and comfortable. A full moon on a crisp dark night. Like plunging into a lake and not knowing how deep it is but feeling glad when you can't find the bottom, your toes tickling each little fish.

I close my eyes.

I reach a sacred cave buried deep in the hillside of stored dreams. At the end of this dark echoey cave I discover a huge, brown, silky, cocoon.

'What do you hide?' I ask. My question reverberates around the walls far louder than I had spoken it.

The cocoon cracks and hundreds of butterflies escape and flutter about in the fragile way that they do. Wanting to absorb this delicate beauty, I capture and then eat them one at a time. Whole and complete. Each little wing hitting the lining of my stomach as if pounding lightly on a drum. It feels like a moving mosaic: a living, breathing, quivering splendour that is all mine.

The beat of the butterfly wings become fainter. Until they are not moving at all. My stomach acid has destroyed them, and they lay rotting in my gut, still and deformed.

This is what self-hate feels like and the only way I can try to describe it.

I open my eyes.

I fumble under my bed until I find the pills. I eat one at a time. Slow and purposeful. I lay my head against the pillow and wait. A big torn ragdoll scratched and bruised. My stomach now full; my butterflies crammed with nectar.

I remove the book from under my pillow and kiss the front cover. I hold it tight against my chest.

I feel the butterflies come back to life in my stomach.

Each one growing stronger, brighter and more beautiful.

They beat - bolder and truer than ever before.

As I sink into the rye.

CHAPTER TWO

Apologies for being alive. A book about my adventures in the underworld or heaven, knowing my luck somewhere unexceptional like purgatory, would be lovely, wouldn't it? But I can't even get death right. I sound so much like Plath right now I'm hungry for some home grown honey-and-drudge muffins that regard me sadly. I hanker for Ted to grope my titties whilst we verse through daddy issues surrounded by colourless poppies and tulips that are way too excitable. You. Do. Not. Do.

In a semi-unconscious state: my body is moved and touched. People sound far away, like echoes in an empty church. A jigsaw of noises and fingers that I must try and piece together. Did I die at some point? I'm not sure – but a cliché memory montage of my life did not occur. There aren't any epiphanies, flashbacks or recollections of happy and significant moments. My near-death experience is like being trapped in a dark tent on Rohypnol with things getting shoved in my nose and throat. A giggly and horrific guestimation- if only!

I'm surrounded by aggravating inaudible voices: as if a neighbour is trying to converse with me through a wall. Not that they would have any reason to do this. The wall detests me, as do my neighbours. As I gain full consciousness, I'll explain why my neighbours despise me via a meaningless interlude of hate and mayonnaise.

A Meaningless Interlude of Hate and Mayonnaise

Once upon a time on a darling summers night, I sat in the garden getting drunk.

Repeat every day for infinity.

The End.

No silly sausage! With it being a Tuesday I thought I'd try and sober up for work the next day by eating a tuna mayonnaise sandwich. As I very merrily sat down to eat, my taste buds were slapped with the realisation that I had forgotten to put tuna in my sandwich: white gloop between two slices of a distinctly average bloomer. As anybody with passion and a mouth for fine cuisine would do at a time like this, a massive tantrum ensued, and not realising the force of my windmill strength arms, I threw the disappointment away from me into the night.

Life is never kind. The 'sandwich' landed on the conservatory window next door. Here Cathie and her chubby lapdog of a boyfriend, whose real name I don't know because he is only ever referred to as 'Sweetie'- sat 'enjoying' each other's company on their separate iPads. Cathie screeched and Sweetie muttered something inaudible. Can I add that the big log of a lad is the exact opposite of sweet, apart from his candy-onion body odour you cannot miss but whiff when there is an Eastern breeze.

'What the fuck was that?' Cathie cried. Her awful bunched-up tissue of a face peered over the fence.

'Is there any fucking need?' she shouted hysterically.

'Sorry,' I said, 'I think I put too much mayonnaise on it. Mayonnaise is so slippery these days.'

'What the fuck is it?' she shouted.

'Just some mayonnaise on bloomer,' I replied.

'Thank fuck,' muttered Sweetie quietly, whom I guessed was behind her, as this had been his position since the day they met, 'I thought it was cum on white.' Sweetie giggled at himself.

'Oh, fuck off Sweetie,' said Cathie, 'this isn't the time for you thinking you're funny, get the ladder and get that shite off my conservatory, the window cleaner only washed them two days ago.'

'I'm sorry,' I said.

'I'm sick of this...if it isn't your loud music and singing at all hours, then it's bollocks like this. I found a human dump in my garden a few weeks ago and I'm going to take an educated guess (don't laugh dear reader) that it was you up to your usual drunken antics.'

'How do you know the dump was human?' I asked.

'That's not the fucking point is it!' she shrieked, 'you're a constant fucking nightmare. Next time I'm calling the police.'

Cathie marched away and slammed the conservatory door. Sweetie muttered 'daft cow' under his breath. I'm unsure whom this slur was aimed at.

Also…I never took a dump in their garden. I reckon it was a Sweetie rebellion.

As for the wall: it is a known fact by all wall enthusiasts that walls hate humans. We treat them like utter shit - covering them with intoxicating paint, hammering, punching, demolishing and constantly acting like they don't exist. Imagine a world without walls – an unthinkable dystopia. Yet you show them no love.

I open my eyes. My housemate, Erin, is sat in a chair next to the bed. Evidently a hospital bed - as my senses are immediately hit with old gravy, stale urine and claustrophobia. When Erin sees I am awake she lets out a long sigh.

'Soooooo' she says and sighs again.

'Erin, please don't act like we're in some American teenage drama,' I reply, 'Shane Junior broke up with Taylor-Marie but I'm sure we'll all get through it.'

'Don't make jokes,' she says, 'you have no idea how worried I've been.' Erin has a sub-mediocre sense of humour: she never finds anything I say remotely funny.

I try to sit up, but wince – my body feels heavy, my stomach and throat sore.

'Are you ok?' Erin asks and shoves a cardboard unidentifiable-looking object under my nose, 'this is in case you vomit again. The doctor said you've probably got most of it up.'

'I can't remember being sick.'

'That's good,' Erin replies, because there are absolutely no other words to reply to my comment.

'If only all memories were optional,' I add and brush away the sick-bowl-thing. Erin simultaneously brushes away my melodrama – a skill she has mastered throughout our years of friendship.

Erin re-fills a glass of water and hands it to me, 'you need to drink lots of water. The doctor said all being well you can leave soon.'

'How long have I been here?' I ask.

'About six hours. You've been asleep for most of it.'

'You haven't told Mother, have you?'

'Not after last time.'

Last time Erin informed Mother of my 'accidental overdose' I didn't talk to her for two weeks. When I finally forgave her, as I needed to borrow one hundred quid for 'an unexpected bill' i.e., drugs - I threatened that if she grassed on me again, I'd publish her search history on social media. Erin would hate people to know the extent of her banality as she has possibly the most boring search history in search history's history - ridiculous Google searches like 'what's more fattening an apple or an orange?' and YouTube videos showing 'a step-by-step guide on how to create the perfect ponytail.'

'You should tell her though,' Erin continues, 'when the doctor asked about your family, I said you only have your mother and that she's on holiday, but I'll contact her.'

I sip the water. Sipping water is tedious. I've always felt it is a very tedious task.

'What happened last night?' Erin asks and sits back in the chair.

I shrug. 'I think my drink was spiked or something.'

'You had an empty pill bottle by your bed.'

'I'm not sure then,' I shrug.

'You're lucky I found you in time, I only popped in your room to switch off your lamp, (Erin hates to waste electricity) ….and there you were.' Erin bites her lip to try and steady her emotions. Her eyes show concern, maybe pity. I make her life difficult, and it kills me.

'I think I passed out reading,' I lie.

'You were reading that book again; the one about the guy who catches stuff. You were holding it in your arms like it was a baby. You've been told countless times to get rid of it. It's no good for you.'

I quickly change the subject, 'I think it was a mixture of alcohol and perhaps being spiked. Oh yes, I remember now.' I stare at the drab hospital ceiling as if it's helping to recollect. I nod my head with conviction, 'I flushed all those pills down the toilet because I'm feeling so much better, that's why the bottles were empty.'

'You have seemed a lot happier lately,' Erin says, 'that's why I was so shocked and I...I...just didn't know what to do.' She bites her lower lip again.

'I'm sorry,' I say, 'I must have left my drink at the bar when I went to the toilet. There were some real phonies in there last night, the sort that would spike for a grope.'

'Amber, you'd had at least a bottle of prosecco before you left,' Erin says sternly. She awaits a response, but I don't say anything, so she continues: 'You need to stop drinking so much.' If only she knew about the other substances that frequently abuse my body and mind. 'So how was the date?' Erin asks, realising she isn't going to get any sort of acknowledgement, confession or justification.

There is a sudden disturbance in the curtain. Michael Myers appears and stabs us amidst screams and pointless wriggles. Jokes. It is a harassed-looking lady with a fleeting resemblance to Lorraine Kelly.

'Good afternoon, Amber,' she says, 'I am Doctor McCreary. Glad to see you're awake. I'm just going to check a few things with you.' The doctor removes an electronic device from her front pocket. 'Your name is...'

I refrain from saying Slim Shady.

'Amber Elizabeth Grant.'

'Your date of birth is....'

'Twentieth of May Nineteen Eighty-Six.'

'You currently live at....

'Six Bullhorn Road.'

'Your memory seems fine. How are you feeling?'

'Bit of a headache, sore stomach and throat, but I'm ok.'

'So Amber,' the doctor says, 'last night you took more Valium than you should have. They are part of the benzodiazepine family; your notes say they're to help you sleep.'

'Yes.'

'The Valium plus alcohol resulted in an overdose. Nothing serious thank God. I'm sorry to have to ask you this, as I realise it's sensitive, but did you take the pills on purpose?'

'No of course not, I was really drunk and must have taken more than I realised' I reply. Re-lie.

'So, to confirm for our records, this is an accident and not a suicide attempt?'

'Oh absolutely not,' I feign shock, 'I reckon what happened was I took two pills before I went out and two more when I came home. Then I must have forgotten I'd taken any, because I was drunk, so I took more.'

'Did you take any other drugs?' she asks.

'No' I reply – shocked and hurt. Doc, if you cut me open my blood will be pink. To a tiny insect the inside of my nose is as exhilaratingly bumpy as the Himalayas.

'Ok that's fine Amber,' the Doctor types into the device, 'because if this is a cry for help, we do have experts to deal with any issues you may have. Whatever you disclose to them is always confidential.'

'I'm great, honestly' I reassure, 'I feel silly about all this. It's an unfortunate accident.'

I refrain to add that my whole life has been an unfortunate accident. Doctor Fake-Lorraine-Kelly will be used to dealing with patients with 'real' problems. Those with mental health issues, addicts and suicide enthusiasts will appear trivial in comparison. They are merely playing a game of self-indulgent sorrow, whilst others are desperately trying to stay alive.

'It says on your medical notes,' the Doctor continues, 'that you've previously tried to commit suicide.'

'I used to be in a bad place, but now I'm really good,' I look over at Erin for support.

Erin nods in agreement, 'you did seem a lot better.'

The Doctor smiles at Erin and then looks at me. Her face is expressionless, but her eyes judge: nuisance, druggie, alcoholic, a degenerate waste of space.

'It's a good thing your housemate caught you in time,' the Doctor says and looks at Erin with what appears like genuine awe. Oh, Erin you bloody martyr! Please come down from the cross you are impaled on as you burn in flames. Please grace me with one fucking sentence about your mundane life, whilst you dribble stigmata into my sorry vice-abused mouth.

'Will you be with Amber tonight to keep an eye on her?' The Doctor asks Erin, 'she should be absolutely fine, but any concerns just bring her back in – I've given you the number.'

'Yes of course I'll stay with her,' Erin replies in her usual Miss-goody-two-shoes manner.

The Doctor turns to me: 'if you feel fine, you're free to go. There could be side effects from when we pumped your stomach- coughing up phlegm, wheezing, chest pain, fatigue, minor bleeding and fever. These could be signs of aspiration pneumonia, so get in touch if you have any of these symptoms. I suggest drinking lots of liquids, no alcohol. Eat soft foods for twenty-four hours – soup, ice-cream, mashed potato – things like that.'

'Will do,' I reply.

'That's great thank you,' Erin adds, even though the Doctor is addressing me. Erin smiles widely: sunbeams spring from the minuscule gaps between her veneer.

'Leave the gown on the bed and tell the ward receptionist when you leave so we can get your bed ready. We're always very busy here.' The Doctor lets out a little snigger-laugh. 'Fuck off Amber, so we can get the bed ready for someone worthy of our help' – her snigger-laugh implied. 'You need rest Amber,' she continued and put the electronic device back in her breast pocket - against her right breast if you're interested.

'If only I could take a rest from life,' I mumble under my breath as the Doctor walks away.

Erin lets out a small tut. She is a constant spectator to my morbid dramas and declarations and is rather desensitized to it all. What's a couple of suicide attempts between friends!

Erin reaches under the bed and produces a carrier bag with clothes for me to change into: underwear, black leggings, a plain black hoodie and fuchsia pink basketball shoes. How dare she leave my bedside, my deathbed, using the excuse to fetch fresh clothes- when really, she went home to take her daily vitamins and give Will a quick hand-job. Erin doesn't give a hoot if I leave the hospital wearing nothing but a shit-stained thong.

'I told the nurse to bin your dress because it was ripped and covered in vomit,' she says.

'How 90's grunge of me.'

'Everything is just one big joke to you isn't it?' Erin fumes.

'The exact opposite Erin, but don't worry your pretty little head about me. Let's get out of here before the harsh hospital lighting makes you look a mere nine out of ten.'

Erin aggressively shoves the now empty carrier bag into her oversized peach clutch. Coincidentally - if I had to describe Erin as a fashion accessory - I would choose the words – Oversized. Peach. Clutch. And I would say these words slowly and purposefully.

Erin phones a taxi and we leave the ward. I am now wearing the clothes that Erin brought, in case you wonder. I'm not sauntering around in my near-transparent hospital gown. Why the entire ward would be in a sexually aroused frenzy. Tearing and grasping at their own and each other's sexual organs for some sort of release. The nurses would run into the ward to find an amalgamation of sweaty glistening bodies -a stirring and moaning re-enactment of Gustav Vigeland's Monolith.

On our way to the exit, we go past a Community Art Gallery – the type that displays projects by disadvantaged children, people with disabilities, groups trying to reform i.e., the drunks, druggies, sex offenders and other bad 'uns. This goodwill exhibition shows the unsophisticated scrawls of various 'flowers' growing underneath the smiling faces of various 'suns.'

'Why would anyone on their last legs want to see these shit drawings?' I ask, 'they were probably created by relatively healthy individuals with their entire lives before them.'

Erin let out a large, aggravated sigh, 'it's pretty Amber, people like to look at things that are pretty.' Pretty like me – I bet she secretly wanted to add. Erin's voice has risen. This means I have overstepped some boundary of disrespect in her usual impartial eyes. She will no doubt bring up my comment later amidst some unconnected argument.

Erin looks ahead. Jaw clenched. Hands firmly clasping her disgusting pastel clutch. She walks faster towards the exit – away from me.

With friction and in silence we get into the taxi.

I stare out of the window and contemplate hospitals; they are constantly stuck in a shit limbo. A nightmare-like purgatory state between death and life, joy and sadness. Like three in the afternoon on Christmas Day at your grandma's, after lunch when you're bored of your presents, bored of eating, bored of your family and slowly but surely becoming bored of being alive.

I greatly admire and am grateful for the people that work in hospitals. Who are the regular Pete's and Norma's who go from eating toast and tea in their pyjamas to saving all the humans? Let's look into their imaginary eyes and see.

Eric is an A&E Medic: this morning he wiped the dripping snot from his little girl's nose before she skipped into the school playground. Another successful co-parenting weekend. Eric now wipes blood from his hands. Slowly and solemnly. Priming to tell a weeping mother that her daughter is the fatal victim of a knife attack.

Lisa is an Orthopaedic Nurse: she was out last night getting pissed on Jager-bombs, her vagina still a bit sore from a midnight finger blast in a neglected bus stop with a pizza delivery guy called Tony. Lisa now gives her patient a shot of insulin, her hand trembling at the vein, cursing every one of those fifty-six herbs, blooms, roots and fruits.

Tom is a Senior Surgeon: he was up at four in the morning to walk his beloved German Shepherd. An hour at the gym with his personal instructor. Protein shake. A shower. A wank. A haircut scheduled for ten. A run. A shower. A wank. A superfood salad whilst watching and mocking a medical drama. Then an hour's nap before he performs a triple heart bypass at three. Tom is now wrist deep in human tissue.

Normal human beings saving normal human beings. Where would we be without them? Gods in cotton.

◆ ◆ ◆

The delicious silence lasts until we get home. It is as Erin puts her coat over the banister, that she releases her anger. As if the soft corduroy touching oak presses a button from within which unleashes some sort of personality or passion that we were both unaware of and that she has indeed been lacking or hiding since birth.

'I'm sick of your lying,' Erin shouts uncaringly, 'you weren't spiked, you took those pills. Why can't you be honest?'

I shrug.

'This is the kind of stunt you usually pull over some guy. Did he treat you bad?' she asks.

'He did not murder me and there was no rape or general mutilation involved. He was just a jerk.' Erin goes to say something, but I cut her off. 'Don't you dare fucking say that there's plenty more fish in the sea. I just want to forget about it. No fish right now.'

Erin bites her lip. I instantly feel remorse. I mean she did rescue me, albeit it from a life I don't want to live.

'Thank you for all your help, Erin,' I say gently, 'I really do appreciate you putting up with me. I'll treat us to a nice takeaway tonight as a thank you.'

'I can't tonight. Will has got us tickets to see that new Mamie Blumer film,' she replies. I could have died a few hours ago, yet

I'm positive that Erin is going to experience something more horrific. Erin's eyes widen and she squirms as if in pain, 'what am I thinking...the Doctor said you can't be left alone. I'll have to cancel.'

'I'll be fine,' I reply. 'You have your phone if anything happens. Which it won't. I'm just going to sleep and rest.'

Erin takes little persuasion. Spending time with Will is her be-all and fucking end-all. I turn to go upstairs, to leave Erin in blissful daydreams of sitting next to Will on plush velveteen cinema chairs, his arm firmly around his gal, her head snuggled into his stubble-free struggle-free neck.

Erin forcefully grabs my arm. 'Amber, I love you, you're my best friend.' She turns my body to look deep into my eyes- a pointless gesture. The once exquisite azurites (lol) now mercilessly reduced to lifeless blue pebbles. 'I only get angry and upset because I can't bear to see you like this,' she continues, 'Please get help.'

'I will,' I whisper.

Erin hugs me. 'Everything is going to be ok you know. You're a good person.' She pulls away with a sad smile on her face and walks into the kitchen.

In my bedroom, I hide under the duvet and have a little cry. Sincere human contact always gets to me. If only Erin could understand. Nothing is going to be ok. It's all about what isn't said: the daily Sisyphean struggles. Imagine I dramatically blurt out to her in the ad-break of Coronation Street: 'Erin help me ... nothing can make me happy. My life is like looking out at a dark stretch of water with no reflection. I am unable to appreciate anything: art, words, music, a grapefruit pink sunset - and this makes me so fucking sad that I want to disappear. Ok so not always: sometimes the switch can be flicked up and I can fully respond to life, but the switch will undoubtedly go back down. I am never sure when that will it be. But it will be. The shadow created by the sun. The inevitable fall. 'A special kind of fall' - to quote Mr Antolini from *Catcher in the Rye*.

Erin will not know how to respond and will fake a sudden

episode of diarrhoea to avoid me. She can then spend the night in the toilet playing Candy Crush until I retire to bed. Hopefully in the morning my little outburst will be forgotten. The truth will be forgotten. Continue life as before.

The true pain is seeing how my depression and behaviour effects those around me. I shouldn't have to see that sad smile of Erin's or cause a bitten lip. How could I ever explain it to her without sounding pathetic? I haven't lived through a war. I do not fear for my life. My life is comfortable and plain. No major tragedies, violence or hunger. Sure, there was Covid-19, which was challenging for many, but for me it was a relief that I didn't have to be around people. Whilst Erin wept and missed everyone terribly, I was glad to work from home and not communicate with humans. My unsociability could at last be celebrated, a pat on the back for my dedication to avoiding others. If anything, the pandemic meant I could relate to others for the first time in my life: the whole world was miserable. Welcome to my life people - the forced smiles and heavy eyes. I don't mean to play down the horrific effects of the virus. Millions died. Millions are still recovering both financially and emotionally. I'm grateful that it did not devastate my life, I really am.

All I want to do is crawl through the rye, on my stomach and to feel…

There is a gentle hum vibration like an irritated wasp. A Facebook notification. Guess what folks…a year ago today I went to Pizza Land with Maisie from work. Whoopie Fucking Doooooieeee! Abort my fucking brain.

I look through messenger and go to the last message Holden had sent me: 'Can't wait to see you tonight gorgeous !!!!! xxx.' Three kisses. One for each stab. Also why overuse the exclamation mark?

I scan our conversation history. It had started shyly and formally and progressed into deep conversations about films, books, and life. What a joke. Bet he has another ten girls on the go. We really do accept the love we think we deserve. I delete the messages. All those empty words. Meaninglessness. Words are important to me. I know people say 'actions speak louder than words' and heck I love cuddles and affection and intimacy, but when I have a profound conversation with someone, when I connect, I know that every word I say is true and I expect the same of them. An ex-counsellor said I have unrealistic expectations about relationships: I like to think of it as beautiful optimism.

I go on his Facebook page. We haven't added each other, but you know the score, everyone does a little light stalking. There is a new photo of him holding a pint and grinning with his old college friends/acquaintances – the ones we had called phonies. The post is from 12.23am last night, or this morning, however you want to look at it. 'What a fun night!' he had written underneath and then silly bitch Jane Jones (a superhero name to boot) had commented with a sticky-out tongue emoji. I hope that emoji wasn't directed at me. Anyway, who even uses the sticky-out tongue emoji.

I bet they are in bed now, naked and giggling, spooning to high grossing vapid films and fiddling with each other, with greasy take-away hangover fingers. They had decided to get a kebab, after all, to soak up everything, and I mean EVERYTHING. They laugh about me, and Holden will call me 'psychotic' or 'needy' or some other horrid slur that guys label women when we confront their shit behaviour. He will snuggle into Jane's coconut fresh hair and say, 'I'm so glad you were there so I could escape.' They will laugh and do impressions of me. Possibly of when I pretended to blow my brains out or when I called Jane a cunt – they are my personal highlights from the night.

I pick up the book. They don't matter to me. They'll never understand us.

My phone buzzes. It's a message from my friend Jen: 'you must come to my party tonight. Feel free to invite a plus 1, or Erin, we all know how much she loves to party.' Thumbs down, laughing face, kiss, kiss.

Interlude about Erin and loneliness

Erin is one of the most clean-cut people in the world. She is the living embodiment of the antonym for 'party.' Erin is nice. What an awful adjective, sorry. I've known Erin since secondary school. At school, Erin and I stuck together as we were both considered weird. I am gloriously strange, but Erin was shunned because she had braces, bad acne and was so tall she hunched over to appear smaller. Like any classic Hollywood teen movie, she got her I'm-really-a-total-knockout revenge, because as soon as we went to college she blossomed into an absolute stunner and has grown more physically beautiful every day since.

I love Erin but she has never been the friend I needed or wanted – the cool alternative girl to have adventures with. She was never my Rayanne Graff, Erin Horvath or Lindsay Weir. We didn't colour each other's hair blue whilst listening to The Smiths and kissing posters of Kurt Cobain. Instead at school we just talked about school stuff and then at college we just talked about college stuff. I couldn't confide in her about the usual teenage dramas: periods, masturbation, self-mutilation and the like.

I'm never going to find her now. The best friend. You get to a certain age, after university, when you are forced to become a 'real' adult with a 'real' job and 'real' responsibilities, and you realise - I'm never going to find her now. So, you just go to work and hang out with mediocre people and have mediocre conversations about mediocre things and instead put your mind and heart into finding your life partner. They don't come along either and you're lonely. So lonely. Surrounded by so many people. At night, you sadly look at the stars and they sadly look back down at you knowing you will never see each other alive. The song 'Somewhere Out There' from An American Tail is stuck on repeat in your head, and you hope that special someone really is 'sleeping underneath the same big sky.' You finish off your bottle of prosecco and have two hefty lines of coke and for a moment you are vaguely content thinking about a future that may exist someday.

My phone pings – it's Jen again. 'You must come though, miss your face xxx.'

Why is Jen so desperate for me to attend her god forsaken party? To feel smug about how well her life is going compared to my shit-fest? I haven't seen her in months – and even then, it was a brief, 'hello, how are you, can't talk I'm in a rush' - kind of thing, in the condiments section of Tesco. Getting away from me undoubtedly being the source of the rush.

Should I go to the party? I do feel kind-of ok. I'll only be stuck at home by myself whilst everyone is out enjoying their lives. FOMO. My last counsellor did say to socialise more. Perhaps Jen getting in touch was some sort of sign. Oh, universe is this my time? If I don't go, will you bitch slap me through the rye?

I open my wardrobe and pull-out shoe boxes that conceal and secure darling bottles of prosecco. I take a bottle to bed. Unscrew the top. Take large life-saving gulps. Never buy bottles with corks – they only result in anxiety, upset, spillage, accidents and death. I turn on my laptop and log into the dating app I had been using up until a month ago when I met dickhead, optimistic that I had found someone for keeps. I find it disrespectful to chat to more than one person at a time: I know that's how people play the game – but the heart isn't a game, people aren't games. I prefer to focus my attention on one person at a time.

There are fifty-four messages from the usual specimens:

1) Pervy-lads asking to be tied up and spat at....and worse.

2) Jock-lads with pictures of them living the clean life - climbing up mountains or playing football with other clean cuts.

3) Chav-lads with tans and high neck tops holding up shots on nights out with their mates. When there's a group picture, how are you supposed to know which one is the wooer.

4) Car-lads with semi's because they're stood next to some shiny flash car.

5) Gym-lads with their tops off showing their six packs and muscular frames.

6) Abhorrent nerd-lads with their lists of qualifications and

employment specifics – often working in IT and always mentioning their wage.

7) Fake-saint-lads holding furry animals or playing with children to appear sensitive– all accentuating in their lifeless 'About Me' profiles that the kids and animals are DEFINETELY NOT theirs.

I am left with three contenders:

1) Jimmy is thirty-two, six foot three and a business manager. I click on his 'About Me' section: 'I am an easy-going and down-to-earth guy who is trying to find his forever mate, or a bit of fun, whatever. I enjoy walking my dog, playing basketball and watching TV. Want a nice girl to spoon and travel with.' (Surely Jimmy doesn't want to spoon and travel at the same time – I shan't be exploring the Grand Canyon with a man snuggled into my back!) 'If interested, message me, no time wasters.' His photos show a handsome, dark blonde, man with a cheery disposition. I click on the message he has sent me: 'hey you sound like a nice girl, have you had a nice weekend?' How very nice of this nice lad to nicely message to ask something nice. How should I nicely reply to that: 'not the best weekend if I'm honest Jimmy – my heart got broken and then I tried to commit suicide – fancy a coffee or a shag next week?' I delete his nice message. Which isn't nice.

2) Ray is twenty-eight and works in a bar. He likes football, hanging out with his mates and is into 'all sorts of' music. Avoid an 'all sorts of' person – be it music, TV, film, food, books, sex – if they can't be more specific about genre or names then they are dead inside. The only thing Ray writes in the 'About Me' section is: 'I'm rubbish at writing about myself, so just ask.' Generally, men who don't reveal anything about themselves are just wanting a shag and/or may already have an unsuspecting girlfriend/wife. I delete his message without reading it. Bet it says something like, 'How are you?' Monosyllabic moron. Insert caveman grunt between each word.

3) Martin is twenty-eight and a chef. Average looking, regular

build, with short brown hair and lots of stubble. On the photo he is wearing an I Love Kubrick T-shirt, so I instantly click on his message. 'Hey, how are you? I'm a (hopefully) funny guy who loves watching comedies - It's Always Sunny in Philadelphia, Curb your Enthusiasm and South Park are some of my faves, love GoT and anything sci-fi or fantasy. Love to read – sci-fi mostly and I'm currently writing my first sci-fi novel. If you think I don't sound boring, message back.' Overall, he has some lovely interests.

The message is dated seven days ago so I type back an absolute lie. 'Hi Martin, sorry not replied sooner, I've been visiting a friend's villa in Spain, it was up a mountain, so I didn't have internet connection - brutal! Well, you had me at sci-fi. Serious sci-fi geek here! What's your favourite shows/books/films?'

Should I have added a smiley face emoji and perhaps a kiss? It's the little things that keep you up at night.

I put on a short simple black dress in a slightly clingy fabric which shows ample cleavage and enough leg to attract both a breast and/or bum and/or leg enthusiast. I then apply lots of makeup. One of the many advantages of being female is that you can hide your ugly face and a thousand flaws with layers of the stuff. I can easily go from a two to a six in five minutes. But if a guy is a two, he's fucked. Perhaps with some nice clothes and decent smelling aftershave he can progress to a three, and if he works out perhaps a four or five, but other than that he must endure his hideousness. Of course, it's not all about physical attractiveness - personality, kindness, intelligence and wit can add points, and a guy who is a ten physically can soon become a two due to rudeness, vanity, dullness, and lack of intellect.

I bask in the light of realisation and repulsion when a guy wakes up next to me the morning after the night before: makeup streaming down my face, my hair extensions lying on the floor, along with my pull-in pants and push-up bra. I sincerely hope he rues the day he slept with a two pretending to be a six.

I phone a taxi, gulp down prosecco and get my bag together. The taxi pops up out of nowhere, so I rush. I bring both bottles of prosecco, along with an emergency bag of coke I keep hidden in my knicker drawer. A shit life being the emergency.

It is eight forty-five in the middle of a summer's night. The best time of day because everything feels and looks magical, the world is picturesque yet strange as the cold night air creeps in taking over the warmth of day - not spoiling, merely changing, refreshing.

Jen and Noel live in a three-bedroom suburban cul-de-sac in Ingleby Barwick. Jen is a Primary School Teacher and Noel works at Barclaycard. They both live the dream: a dream they had not wanted ten years previously.

What were my dreams and aspirations ten years ago – you yearn to know!

Interlude of dead dreams

I planned to write for a magazine – to start as an assistant and make my way up to journalist extraordinaire. There were few opportunities in Middlesbrough, so I applied for writing jobs all over the country and indeed world – Manchester, London, Glasgow, New York. I said I could move and that I was willing to do anything. Hell, I would have been happy making cups of tea and running errands for over-privileged wankers, if I was in the arts industry and doing something I believed in.

Rejection after rejection came my way. I didn't have the right connections. The jobs go to the Emilia's and Camilla's, the kind of girls whose mothers once sat on the editor's face way back when (be it male or female) after some debutante party. The kind of girls who had been to private school and would marry lawyers or doctors and job share whilst they shove out shitty bore hole brats. Women like me - partner-less and child-less, possibly for life, we, WE could have had their jobs and would have worked bloody hard at it. Fuck you, Emilia. Fuck you, Camilla.

After numerous rejections Mother pressured me to take an admin job for 'a bit of money' and it really was a 'bit.' I did as I was told to shut her up but argued that I would write every night and eventually get the job I wanted. Mother and the system would not trap me.

Working a 'normal' job was (and still is) truly awful. At night I was in heaven writing stories and immersing myself in something I was passionate about, but then the next day I would be filing papers and taking minutes. It was as if I was two people existing in one body. A cycle of pleasure and pain. Ecstasy followed by mundanity. It was three months into my new job, and after numerous articles and job applications were rejected, that I had a breakdown. I woke up one morning and couldn't move. When Mother realised, I would be late for work she rushed into my bedroom asking if I was ill. When I explained how I felt, she couldn't understand. She said that nobody wanted to go to work, but that was the way of life. When I questioned this, she merely shook her head and said I was being awkward. Then she went on and on about how hard her life has been and that she had no choice but to work 'when that tosser left us.'

I screamed. Full force, without barriers, as if I was getting stabbed. I just wanted to see if I could scream - there's so few opportunities to release oneself in adulthood, why should children get all the fun. Mother responded by sobbing loudly, and after a glass of wine, she phoned my former therapist. You see this was the perfect opportunity for her to talk, yet again, about her own problems and how I made her suffer. Mother didn't know what to do with me, she never had.

My therapist came to visit that afternoon. I had stopped screaming by then. Mother wailed and wittered on downstairs - retelling the same old stories. I was diagnosed with a mental breakdown- although they don't like to use that term anymore. I was given some strong anti-depressants and had to go back to counselling.

My depression was nothing compared to the pain my mother now felt daily. How brave and wonderful she was to cope with me. I mean she just coped people. With her own daughter. The bloody saint.

I took the tablets. I went to therapy. I gradually felt better. 'Better' as in not screaming. Well not screaming aloud. I constantly scream inside.

I was younger then and optimistic about my future. That I would find sense and purpose in my life and eventually be happy. But now I know that the future is where dreams go to die.

Every day I long to lie down in that field of rye. To close my eyes and wait. For days and nights. I'll ignore everything. The hunger and thirst. The cold and rain. The sun and the insects. Until I feel nothing at all. Nothing matters. It is all over. I have won.

I am finally at peace in the rye.

CHAPTER THREE

Taxi Intermission

Taxi journeys. Sigh. They're awkward if you talk to the driver, and awkward if you don't. There's no 'win' in the situation. I can either: speak to someone on my phone - but I don't like talking to anyone, pretend to be distracted – again on my phone, or I can sleep/close my eyes. I shan't do the latter because the driver will assume I'm drunk and hysterically ask every twenty seconds if I'm going to vomit. This will be followed by a stern penalty fine warning and a plethora of tales regarding previous puking passengers. For the rest of the journey the driver will glare at me from the rear-view mirror and make me feel uncomfortable and criminalised. I can't daydream or play a game on my phone, because I'll undoubtedly be jerked to the present with a loud, unnerving, heart-palpitating - 'am I going the right way?' Taxi drivers always expect you, yes YOU, to know the destination and route. You do half their job, yet they take offense when you hand over only fifty percent of the fare!

I always leave a taxi wishing I'd set off three hours earlier and walked. Or hitchhiked and risked rape and/or murder.

I rest my arm on the armrest: utilising it for the very name it has been given. I hold my chin between my forefinger and thumb – a gentle V. I look out of the window and frown. I need to appear like I'm mentally distressed and about to cry. Thus the driver will avoid communication i.e. talking, gesturing, singing, looking, grunting.

I'll use this taxi journey for a meaningful interlude about me and Jen.

A Meaningful Interlude about me and Jen

Jen was my girlfriend for a short period when we were at college. We were in the same English Lit class and connected over our shared passion for Sylvia Plath. We fell in love. People would stare at us in public, but we didn't care. We let our lips linger for longer just to provoke them. We felt powerful and cool and subversive. Fuck the system. Fuck the parents. Fuck heterosexuality. Fuck the fuckboys.

I was nervous the first time we had sex because I had never done it with a girl. But it was perfect and intimate. No harsh male fingers chafing my clitoris to distress or lacerating my vagina walls like a cat relentlessly testing a new scratching pole. I wasn't bent into weird positions as if trying to recapture some favourite porn movie. It was candles and kisses and loveliness.

I don't want to think about it. It makes me sad.

Prior to this, I had only had sex with a few guys. It was awful. Sex can be awful.

An Interlude within an Interlude: Sex can be awful.

I lost my virginity at fifteen to a guy I was 'seeing.' We were 'seeing each other' for about a month when we had sex. His parents were out at Mecca Bingo, and he had put on some awful Vin Diesel movie – which should have been a sign to drop him immediately, not my knickers. We drank cheap cider from his parent's liquor cupboard. Afterwards, my vagina hurt but I felt 'normal'. Two days later he dumped me. It was the first time I'd heard the infamous spiel: 'it's not you, it's me.' The first time that a guy had made me feel broken and used.

I was thankful he did not attend my school because then everyone would find out, even the teachers. I would get called names and labelled and laughed at. But not that git, he would be deemed a god damn prince. The guys at school would ask him all sorts of personal details:

1) What does Amber's vagina smell like?
   Walking into Lush. + 1 point
   Fish stall in Morrisons. +1 point

Fridge full of ready-to-be-barbequed meat. - 1 point

2) What is Amber's vaginal hair situation?

Little bald man. +1 point

Well-maintained landing strip. +1 point

Hairy caterpillar. 0 points

All over hair but well maintained. +0.5 points

Chewbacca. -3 points

3) What is Amber's flap situation?

Tiny, practically non-existent. +1 point

Droopy but still doable. 0 points

Hanging over like a dog's wagging tongue. -1 point

4) How are Amber's tits?

All tits are good. +1 point (trick question)

5) How was Amber's overall performance?

Tried multiple positions and made noises to encourage performance. +1 point.

Had a go, but her heart wasn't in it. 0 points

Laid there in silence with little participation or vocal support. -1 point

6) Did Amber give you oral?

To get the party started, but stopped at the ideal time to stick it in. +1 point

Pushed head down in that region but she didn't get the hint. -1 point

Shit technique. To stop the embarrassment show I dipped it in quick. 0 points

7) Did Amber get anal?

Yes, she fucking loved it. +10 points

Attempted but it hurt her too much, maybe next time. 0 points

Flat out refused entry into the brown zone. -1 point

8) Did you cum?

Like a lord. +3 points

Did she cum … (hahaha who fucking cares).

9) Did you use protection?

Assumed she was on the pill. +1 point

Asked me to pull out when I was near. So, I cum on her face and tits. +1 point.

Let me take off condom half-way through because it felt shit. 0.5 points

Made me wear condom. Fucking party-pooper. -5 points

FYI, I scored 7 points.

My second sexual experience was at a friend of a friend's (FOAF) housewarming/baby shower. She became pregnant at sixteen, so the council gave her a shithole of a flat in an urban crime hotbed. FOAF said that women should only drink fourteen units a week (she'd read that on an AA poster in the bus stop next to the off license) so in her delicate predicament (she did not use this term, in fact, she struggled to pronounce anything longer than two syllables) she could only drink half of this – i.e., seven cans of lager. She assumed that a can was one unit, and I didn't want to reproach or contradict this belief as she looked like a violent hound of a girl.

I was relieving myself in the bathroom when there was a knock on the door. It was a guy called Gav, I didn't know him. I pulled up my knickers and opened the door. 'There you go' I said addressing the now vacant toilet and not my body. He pushed me back into the bathroom, closed the door and threw me up against the wall. His tongue barricaded my throat. I pushed him off at first but then went with the flow. I was drunk and thought 'a snog's a snog'. Then he stuck his bony digits up me. I told him not to. He whispered breathlessly, 'you're so hot,' as if we were in the middle of some great porn shoot. He unzipped his trousers, flung me over the toilet, and fucked me doggy style over the seat. I gripped tightly onto the toilet bowl, so I didn't fall into the murky pool of urine-and-worse below. I thought 'well isn't this what teenagers do at parties – get drunk and get laid'. Once upon a time, I tried to follow the crowd. It didn't work out well for me.

Later that night I sat on my now sore vagina and watched the party people eat pizza. Gav took a slice and then shouted over to me 'eeya what's your name, you have some.' He didn't even know my name. Modern love story.

A Meaningful Interlude about Me and Jen: Continued

Jen and I had been together for about six weeks when Helena joined our class. She had a dyed yellow blunt-cut fringe and an asymmetrical black bob. She wore vintage band t-shirts which were always torn - not through age or the consequence of a brutal mosh pit, each cut was perfectly placed by her very own scissors. Rock on with authenticity.

Helena knew what to say and how to act to interest people. She wasn't a horrible person, just a phoney. She didn't really enjoy the bands or books or films she pretended to like. She posted hourly selfies on social media with self-deprecatory comments to attract sycophantic replies. To each arse-licking she would 'like' and comment 'no you're beautiful, I'm the one who's ugly darling xxx' And other stupid fake bore bitch shit like that.

It wasn't long before Jen and Helena were an item. I don't remember how it all happened now or how I found out about them. I cried a lot. I hoped Jen would see Helena for who she really was. But when someone is cool (however phoney) and beautiful, you can't look past that, you've found what you need. Love, loyalty, intelligence, kindness and humour - these qualities can be overlooked. Come on now, I never stood a chance against that fringe!

Their relationship lasted until Helena went to Edinburgh University. After this, I'd occasionally see Jen on nights out and we'd hug like we were the closest of friends and say we loved each other and pinkie-promised we'd catch up soon. But we never did. Then she met Noel.

Arrival at Destination.
End of Taxi Intermission & Interludes within Interludes within Interludes.

Noel answers the door.

'Well hello Amber,' he smiles and embraces me with a barely

friendly and circumstantially forced hug.

I wonder if Jen has told Noel (and indeed others) about our previous and brief romantic relationship. I hope not. A rumour will then ensue that I am a lesbian and that all daughters, aunties and grandmothers must be locked up instantly as I have no morals or boundaries and will surely scissor them all in a frivolous frenzy with my voracious vagina.

Noel is tall and dependable. Always up for work at seven on the chime, shirt and tie ready. I'm certain he came out of the womb all buttoned up and raring to go. He is ready for work. Ready to be in a committed and loving relationship. Ready for life. Ready for death. Ready for all that happens in-between. Jen said he has a big dick.

'Jen is somewhere chatting to someone' Noel says. He notices my bottles of prosecco, 'how kind, just put them in the kitchen.'

Thanks Noel, but I'm being kind to myself, as they are both mine to consume.

The lounge is full of people I barely recognise, yet we have probably been introduced at some point throughout the years. They are the type of people who leave little impression. I notice a guy in the corner, Teddy, a friend of Noel's who's always had a thing for me - as in 'oooooo I like a kooky girl who's a bit different.' Is mental instability considered kooky these days? Teddy always calls me 'little red' on account of my dyed auburn hair and height insufficiency. Every time he sees me, he nudges my breast in a libidinous manner and calls me that awful pet name. He considers it a term of endearment. I consider it ball-smacking material. He catches my eye and waves. I wave back and smile but quickly move into the kitchen.

Jen is there talking to two plain clothed mammas. 'But we can't work miracles,' she says, 'what do they expect?' When Jen is with these people, she mostly talks about work, and it is very tedious stuff.

Jen's face lights up when she sees me. She rushes over and engulfs me in a wine-induced bear hug. 'I'm so glad you could make it' she exclaims. She turns to the mammas, 'Wendy, Jo, this is Amber - an old and dear friend from College.'

'Hello' they both reply. I 'hello' back.

'We are just talking about work,' Jen says, 'it's so full on at the moment, everything's targets, targets, targets.' Mamma Wendy and Mamma Jo mumble in agreement. Jen continues to talk about the issues they face at work.

I zone out. I remember the way Jen used to be - strawberry blonde curls with wash-in wash-out streaks haphazardly splashed through, a different colour every week it seemed. The septum and lip piercing (taken out years ago) and the huge Courtney Love tattoo on her arm which she recently removed. Jen used to play guitar and sing, she did a few gigs, and she was awesome. She was a charity shop clothes horse and I loved her for it.

Jen now stands before me with an excessively straight, mousey brown, chin length bob, minimal makeup and a beige bodycon dress. She is the human equivalent of a salad without dressing. She accessorizes the outfit with a diamante cross necklace, matching earrings and beige wedge sandals with diamante's scattered on the toes.

'Amber?'

'Yes,' I reply, and hope they hadn't noticed I'd drifted off.

Mamma Wendy is speaking to me, 'so what do you do for a living?'

'I'm in admin.'

'Oh great,' Mamma Wendy replies with fake enthusiasm. The profession can never generate a passionate response as everyone knows it is really a euphemism for 'monotonous incarceration.'

'Amber was a great writer' says Jen, 'she really captured that teen angst vibe. Do you still write hun?'

Why is Jen trying to sell me to her friends? I'm inadequate and that's fine. I've gotten over my life failings a long time ago. Haven't I?

'I haven't written in years,' I reply.

'Oh you really should,' Jen says, 'then I can say I'm friends with a famous writer.'

They all laugh. I join in.

'I wish I was creative,' says Mamma Jo. Of course you do. Mamma Jo in your pink paisley playsuit.

I must act normal. I must try and fit in for Jen's sake.

'I'm over all that now,' I say, 'who has time to write with work and everything.'

They mumble in agreement and smile at me. I feel part of something. Do I fit? Could these be my new friends? Yoga followed by sushi rolls and a white wine soda whilst watching the Great British Bake Off.

'We all do strange things when we're young,' says Mamma Jo.

'I could write a trilogy, let alone a book, about all the stupid things I did as a teenager,' says Jen, 'when Amber knew me, I was a mess. I made some horrific mistakes.'

They all laugh. I join in, even though I am one of the horrific mistakes.

'Where do you live Amber?' Mamma Wendy asks.

'Just in Linthorpe, near the town centre.'

'Just you and your partner?' asks Mamma Jo.

'Just me and a friend, but she's saving up to move in with her boyfriend.'

'Don't you have a boyfriend?' asks Mamma Jo.

'No.'

Mamma Jo looks at me with grave concern. As if I said I have terminal cancer. Judging by their faces I wish I had said that. They were the types that could handle cancer better than singledom.

'I haven't had a boyfriend in years,' I continue. I could lie and make it nice for them, say I'm dating a guy or have recently split with someone. But I want them to face my truth as I do every day.

There is silence for about five seconds as they masticate my uneasy words. 'You're better off without them,' Mamma Jo says, trying to salvage my dire situation 'Pete is a real pain in the arse. Socks lying around everywhere. Never considers doing the pots. Watches football constantly.'

They laugh. I laugh.

'You'll find someone,' reassures Mamma Wendy.

'I'm glad I met Noel, or I don't know what I'd do,' says Jen.

The grim reality of my existence is bringing them down. They quickly change the subject and continue their discussions about work. Dreary stuff - so I pick up my bottle of prosecco and mumble that I need the loo.

I go into the back garden. There are a few people sitting around the patio table smoking. I lean against the kitchen wall and pretend I'm doing something important on my phone. The smokers regard me suspiciously. They stare at the bottle of prosecco in my hand. I've been told it is customary to use a glass. I take a big glug out of the bottle, not giving a shit.

I peruse the usual to look busy – Facebook, Instagram, Snapchat, then look on the dating site. Martin hasn't replied. He is online. Probably talking to some bint he deems better than me.

The people at the table laugh about Geoff at work and the time, now wait for it, it's exceptionally funny, give me a second to calm myself to tell this hilarious tale, you see, one day Geoff fell off his chair, no you see, he actually fell off his chair, when he was at work, because the armrest gave way, the actual armrest of the chair, which made Geoff fall onto the office floor, he still had his pen in his hand, even after falling onto the floor, his actual pen, just Geoff on the floor, pen and Geoff. Floor. Geoff. Pen. Thank fuck that after this hilarious anecdote they go inside, so I can stitch my sides back up and continue with life.

I move to the table - elated they didn't speak to me. I hate talking just for the sake of covering silence – you know, inane chatter to shop assistants or people in the queue to the toilet. I don't know you. You don't know me. There's a great possibility we will never meet again. Let's not bother with chit chat. I don't find the silence awkward. It's nice. Conversations about the weather or what they're going to have for dinner, now that's awkward. Completely mundane dialogue comprised of nothingness. They never chat about anything topical or interesting, say climate change or terrorism. That would be a slight improvement. Just slight. Silence is always preferable.

The sky is turning grey. In the distance the moon begins to gently appear. Everything is still and lovely. I drink prosecco. I have two lines. I try to ignore the unending drone of chatter, music and laughter coming from inside. I drink prosecco. I have two lines. I go back on the dating website. I message Martin: 'my faves are Dr Who, Star Trek, anything Marvel and anything dark, you?'

I wait five minutes. No reply. A tick at the bottom of the screen indicates he has read my message. Perhaps I shouldn't have said 'dark'. I log out. I drink prosecco. I have a small key of coke. I begrudgingly go inside.

I look around the living room for Jen but can't see her: she is probably still in the kitchen talking shit with the mammas. Someone taps my shoulder.

'How are things Little Red?'

That odious tone. The waves of repulsion that rise in my stomach. The one and only...

'Oh hi Teddy,' I reply.

Teddy gives me a hug that I don't want to receive. I reminisce fondly about the days of Covid when we couldn't hug each other and had to stay two metres apart.

'So how are you?' he asks, 'long time, no see. What have you been up to?'

If I had a delete button that I could use on people, then right about now my finger would be bruised from hammering the bastard.

Teddy is small and a bit chubby. He slurs his speech when he's drunk. A repulsive trait. His eyes glisten. His chin whiskers are wet from drink.

'Nothing really,' I answer, 'you?'

'Nothing much. I just got a new car - a Mercedes Cleopatra II,' Teddy smirks because he is a smirking smug bastard. 'I've just come back from a month working in Dubai, mint place, loved it. Life's been good to me Little Red. Recently got a promotion and bought a five-bedroom new build not far from here. You should come around sometime for dinner. I make a snazzy homemade Spaghetti Carbonara.'

'Mmmm,' I reply. I cannot give a verbal response to possibly the most repugnant offer I've ever received.

'Are you dating anyone new Little Red or are you still free, single and raring to mingle?' Teddy laughs.

I loathe him. 'Oh, you know me,' I shrug and don't give a proper answer.

Teddy is insipid. The kind of guy who listens to 'rock music' but it's wholesome lightly played shite with Enid Blyton-type lyrics and the occasional 'fuck' thrown in to appear edgy and obtain a parental warning label on the CD. Not that people buy CD's these days. The music equivalent of wanting to watch hardcore porn and putting on *Fifty Shades of Grey,* the censored version, with the sex scenes deleted.

Jen comes out of the kitchen. I catch her eye and she walks over. Then some suited-and-booted pulls her aside and they commence conversation.

Teddy puts his hand on my back and leans in closer. 'What plans have you got this summer?' he asks.

To avoid thee, good fellow. 'Not many so far.'

'Me and the lads are off to Mexico next week on a stag do. We were meant to go last year but couldn't because of Covid. It's going to be craaaaazy.'

'I've never been,' I reply.

'It's amazing,' he says, 'I've been three times. I'll take you some day. My treat. I know you don't have much disposable income.'

Murder in the Rye?

'Thanks,' I reply.

'Where are you working these days?' Teddy asks. His breath smells like he uses sugary drinks to try and disguise gonorrhoea.

'Just in an office.'

'Oh really, I'll be looking for a secretary soon, I'll keep you in mind.'

'Thank you,' I gulp down prosecco. Teddy stands so close that the bottle knocks his chin, but sadly misses his daily flossed teeth.

'I see you're on the whole bottle Little Red,' he laughs, 'I've always said you're my kind of girl, fun-loving and kooky.'

There's that fucking word.

'Are you two having fun?' Jen sneaks up behind me and nudges my arm suggestively. The only useful suggestion in this situation would be if she had slyly given me a loaded gun.

Jen is about to join our conversation and play cupid in the process, but I can't be bothered with any of it, so I say to Teddy, 'I need to talk to Jen in private, it's a girl thing.' If necessary, I was ready to verbalize the 'p' word and hold my lower stomach.

Teddy looks disappointed. 'No problem, later Little Red' he says and shifts away.

Later. Never.

'He's so lovely,' Jen says when he is out of ear shot, 'he's got a good job. Now all he needs is a good girl.' She winks at me.

'Please don't wink,' I say.

'Awww he likes you,' she laughs, 'beneath it all, I think he'd be a great boyfriend.' By 'it all' does she mean, 'his revoltingness.'

'I'd rather slice off my vaginal flaps, pluck out the pubes, make fleshy castanets and become a flamenco dancer, than go anywhere near him,' I reply.

'Why?' Jen asks shocked, 'you're too fussy, you're not getting any younger you know?'

'He'd bore me into an early grave,' I reply.

Jen laughs, 'what are you looking for? No one's perfect. People settle down and are happy. That's what life's about.'

Once I googled the definition of the word 'settle' because people use it a lot in terms of relationships. It said: 'Resolve or reach an agreement about an argument or problem.'

'End by mutual agreement.'

'Reach a decision about.'

'Accept or agree to something that one considers to be less than satisfactory.'

These descriptions make me sad because they are the exact opposite of love.

'Teddy and I are not alike,' I reply.

'Well opposites attract, Noel and I are different, but we get on great.'

How can I explain to Jen that this isn't good enough for me. Teddy could never understand me. We could never talk about books, writing, music, art and movies. We would talk about how our day has been and idle internet gossip. We would laugh about universally humorous memes. He would boast and brag about nothing important. He is a phoney. I would live a life of 'what ifs.'

I shrug, not knowing how to answer. I gulp down prosecco.

'You drink too much,' Jen says, 'You're always absolutely wasted, and it's not good for you. I'm only saying this because I love you, but when you're drunk you get over emotional and loud and argue with people.... maybe you should lay off it Amber.'

'I will when I have a reason to NOT drink,' I reply curtly.

'Teddy would be...' Jen starts to say, but I cut her off because I don't want to speak about that repugnant little urchin.

'Would you like a little pick me up?' I ask. 'I've brought some naughty powder.'

Jen looks disapproving, 'I haven't done that for years, Noel doesn't like it. Who knows what crap you're putting into your body? He's ok with the odd joint on special occasions, but that's about it.'

'What a killjoy. Dump him immediately!' I am of course joking (half-joking) but by Jen's reaction her sense of humour has clearly turned to mush.

'I guess I don't need it anymore Amber. Noel just wants the best for me and I'm happier than I've ever been,' she replies in both a defensive and condescending manner.

I smile at her and hope my suffering is invisible.

Noel taps loudly on a glass: – 'Right I have an announcement, is everyone here? Bring in the mucky smokers.' Noel considers smokers to be complete dirty bastards. If only he could rifle them down on arrival into his fresh Gardenia scented, rosy, pink lung of a home.

'Right,' Noel says once everyone is present. He looks around the room with his bland over-ironed clothes and sparkly un-abused teeth laden with ambition and contentment. He sees Jen and ushers her over, 'come here gorgeous.'

Jen giggles into her hand like a stereotypical Japanese schoolgirl and follows Noel to the centre of the crowd.

'Right,' says Noel. He uses this word a lot, because he is so very right in every respect. 'Last night Jen and I went for a lovely meal, which cost me a bloody bomb may I add.'

Everyone laughs and someone shouts, 'I hope she put out.'

Noel continues, '...and at this meal I asked Jen to be my wife...' (dramatic pause for little drama) ... 'and she said yes.'

Everyone cheers and congratulates. Jen and Noel kiss and hug. Smiles corresponding. The perfect picture of happiness. The crowd moves closer. Pats on backs. Handshakes. Air kisses. Laughter. Cooing. Awfulness.

'I wondered why he went down on one knee,' Jen shouts over the crowd, 'I thought he'd dropped his knife.'

Everyone laughs. Except me.

Holden would never propose in a restaurant. Too ordinary. His proposal would be spontaneous. He would act on his instincts, which were superb, and he'd naturally sense when the ideal moment transpired.

We would be on holiday, somewhere beautiful and magical. We would be drinking champagne in the dusk, underneath fairy lights (which seemed to illuminate us wherever we went). Violins play faintly in the distance. The world would smell new. The breeze would gently move our hair to create a picture of love at its best. Holden wouldn't get down on one knee. Too ordinary. He would simply look me in the eyes and take both my hands, first he would put our champagne flutes on the ground, otherwise the drinks could spill everywhere causing stickiness and physical interaction unpleasantness and ruin the proposal which is indeed a two-handed job, and say something like this:

'Before I met you, I was so lonely, living in this world of phonies.

You are what I've been searching for. Please can we be together forever? Can we save each other and be happy together in the rye?'

I would say yes, and we would both cry with joy. We would kiss in between tears and wait for the night to arrive and our lives to begin as husband and wife.

Wanting to fit in, I go over to Jen and Noel to congratulate them. But they are busy talking to everyone who matters. People ask the usual wedding questions – the where's and what's. Dare I ask why – teehee.

Jen turns to Mamma Jo and Mamma Wendy, 'I want you two to be my bridesmaids along with Noel's little niece.'

They whoop with joy. Well fuck you, Jen. 'You're my oldest and dearest friend.' Bollocks. A few years ago, you were eating me out. Now I understood why you were so eager for me to attend this little soiree. To kick me in the mouth, heart and cunt.

I need to be alone. I go into the kitchen to put my empty prosecco bottle in the bin. I open the other bottle I'd brought and pour myself a glass, since drinking from the bottle was clearly frowned upon at this sophisticated get-together. I go outside. I sit at the table. I drink. I have a line.

I am happy for Jen and Noel. Slightly. While Noel was on one knee proposing to his new fiancée, ready to start their life together, I was trying to end mine. I check my phone and log onto the dating site. Still no reply from fuck boy. He is still online. So, I have a line.

How have I had ended up like this? I want to blame something, someone. Was it my dad for walking out and making us a broken family? No, I was weird before then. I remember being at nursery and looking at the other children as if I was watching a film. Never feeling part of anything. An unnoticeable extra. An irrelevant member of the film crew. An unremarkable and ineffectual director. I would try and fit in at school, college, university, work...but I never did. I was always just looking in.

Sometimes I imagine having a 'normal' life- the husband, the children. Would I feel complete? What if they grew up to be like me, how could I cope with that? Beautiful children having dark seeds rooted from conception, just waiting to sprout. That first insult. That first heart break. That first rejection. You can't deny nature. As they get older, they'll think I am irresponsible for having reproduced. I can only apologise and hope that they will somehow find happiness.

How soon will it be before I have a breakdown? When my husband and children see the real me? The days in bed. The fatigue. Unbrushed hair and stained pyjamas. The inability to speak or move. The comfort of blankets and silence. Or the antithesis. The hysteria. The panic. The tears. The alcohol and drugs.

Holden will stay by my side. He will understand and reassure that everything is going to be ok. He will bring me soup to eat and a flannel to wash my face (on my most crazy days, I will eat the flannel and wash with soup). He will distract me by talking about books and TV shows. How when I am well, we can go to a café for coffee and cake. We will plan a holiday. He will leave the book on my bed with a little note in it 'these words and my love will give you strength.' Slowly I will come back. We will be happy again. Until next time.

Loud music breaks through my thoughts as people come into the garden to smoke. I down the remaining slurps of prosecco and go inside for a refill.

The kitchen is ridiculously hot because some sort of food is being cooked. It smells like charred penis with peppers. Mamma Jo and Mamma Wendy are pouring drinks. Single measures obviously, they have husbands to breastfeed.

'We're doing celebratory shots if you're in?' Mamma Jo asks excitedly.

'Good move, 'I reply, feeling absolute pleasure in the fact they aren't complete panna cottas, and we perhaps share a common love.

They hand me a bright green, acidy smelling substance. I hoped for straight vodka shots, but don't complain.

'These things are gross,' Mamma Wendy says. She sniffs the glass and pulls a disgusted face.

'Are you ready?' asks Mamma Jo, 'One. Two. Three. Down the hatch.'

We stand together, the absolute best of friends and clink shots. 'To Jen and Noel' she adds before we down the little rascals. We slam the plastic shot glasses down onto the kitchen counter and screw up our faces at the fake fruity aftertaste.

'The pizza will be done about now. Pepperoni pizza yum-yum,' says Mamma Jo. She sticks a tea towel between her hands to open the oven.

'I love pepperoni,' Mamma Wendy confesses, 'I could eat it all day, every day.'

I'm sure you agree that this is a ridiculous thing to say.

Out it comes, amid massive wafts. Mamma Jo places it on the counter and cuts it using a pizza slicer. She obviously knows her way around the kitchen. I'd only been invited to Jen's house once but didn't go as I was having a massive comedown. I lied to Jen and said I had to write a report for work which was needed ASAP. This was a more sensible excuse, which would provoke fewer tuts.

The cheesy ooze drips down the sides of the pizza, a film of grease shines thick on top, making rivers of orange goo among the folds. The round eyes of pepperoni red, pink and brown - little specks of fat flicker through them, like licking the areolas of a fat sunburnt bloke. Come now we've all been there. A good holiday blowmance. Then, possibly because of the visualisation above, I vomit on the kitchen floor.

'Oh my god,' cries Mamma Jo.

'I'll go get Jen,' says Mamma Wendy and dashes out of the kitchen.

I try to call out to her – 'stop, don't, I'll clean it,' but instead of words, out comes more puke. The world spins. I hold on tight to the kitchen counter.

Jen rushes into the kitchen and without saying a word

yanks open a cupboard underneath the sink and brings out an assortment of cloths and cleaning products. She aggressively mops up the sick and scrubs the floor.

'I'm sorrrrrry,' I slur as I try to stand up straight. I fall on my hands and knees next to Jen. 'I am sorry. I'll do it,' I say. I try to take the cloth from her.

Jen grabs it away from me, 'what the hell have you been drinking? It fucking stinks.'

'I'm sorry. I don't feel well.'

'Look at you, you're a state. Amber, you need to go home.'

Jen is really angry. I've never seen her like this. There was a time when she would have found this funny. Back then she would joke around and pretend to slip on the puke. But then she would accidentally fall next to me, and we would both laugh hysterically. She would stroke my hair to make me feel better, which may have ended in tongues and a finger fuck, dependent on how dizzy I felt and the rancidity of my sick breath.

'Someone phone her a taxi,' she orders. Jen stands up abruptly as if she can't bear to be near me. She throws the sick covered cloths in the bin, and then washes her hands. Not the symbolic washing of the hands.

'I didn't think I'd be washing sick off my hands tonight,' Jen says angrily, 'especially wearing my new engagement ring.'

I grab onto the cupboards and try to stand up. My hands slip. My throat burns with acid. I can't move. I just stay there on my hands and knees.

'I am so sorry,' I say again.

'Amber, why can't you act like a fucking adult?' Jen shouts quietly so only the people in the kitchen can hear, 'I only invited you because we've been friends for years...and now this. And bringing class-A drugs into our home!' There is a soft gasp from the Mammas. 'Noel was right about you' Jen continued. Of course he was. Right. Rightie. Righto.

The Mammas are motionless. Probably with shock from 'class A drugs.' All I can see are feet and legs - as if I am in the Muppet Babies. You know the episode where Animal fucks up his life and then fucks up his ex-girlfriend's engagement party. AMBER-MAAAAAL. Gravelly laugh. 'Drums are food,' I shout and thrash my hands about as if violently playing the drums.

I don't really do this. It would be ridiculous and inappropriate. Given the circumstances.

'Look you can't even get up,' Jen continues.

AMBER-MAAAAAL.

Mamma Wendy helps me to my feet. Then to make matters worse, a lot worse, significantly worse, Noel enters the room.

'What's happened?' he asks and kisses Jen on the cheek. He puts his arm around her waist, 'you look distraught my darling wife to be.'

'Amber has been sick everywhere,' says Jen.

'I'm so sorry,' I mumble.

'The taxi is on its way,' says Mamma Jo.

Jen and Noel look at each other. The 'parents' look.

'I'm so sorry,' I say again.

'There's no point saying you're sorry Amber,' Jen says, 'all you've done tonight is ignore everyone, down bottles of prosecco and snort cocaine.'

'I'm sorry.' I am so wrecked that these are the only words I can manage to get out of my mouth.

Jen shakes her head, 'Amber when you did this in college it was funny, because you were eighteen, but now you're in your thirties. When are you going to pull yourself together and start to act like an actual adult?'

With a sudden surge of clear-headedness I put my bag over my shoulder and check I have my money, phone and keys. I will wait for the taxi outside.

'You don't know me Jen. You're the one who stopped having fun, bully for you. You have a great life, bully for you. You can't stand there and judge me. You're all a bunch of boring phoney bastards. Well enjoy your boring phoney bastard jobs and your boring phoney bastard weddings and your boring phoney bastard children and your boring phoney bastard lives.'

I stomp out of the kitchen (carefully, so I don't fall on the wet floor and make the whole incident even more tragic and pathetic) out of the lounge, and outside into the cold night air. I will be like this forever and I will be alone.

Alone in the rye.

CHAPTER FOUR

I am continuously impressed with myself. Why not? Why shouldn't one be impressed with oneself? You see, no matter what state I get in, I always remember where I live and get home safe. On the spectrum of genius – unsure. I bet Einstein couldn't remember where he lived after a crazy night on the cobbles.

'Wo zum teufel lebe ich?' he did shout in anger, theoretically speaking.

Erin is in the lounge watching a lame arse reality programme. The type which focuses on relationship problems of the romantic kind, whilst simultaneously promoting unrealistic standards of beauty.

'Where have you been?' she bellows as the front door clicks shut. 'Come here.'

I walk slowly and fearfully into the lounge like a naughty teenager who has been caught doing something fun they shouldn't be doing. Erin pauses the TV show. On screen some blonde cartoon of a girl blows into a handkerchief. Tears stream down her face - matching my exact internal sentiments.

'I've tried to ring you, but it keeps going to voicemail' Erin stands and puts her hands on her hips. A wagging pointed finger may be added at some point for effect. The effect being superiority and condescension. 'I only
realised you weren't home about twenty minutes ago. I thought you were asleep in bed.'

The toilet flushes and Will comes out of the downstairs bathroom. Erin always needs someone with her – a boyfriend, mate, work colleague, family member, someone on the phone to talk to. Even when Erin is asleep, she must have music or an audio book playing in the background. She can barely exist alone. She must not have time to contemplate her own banality.

'Hello Amber,' Will says and brushes past me. He sits down. He huffs - annoyed that Erin has paused the TV show: that I have caused a pause.

'Where the fuck have you been?' Erin continues.

'I went to Jen's party,' I reply, 'just to say hello, I wasn't there long.'

'A party!' Erin cries, 'Amber, you're crazy...what's wrong with you, you just got out of hospital.'

I don't say anything.

'You're drunk,' she shouts, 'I can smell you from here and you can barely stand straight. What did the doctor tell you? What would your mother say?'

I shrug.

'I wash my hands of you,' says Erin (not another symbolic hand washing!) 'I'm sick of worrying. If you don't care about yourself then why should I? The sooner I move out of here the better. Then you can go back home and be your mother's problem.'

'Sorry,' I reply. Well, what else could I say.

Erin angrily flops down on the sofa next to Will. He huffs. I use all the flopping and huffing as a chance to escape.

As I walk upstairs, I can hear Erin's irate screech and the odd mumble from Will. Then the TV show is turned back on. They're not bothered anymore. I am merely a dramatic interlude that has now finished.

Exhausted and ridiculous I go to sleep.

It is Sunday. I spend it in the usual fashion: in bed, hungover, hating life and wanting to die. Is it really Sunday if you don't contemplate ending your life? 'I'll have a bit of turkey, beef, a Yorkshire pudding, carrots, beans, mash, cauliflower cheese, roasties, gravy, mint sauce and a noose please. Ooooo actually what the hell it's Monday tomorrow... I'll have some arsenic, two bullets and a gun.'

On Sundays I move for three reasons: 1) toilet needs 2) to obtain fizzy drinks 3) to answer the door for takeaway. I lay in silence. I want to sleep and forget, but my mind is wired with drugs, I can't keep my legs still: they move against the soft fabric of the bed in a soothing manner, wriggling for attention, relaxed by the familiar feel of the cotton. What do you do – when the body is tired, but the mind is fired? Or is it the other way round?

I scroll through social media in the hope of reaching such a high state of anxiety, by comparing my life to the seemingly happy and successful lives of people I hardly know, that I pass out. Those glorious strangers - going out for Sunday lunch, taking their children to the park, visiting relatives, drinking with friends in beer gardens (the two-pints-after-all-it-is-Sunday bores).

Photos have been added of Jen and Noel's engagement party. Everyone pretending to have fun when really it was a total chore. Or maybe the pack of phonies did let loose when I left? Maybe I am the chore? The delinquent outsider. The drug fuelled wench. The under-achieving, un-married and unhappy un of huns.

I check my online dating app. Still no reply from Martin. He is online. Men aren't good for my mental health. I allow them to ruin my life. Well allow them to help me ruin my life. The cheeky collaborators. I have what I need under my pillow. I can hold it in my hands. Smell it. Feel it. Holden is in my head and heart. I don't need those pigs. I delete the app.

With a flask of strength-giving coffee in-hand, I google the usual Sunday madness- how to cure depression, positive thinking, mindfulness, anything that can help me through the day or at least keep me alive for a little longer.

Interlude about the universe hating me

I read a book a few years ago about positive energy and the importance of being grateful for everything you have in life. That this will make the universe work in your favour and give back to you in wonderful ways. You're supposed to tell the universe what you want: visualise it, believe it is happening, and it will transpire. I sincerely want to believe in bollocks like that. Apparently, you can positively believe yourself anything. The ideal house. The ideal car. The ideal partner. The ideal life. You can even believe yourself back to health. If only cancer knew.

At the time I wanted to believe that there was a cure for my depression and general fuck-upness. I tried to adopt a positive mindset and began to be super nice to everyone. I even wrote a daily gratitude journal. I racked my brain to write grossly untrue statements like …

…'I'm grateful for a lovely lunch with my work mate Maisie.' Should have read…. 'I'm grateful for resisting the urge to repeatedly stab Maisie (with the knife used to butter the granary roll which accompanies her bowl of low-fat chicken noodle soup – a simple concoction she eats every single day) because she is an exceptionally bland person who consistently talks about her dog Pitta like I give an actual fuck.'

'I'm grateful for having a really positive day.' Should have read…. 'I'm grateful for making it through the day, with less frequent thoughts of suicide and no alcohol and/or drug use.' This obviously didn't happen. I cannot go a day without some sort of abuse to my body.

'I'm grateful Mother rang to 'check in' and invite me to hers for Sunday Lunch.' Should have read…. 'I'm grateful Mother rang to nose in on my personal life, then invite me to hers for Sunday lunch so she can check how hungover I am from the night before and say bitch-bite little comments about how I constantly try to ruin my life…and of course hers.'

With a more positive, albeit forced, mindset I purposefully spent more time with my Mother and 'friends' in an attempt to form real connections with people. I tried harder at work and imagined that I could have some kind of exciting future working in administration. Could I become the next Senior Administrator? The next Office Manager? The next Chief Exec? Make my way up to the highest rung in administration insipidity.

But here's what happened. My hard work got me promoted to a new team, and I began to 'date' my manager, Keith. I obviously never wanted to 'date' someone called Keith. Well, I thought we were dating, but what was happening and has occurred ever since is the following shit-fest: Keith takes me out for drinks until I'm absolutely hammered and require a shag. He never mentioned his wife and two children. I found out the truth a few weeks into working there. I confronted him. The poor blighter had a real sob story - he married young, she got pregnant, she didn't understand him. Clichés to the death. I regretfully confess that I longed for him to leave his family and be with me.

It soon came to my attention that I wasn't his only mistress. Urgh as if I was a mistress. Eight months ago, Keith moved in with the luckiest mistress of them all, Nina. He got a quick divorce and then got engaged to said lady. Rejection, even if it is from someone who is an absolute massive arsehole, is still rejection. You feel second best, or should I say third or fourth best...maybe even further down the line, who knows. I wanted to be Nina: to be worthy enough for him to leave his wife and children.

One night I got drunk and messaged Keith asking what he was playing at by marrying Nina when he'd been 'seeing' me. I'd deleted his number a few weeks before, but there's always a way to find a deleted number isn't there! His reply went something like this: 'you're an amazing person Amber, but Nina is the love of my life. I hope you find someone. I always enjoyed your company.'

Enjoyed. Past tense. Dead. Worms nibble. Spider's bite.

That night I slit my wrists. I just didn't know what to do about it.

The universe and positive energy thing never worked out well for me. Keith had a nice time though. The universe loves that bastard.

Here comes the real laugh-out-loud part of the story ...my self-esteem is so low I still sleep with him. I'm hooked on Keith:

what can I say, I have an addictive personality. I need affection, however temporary. I tell myself it's some sort of female empowerment, that I'm using him for a quick orgasm, to be fair he is good in bed. He has light, quick fingers and a pleasant penis. However, he says off-putting things mid-coitus like, 'I wish Nina could blow me like you', 'I wish Nina had a tight pussy like you.' It's so disrespectful. Imagine your partner speaking about you like that, whilst screwing their mistress. It's hammer-to-the-nuts bad.

About a month after I was released from 'hospital' (for the whole slitting of the wrists thing) I slept with Keith again. He tied me up and started to lick the scars on my wrists: 'did you do that because of me you horny girl?' Then he went down on me. What a douchebag. I am too. For letting him eat out my vagina and heart.

I can't go to work tomorrow. I can't face them all. I will phone Keith in the morning and say I am unwell and will be off work for at least a week. Keith won't say anything. He's scared I can damage his reputation and marriage. That I could blurt out loudly in the Any Other Business section of the Monday team meeting: 'I just want to add: … Keith fucks my pussy to bits on the reg.'

Tomorrow morning I will phone the doctors for a sick note. I will then meet Mother on my dinner hour as we do every Monday – she must not discover I am on the sick as this will make her displeased and irritable. Over lunch I will be charming and polite and she will look at me with pride and love. It will be a delightful time. Mother will thank the lord the condom split that grim night thirty-four years ago. She will then go to the bank and transfer money into my account for my trip to New York.

That's right I will go to New York. Where else will I find Holden? Where else will I be happy in the rye?

Mother and I always eat at an Italian restaurant near where I work. The lunch-hour weekly get together is a great idea of mine: it means I have about forty-five minutes to spend with her per week. A short, sharp shock: like electroconvulsive therapy but with the adverse effect.

I wait for Mother outside. I hope we don't run into anyone from work - as they could expose me to both Mother and management. I can see them all scrabbling over each other, yanking at ponytails and aggressively seizing knicker elastic to be first into the manager's office. They will tell on me: 'well she was well enough to eat salmon tagliatelle, so I don't see why she's not well enough to come into work.' You know what office types are like – bored and lacking in empathy, lacking in everything, except paper. God bless the papyrus plant- their saviour and yet their enemy. Damn those paper cuts, that itchy scratchy stimulating tease.

Of course, management aka Keith will do nothing about it (because of potential penis-into-pussy blackmail) so they would be wasting their filing-and-answering-telephones energy. But if Mother finds out I am off work 'ill' she will be furious. She believes that you go to work no matter how dead you are. And you see I'm not fucking my mother, so I can't blackmail her.

Mother arrives seven minutes late, laden with shopping bags.

'Hello,' she says half-arsed, 'there was a queue in Marks and Spencer's because of this stupid woman returning something. She was wearing an awful red beret and had chipped black nail polish. The whole thing was awful.'

When Mother and I meet we never kiss or hug, it's always a simple hello followed by some sort of complaint. Hugs and kisses are saved for birthdays and Christmases, maybe even for an unexpected family death or exceptionally bad news, but even then, it is forced and rigid. A hand on the shoulder. Lips that barely skim the cheek. Limbs that want to escape. Eyes full of hostility. Thoughts that can never be verbalized.

Mother is sixty-three and attractive in a broom-like way:

tall with shoulder length blonde hair, always tanned and well put together - makeup, polished high-heels, perfume, expensive spotless clothes, acrylic nails. She looks business-like, professional, even when casually shopping at Marks and Spencer's. Hell she'd look like an upper-class tart if she was shopping at Poundland – not that she would ever bring herself to shop at a discounted goods store.

Mother was born in Durham and tries to hide her strong Northern twang with a fake accent which she assumes sounds posh. She sounds peculiar: like two people in one body. Imagine it's the early twentieth century and the Lady of Durham Manor is having sex with the scullery maid- but they're both very talkative and keep cutting into each other's sentences mid-scissor. Well, that's what she sounds like. Hope you enjoy the visual more than the audio.

Mother was the manager of a local hotel – she began as the hotel receptionist and worked her way up. This has given her a fierce superiority complex. You see she started from nothing and 'had no choice but to work when that tosser left us.' A phrase she manages to get into every conversation with every person she's met since 'that tosser left us.' After my last suicide attempt (now second from last) Mother left work to look after me. She was due to retire in ten months, but this way she could leave earlier than planned, make me feel bad about it, and evoke pity from others. Win. Win.

'Have you been waiting long?' she asks.

'I just got here a minute ago,' I reply.

Mother walks inside, bored of the fact I am replying. She asks for two seats, and we follow the waiter. We sit down. I hate to state the obvious, but that's what we did.

'Two iced waters,' she says to the waiter, 'so how's work?' She asks this without a pause. For a second the waiter looks confused. He opens his mouth slightly as if about to embark on a derisive review of the hospitality industry and the mistreatment he has faced- the long hours and poor pay - but then realises Mother is addressing me and carries on in his servitude.

'Great,' I reply.

Mother nods and examines the menu. She believes my job inferior to my once-upon-a-time-ago potential. She is not proud of me. She wanted me to be a lawyer or some other awful profession she could show off to her friends about. She pretends to them that I have a senior position in the office. To be fair, I am senior cocksucker.

'You look healthy, have you been eating well?' she asks looking at the menu. Then realising her comment (I had an eating disorder as a teenager) she looks at me with a blush of embarrassment in her cheeks, she backtracks and adds: 'healthy slim not healthy fat.'

'Just the usual.'

'Have you been going to the gym?' she asks.

'I try.'

'The doctor told you to go at least three times a week, for the endorphins to help your mental problems. I'll go with you if you want, if I can fit it in.'

Since retirement Mother has joined lots of groups – art for seniors, yoga, pottery, horse riding, a walking group, a luncheon group, night courses at the local College studying French for Conversations and Beginners Acrylic Nails (why don't they merge the two and learn French over nails? – 'J'ai demande des bords arrondis, stupide salope) ' Mother also volunteers at a snobby charity shop in Yarm, just so she can philanthropically nose out of the window to see if she knows anyway walking past. She can then usher them in to chat and complain about her life 'since that tosser left us.' She will try to avoid talking about me. If a friend asks how I am, she will merely swat away an imaginary fly and reply 'Amber's, Amber you know.' They will nod, perhaps let out a nervous little titter/giggle, but dare not ask anything further.

'No it's ok. I will go to the gym more, I've just been busy lately,' I reply.

'Oh, what have you been up to?' Mother glares at me and raises her right eyebrow, Vivien Leigh style – probably practised to perfection in the mirror to be like her bitch-twin Scarlet O'Hara.

'Just work and stuff.'

'Got yourself a nice man yet?' she asks.

The waiter comes over and she orders two Chicken Caesar salads. I really don't fancy a garlic-y chicken-y mayonnaise-y concoction but have not been given a choice. What's good for the gander is good for the gosling.

'You do still like Chicken Caesar?' she asks as the waiter walks off. Before I can reply she continues, 'so, do you have a gentleman friend?'

'No.'

'Miss Independent,' she says, trying to put a positive slant on a dire situation, 'you get that from me. I had no choice but to work when that tosser left us. I had to stand on my own two feet and get on with it. I had to pay the mortgage and bills whilst looking after you.'

I nod.

'Your father leaving was the best thing that's ever happened to me,' Mother adds.

I nod.

'It made me realise how strong I am. I don't need a man, what have I always said to you...'

'Always depend on yourself,' I say and nod.

'Absolutely,' she nods. Our meetings are always very noddy. 'I had no choice but to work when that tosser left us. But that push made me realise and reach my full potential. I went from a receptionist to hotel manager in ten years. I bet he couldn't do that.'

I shook my head. You know to shake things up a bit- wah-wah-wah. A sympathetic shake.

'Have you seen him lately?' she asks. Mother MUST know about every interaction between me and dad.

'I saw him last Christmas,' I reply.

'Oh yes,' she interrupts, 'you went there on Boxing Day didn't you. To have festive 'family' buffet whilst I was left alone.' She said the word 'family' in a disgusted tone, like you might use to say the word 'paedophile.'

Dad remarried Lucy twenty-two years ago. It is unknown, but constantly up for investigation by Mother, if he was seeing Lucy whilst married to her. Lucy has a daughter, Esther, who is a year younger than me, she is a nurse and lives in Australia with her husband and two children. Perfect people always have two children. Lucy and Dad have a son together, Charlie, he is fifteen and has autism. I adore him, but we rarely see each other.

'I went to see Charlie, I felt sorry for him because Esther and everyone couldn't get back for Christmas,' I reply.

'She probably didn't want to spend time with them: two bastards and their ludicrous son,' Mother scoffs.

Mother is cruel and unfair. I often want to slap her very hard. Or worse.

'Dad phoned me about a month ago,' I confess.

'What did he want?' she snorts like a hungry pig with an apple dangling in front of its snout.

'Just asking how I was,' I reply.

'He didn't care less when you were on your deathbed in hospital, he was sunning himself in Australia with his new 'family.'' Mother again said the word 'family' in a disgusted tone, like you might use to say the word 'paedophile.'

'He came back early from his holiday,' I say.

'Only because I made him. I told him that his own daughter was seriously mentally disturbed, and it was most likely his fault because he walked out on us, the tosser. I said that whilst he was over there in the scorching heat, not giving a shit, eating barbeque and surfing like a bloody Neighbours extra, his own gravely mentally ill daughter was trying to end her life. What a tosser.'

Our salads arrive. Mother stops and shoves a forkful of food into her mouth. She crunches the croutons with her over sharp teeth whilst lapping white dripping lettuce into her mouth.

'Anyway, let's not talk about him, you know I don't like to speak about him,' she says.

I nod. I eat.

'No dates in the pipeline?' she asks.

'Not that I'm aware of.'

Mother looks at me blankly. Hating I exist. She remembers that I am unfortunately her daughter and snaps back to reality – reality being our true source of pain on this earth.

'You know who I went for coffee with the other day, remember Kendra McLaren, mother to Claire?'

I nod. I went to secondary school with Claire. She was the typical little miss popular: the girl in the cool gang who all the guys fancied. She was also my nemesis in English, which was annoying as she hated reading. Claire didn't give a damn about the beauty of a good book; they were just there to use as a coaster for her Mocha Chocka Latte Bratte. She is the kind of person who meticulously read York Notes and not the primary text. People like this do well in life – yet this very action sums up exactly who they are.

'She's Claire McLaren-Black now. She got married three years ago, a gorgeous ceremony in Italy. Kendra showed me the photos. Claire looked stunning, and her husband, very handsome, tall with dark hair and a buff physique, practically bursting out of his wedding suit. He's a firefighter, I think Kendra said, well anyway, she's just had twins. Claire not Kendra.'

'I saw on Facebook.'

'Facebook,' Mother looks puzzled, 'but I thought you and Claire didn't get on because you're so completely different.'

'We don't. To be honest I hate most of the people on there,' I reply, 'Facebook friends' doesn't mean anything. It's just what you do, add people you hate so you can see their annoying pictures and smug statuses. Then you can make comparisons between their seemingly incredibly happy lives and your own bleak existence. This is why relationships and communication-ships are dying, because everything is a lie. We have become a status, a shared link, a like, an emoji. We will all rot in hell and not know how to have a basic conversation with the demons next to us. We will sit there in silence for all eternity, being licked by the flames and begging Satan for just one peak at Facebook so we can see how many likes and crying face emojis we have received regarding the news of our death, so we can find inner peace for just one second. But Satan refuses because you see this is Hell and He has modernised his torture treatments for the new age. There is no social media in Hell. How we bore Satan.'

Mother looks disturbed. 'Kendra is so happy being a grandma' she quickly changes the subject. She does this if I say anything dark. She's scared my dripping tap of a mouth will become a rushing faucet and all my hate and anger will pour out uncontrollably. 'Claire is Mother to Tony and Tori, isn't that the cutest. Kendra said Claire was glad that she had a girl and a boy so she doesn't have to have any more children and can concentrate on getting back her figure and career. Claire's an English tutor at a private school you know, but Kendra said she'll be head of department soon. Hasn't she done well?'

I nod. Thankful for the chicken in my salad which I chew slowly so I don't have to reply.

'Did she do her degree with you?' Mother asks, 'I'm guessing she studied English too.'

'She went to a university down south.'

'Well she's certainly done well for herself,' Mother continues.

'Well she certainly doesn't deserve it,' I say.

'You get out of life what you put into it, I've always said that to you,' Mother says snootily.

Stick that nose in the air just a tad more Mother and I'll nail it to the fucking wall.

'If I wasn't the way I am, I may have got more out of life,' I reply, 'because I would have been able to put more in. Instead, I'm crippled by my thoughts.'

Mother smiles, 'you're doing well lately Amber.' The term 'well' seems to stick in her throat. She takes a sip of water. 'Your turn will come.'

'Will it?' I ask, 'but what if it doesn't?'

We finish our salads. The waiter clears away the plates.

'Do you want dessert?' Mother asks as the waiter hovers. The waiter looks at me.

'You're both sweet enough,' he flirts with an exaggerated Italian accent. Compliments for tips, what a disgusting exchange. Also, no Italian speaks that Italian. I bet his real name is Bob and he will take our plates into the kitchen and shout in a strong Middlesbrough twang 'Eeya lads get these bloody plates washed.'

'I'm full thanks,' I reply.

'Just the bill,' Mother commands with a dismissive flick of her wrist. 'I'll get this,' she says, pulling out twenties from her purse. 'Same place next week?'

'I won't be here next week,' I reply…wait for it…. 'I'm going to New York.'

'New York!' Mother exclaims, her face squirms. 'When did this happen?'

'Yesterday, it was a last-minute decision.'

'Who are you going with?'

'Just myself.'

'Alone! You can't go to New York alone.'

'I'm thirty-four.'

'It's a dangerous place,' she says, 'very busy, you won't like it. It will do nothing for your mental health. If you want a break, why don't you just go to a spa or something?'

'It's all booked now.'

'I'll come with you,' she says.

'No, I want some me-time. Anyway, you have that charity fundraiser next week.' I reply.

'New York is the last place you want to go with your issues,' Mother says, 'it's horrendously busy, noisy, dirty, criminals, drug pushers, pimps. Oh, it's awful Amber, please don't go.'

'You've never been!'

'I have a TV, I can see what it's like,' Mother exclaims.

'You never know, I might meet someone like me there, 'I reply.

The waiter arrives with the bill. Mother hands over a twenty and tells him to keep the change. As if the one-pound tip is a real life saver.

'New York!' she says sharply. She puts her finger in the air and gives a little nod. This usually meant a small switch has been activated in her brain. 'This is about that book, isn't it? The one your psychologist told me to read. The one you were obsessed with. That awful pointless book about that boy... Harry Crawford.'

'Holden Caulfield.'

'Amber, you said you'd got rid of all your copies,' Mother shakes her head, 'it was part of the agreement so you could be released for Jackie's twenty-first.

Jackie is a second cousin thirty times removed, or some sort of barely related shit. 'What will people think if you're not there' – mother wittered on and on. She said she couldn't lie and say I had the flu or was on holiday, because her eyes would give her away. They always did, apparently. Hilarious. After numerous to and frows - I said I didn't want to eat canapes with wannabe middle-class cunts and that the patients in the mental health hospital were preferable company. Mother sobbed.

I went to Jackie's fucking twenty-first fucking birthday fucking party. But I had to pretend I was well. Destroy the books. Get over Holden. Give up.

'I did get rid of them,' I lie.

'Your psychologist or psychiatrist, whatever they're called nowadays, they told me you were obsessed with meeting Harry in New York and living happily ever after.'

'I'm over all that now,' I lie, 'I've just always wanted to go to New York.'

Mother puts her head in her hands. She sighs. 'You're not ill again are you Amber, tell me the truth?'

'No, how can you think that. I just want a new life experience that's all. I was going to go with Erin, but she can't get time off work, and it's too good of a deal to miss. It's only for a week.'

'I thought you were in tons of debt from when you stupidly ran off to France.'

Interlude about when I stupidly ran off to France

What Mother unkindly refers to, is the time I met a guy online called Holden Leru and we fell in love, so I moved to France to be with him. I later found out that he hadn't even read the book and his name was in fact Jean. He called himself Holden because he was a big fan of the French band with the same name.

I stayed with Holden-Jean for three days. He was attractive but his breathe reeked of mud. He spoke to me in broken English (he was obviously using some sort of translation software when we spoke online) which was annoying as we couldn't have any real conversations – it was just lots of pointing and horrid nervous giggling. Due to my dyed red hair, he would call me 'his leeeetle freckle' because he found the English word 'freckle' funny. I don't even have freckles.

In reality, reality being the true source of all our pain on Earth, I hadn't spoken to Holden-Jean for long on the net. In fact, we only started to converse two weeks before I moved to be with him, but when he impishly wrote: 'come to France and see me leeeetle freckle,' I thought - I bloody will, life is about taking chances and it could turn into the most beautiful of love stories. Afterall, his name was surely a sign.

In bed on our first night, I asked what were his favourite books and movies, to which he replied, 'I do not watch TV or read books, I do life.' This could have been an attractively profound response, but what Jean meant by 'life' was working day-in day-out on a farm. He lived there with his moody family in the middle of nowhere. The farm smelt of the worst kind of pig-shit and garlic. Every evening (all three I was there) we went to the nearby village to play cards and drink wine. I had never been so bored. Even the sex was terrible, and he was French. After six games of being beaten in poker and four unremarkable sexual interactions, I told Holden-Jean that my Auntie was ill, and I had to rush back to England.

I couldn't face going home for all the I-told-you-so's (via Erin as no one else knew I was there) so instead I went to Paris to be all cultural. Paris is an expensive city; so, I stayed in a dive of a bed and breakfast, about twenty miles from the city centre, and tried to avoid hookers and criminals, which were plentiful in every direction.

I travelled daily to visit the museums, galleries and tourist attractions. I ate cheese and bread and drank wine and loitered around the Sienne. I spoke to artists and told them I was a writer and they thought I was cool, and we hung out. It was a truly beautiful and magnificent time.

I'm lying. I didn't travel to the city centre. However, I did stay in a dive of a bed and breakfast on the outskirts of Paris. I laid in bed most days, completely depressed and wanting to die. I only ventured out to the corner shop for bread, cheese and wine, so the cuisine bit is true. I wanted to visit all the attractions and hang out with cool smoking Parisians, but I couldn't move, apart from purchasing the necessities above – specifically the wine.

I didn't converse with artists because I didn't see any. If I had, I wouldn't have spoken to them, because everything seemed so pointless: to talk to strangers about dreams that would never materialise.

A week later and my money had nearly run out. I phoned Erin for assistance both financial and physical. I was too anxious and depressed to consider travelling alone. I needed someone to come and help me. Erin didn't have any money; she was saving up for a holiday to Cyprus with Will, and she couldn't come and get me because she was busy at work. She said I should try and get a job in Paris until I felt better and had made enough cash to come home. Silly cunt. I didn't speak French and I didn't want a job.

I spent another week in bed using my overdraft to pay for the room and buy wine. I was trapped in a disastrous cycle of drinking by night and depressing by day. A Parisian noir life. Bet you can't see me for the cigarette smoke.

One night I had finished a bottle of wine and decided to get another from the shop. Outside the B&B I stumbled with drunken stupidity and dropped my purse on the pavement below. As I picked it up, a miracle occurred, probably the only time something good has happened in my entire life. There in the corner of a nearby doorway was a little bag of white powder. Was it beautiful, delicious cocaine, fallen out of some hooker's cleavage or accidentally dropped from the pocket of a recently stabbed pimp? I went over, looking around to make sure this wasn't a trick and that I wouldn't be raped and robbed mercilessly in a Parisian doorway. Although if this did happen what a great story to tell the grandkids (or psychiatrist/prison guard) about corrupt underground Paris when Grandma was young, wild and free.

No one was around, it was strangely quiet. Unnervingly so. I kept thinking of the scene in Bugsy Malone when that dude is tricked down an empty alleyway thinking he can hear a cry for help, only to get jumped and splurged. Was I to be splurged? Splurged in wonderful Paris?

My motions were slow, cautious. I inspected the bag. There obviously wasn't a label on it saying 'Wonderful Cocaine' so a finger-dab-lick told me it was in fact my ivory princess. I quickly shoved it in my pocket and ran back to my room. Who needed wine when I had my best girl with me!

There wasn't an awful lot, but I managed to make about five small lines. I was then so brilliantly up that I rang Mother and explained the situation, a clean-cut version, and asked her to come and get me. I apologised for leaving without saying a word but that I needed to get away for my mental health. I told her I was staying at a friend's house – a girl called Lottie from College who is now a fashion designer in Paris. I used the lie of Lottie as she is a girl from college, who is indeed a fashion designer in Paris. However, I've never spoken one word to her because she is a stuck-up little bitch who is in desperate need of a slapped or bloodied face. But, if Mother Facebooked searched her, then my lie would appear realistic. I told Mother that I missed home and ... bork .... her, and this had caused severe disabling panic attacks, so I needed her to personally escort me back to good old Middlesbrough.

Mother came for me immediately (within twenty-four hours), but she wasn't happy. I did not let her see where I was staying, but instead got a taxi to drop me at 'dans l'appartement le plus flashy de la ville ' where I waited outside. I told Mother that Lottie had begrudgingly dashed off to fix the shoddy hem of some incompetent apprentice designer – she had a show tomorrow so could not stay for 'au revoir mon bon ami.'

When we got back home, Mother made me set up a debt recovery plan so I could pay her back and slowly but surely get back to 'financial normality.'

My great Parisian love story. Hope you enjoyed it more than I did. Apart from the five free lines of coke that were very delicious.

'I've paid off all my debts,' I lie to Mother.

She shakes her head, 'I think you have more important things to spend your money on than silly trips to New York. That money could go towards a mortgage. Erin will be moving in with Will soon and you can't stay with me forever, you're thirty-four.'

'Realistically Mother, a mortgage is never going to happen on my income.'

'Hopefully you might meet someone soon and then you will have two wages coming in.'

'I can't live off what-if's mother. I might never meet someone.'

Mother's sulk is physically apparent- the folded arms and jutted out lower lip, the aggravated foot. Oh, why can't I just be normal, like good old Claire McLaren now Black. Or like Mother - she never had problems meeting men when she was younger: with her good looks, sense of style, intelligence, wit and bang on mental health.

'When do you go?' she asks.

'Saturday.'

'Where are you flying from?'

'Manchester.'

Mother stands up quickly; clearly furious. 'You better get yourself to work,' she says, 'you can't lose your job as well.'

'As well' as what I'll never know …my mind…my virginity…my

life.

I stand.

'Amber, I think you should seriously reconsider this holiday,' she says sharply.

'And lose all that money?'

'You can try and get it back on the insurance, claim poor mental health, it's not exactly a lie now is it.'

I don't say anything. She grabs her bag and turns to leave.

'I bet you've never even considered holiday insurance,' Mother says under her breathe as she walks out of the restaurant. I follow.

Mother turns to me: 'don't think that if you get stuck over there that I can rescue you like last time. New York is a lot further away than Paris, and I'm living off my pension now. Plus, I'm at a flower gala next week in Cornwall. I have last-minute trips planned for myself too you know.'

'I won't bother you, promise,' I say.

'You'll never understand it Amber, but when you raise a child, you always worry about them, even when they're adults. You can't help yourself, it's like breathing,' Mothers voice breaks as if she is about to cry. She loves me deeply; I've always known that. 'Especially with all your extra issues,' she adds, spoiling any lovely sentiment.

'Will I see you before you go?' she asks collecting herself because she is in public carrying a Marks and Spencer's bag. What would Marks and Spencer's think?

'I don't think I'll have time,' I reply. Not for her to waffle on and try to put me off going to New York.

'Well at least text me when you get there. I know how much you hate talking on the phone.'

'I will.'

'And be careful, keep safe. If anything happens to you...' her voice trails off. Underneath all that cashmere and expensive anti-wrinkle face cream there is a beating human heart.

'I will.'

There is an awkward moment. For a second, I wonder if she is going to hug or kiss me, but she doesn't, she just says goodbye, clears her throat and walks away.

Was this to be our last goodbye?

Before I escape into the rye.

CHAPTER FIVE

I meet Keith at our usual café- a dingy side-street low-cost eatery near Teesside University, mainly frequented by students. Chosen because there is little chance of running into anyone we know. And if we do...well I am merely having a monthly supervision with my manager, over coffee and a generous side order of sleaze.

Keith is there, waiting in the doorway. He kisses me on the cheek. It is such a quick exchange that a passer-by could wonder if it happened, or was it just the lighting, our body angles, perhaps my foot tripped on the step to the entrance, causing our heads to appear close. He quickly ushers me into the café, and we stand in the queue to buy coffees.

'You look well, gorgeous in fact, are you sure you're ill?' Keith laughs: he likes to laugh at his own 'jokes.

'I've brought my doctors note' I reply and hand it to him.

Keith stares down at the large, capitalized, typed letters that dominate the small scrap of paper: STRESS RELATED DEPRESSION AND ANXIETY. TWO WEEKS LEAVE.

Keith waves away his previous comment, 'I was kidding.'

Perhaps he is scared I could sue him for stress related shagging or anxiety brought on by the threat of surprise afternoon anal.

'Cappuccino, right?' he asks.

'Right.'

'You go get us a table and I'll bring them over.' Keith is full of commands as usual.

I find a lousy table – at the back of the café, away from the window – unseen by passers-by. Oh, what a treat, what a treasured experience it would be, if I could ever have coffee or chats with Keith anywhere near a sunbeam.

Keith is all-smiles and flirty time to the attractive young female waitress. The black tears in the coffee carafe mimic my sentiments. I hate him. The way his gingery-blonde chin hair sparkles in the light: a human replica of David from Guess Who. 'Is your character a giant bell end?' 'Is your character a serial adulterer?' 'Does your character give good cunilingus?' Everything about Keith repulses me - the crease on the back of his suit from where he had been sitting, his chubby fingers reaching for the coffee cups, his wedding ring glinting like a blade.

Keith comes over and places our drinks on the table. He sits down. All fucking smiles, fucking smiley smiley smile boy.

'What a day so far,' Keith exhales loudly, 'I had a meeting which took three hours cos this dickhead kept waffling on.' He groans.

'Have I missed much?' I ask, pretending to give a shit, when I very much despise every single person in the office, my job and indeed my life.

'Uhm mm,' Keith moans, thinking. Thinking is hard for him as he lives in the present. But not in a cool Eckhart Tole kind of way. 'Not much. Lyndsey spilt coffee on her laptop and was swearing her head off. And Nat is off work with the flu. So, including you, we're two down.' Keith sips his coffee, 'so when will you be back?'

'I have a sick note for this week and next,' I reply.

Keith removes the note from the top pocket of his blazer. It is now crumpled. He examines it. 'Stress induced depression and anxiety,' he reads slowly. He puts the note back in his blazer pocket, 'so what brought this on?'

I shrug.

'I know you've struggled in the past with your mental health, but the last month or so you've seemed happier. There was talk in the office that you were dating someone.'

'That's not true,' I say and lie, not knowing why I feel the need to protect Keith's feelings. If he has any.

'Emma said he saw you on Friday night, walking down

Linthorpe Road with some guy.'

'He was a friend.'

I sip my cappuccino. I use a serviette to wipe away the white froth moustache that may have formed on my upper lip.

Hello there, I am the white froth wiped onto the paper serviette. Twenty minutes ago, I was happy: an icy cup of milk left overnight in the fridge. Such is life. I am the froth of being and see and hear all. This pale gherkin of a guy has feelings for this soul-pinata of a girl, but he is too afraid, too consumed by his own ego, to ever recognise it. He isn't brave enough to embrace uncertainty or the 'other.'

Keith will always be miserable, constantly after someone or something bigger and better. Amber will one day be happy with a unique and blinding love that she very much deserves.

We will meet again dear reader, but now I must dissolve and dampen this paper. I will end up in the bin and then the sea from which I will appear as foam left in the wrinkles of the ever-moving tide. Ciao.

'Emma said you looked really pissed off,' Keith continues.

'The guy had never heard of J.D Salinger,' I reply.

'Who...the footballer player?' Keith asks shocked.

I groan.

'I didn't know you were into football,' Keith continues.

'It was just a boring night, so I went home.'

'You're never bored with me,' he grins mischievously and squeezes my leg under the table.

'Don't,' I push his hand away.

'Are you sure I can't make you feel better?' Keith looks at me in a smarmy fashion.

'No I don't think you can Keith,' I reply curtly.

'I have an hour spare this afternoon if you change your mind... and I seriously recommend you do.'

'Doesn't your wife shag you?' I blurt out.

Keith looks around nervously. Not knowing anyone in the café, he relaxes and whispers in a trying-to-be-seductive fashion, 'not like you do, you're the best.'

'Wow thank you; my parents would be so proud.'

'Amber, you've been weird with me lately. Snide remarks all the time. I don't know what I've done,' Keith says, pulling a what-the-fuck face.

I look at him blankly, 'you have a wife, Keith. Another wife.'

'Did you want me to marry you?' he laughs. Keith's ego is ridiculous. He undoubtedly thinks I am lying and imagines I go into wedding shops and try on silk and lace meringue-like dresses with him in mind.

'Of course not,' I reply.

Do I secretly want to marry Keith? I don't think so. I really don't think so. But who can ever be sure? Even if an obscene creature like Ian Brady or Ted Bundy asked you to be their wife, you would say yes, just so you didn't spoil a beautiful moment and to relish in that warm feeling of being needed and loved. Then at least you can say that you were engaged, that you were wanted forever. Even if just for a brief time, before you call it off, because you couldn't marry someone who slaughters women and children. Not that Keith does that. To my knowledge. He just cuts up your emotions, your self-esteem, your life.

'You're disrespecting your wife,' I continue.

Keith laughs, 'you know I have enough to go around.'

'Do you love her?' I ask.

'Yeah, of course,' he replies with little passion.

'Because if you truly love someone,' I continue, 'like marry-them-love-them, then you wouldn't consider hurting that person. You wouldn't want to touch anyone else because you've found your slice of perfect. You've got everything you need. That's your best friend and you would never spoil that.'

'I do love her. I married her, didn't I? Keith's voice rises, he puts his coffee cup down with a tad more force. 'What would you know Amber, you've never been married? I've never even known you to be in a relationship. You have no idea what it's like, how hard it is.'

'I know what love should feel like' I say slowly, 'and that if I ended up marrying a man like you, I would kill him.'

'Thanks,' Keith laughs, thinking it a joke.

'My husband, partner, whatever, will be a thousand times better than you,' I reply, 'he will treasure me for who I am, not just something to put his dick in to.'

Keith pulls a smirk-smug-bastard face and scoffs, 'you need to go and get yourself a proper boyfriend. See how treasured you feel then.'

I stand up, 'and you dear sir should go and FUCK yourself.'

I want to dramatically throw the cappuccino in his face, but only remnants are left. So only a little glob of froth would shuffle out slowly and it would be an embarrassing disappointment. Like my relationships and my life. Instead, I stomp out of the café. My heels clang loudly like guns. I can say and do as I please to Keith: after all I suck his dick. Used to suck his dick. Past tense. I'm not sucking anything of his ever again.

I go holiday shopping and buy all sorts of wonderful and unnecessary things. The vain hope - the pressure on that poor plastic wafer, to give us unity and joy via products and treats. Irrespective of the carrier bags next to my bed and receipts that display the contrary - I am still dead inside. Despite having now obtained: a leopard-print playsuit, a vintage lilac floral dress, a black tassel and stud covered large handbag, two pairs of black tights, a faux-suedette pair of cowboy boots, dangly crucifix earrings, mascara, nude lipstick and a pack of sanitary towels - nothing has changed. Apart from having fallen into the void of consumerism.

The items can be taken back. The Angel of Refunds: how you listen to our sins and graciously forgive us. This way I had partaken in only half the crime. Materialistic bulimia.

Exhausted - I drink coffee and eat donuts in bed. I flick threw a shitty girl's magazine that Erin has left in the kitchen.

It is obscenely boring and pointless. I care so very little about this season's 'must have' foundation and the vigorous and time-consuming exercise routine of Kim Kardashian - that I fall to sleep.

I have a dream that I've had numerous times before. I am in public and desperately need the toilet, but there is nowhere to go. I must defecate in front of people. Right then and there. Skirt up, knickers down. Out it pours, tons of the stuff. Strangers all look at the pile on the floor and the brown gunge running down my legs. They don't say anything and neither do I. It's a completely shame free encounter for everyone involved.

' Oh, Freud what does it mean?'

'Amber it meanz you envy da penis,' Freud chews on his cigar. His beard smells of ancient tobacco fumes and excrement from the words that constantly flow from his misogynistic mouth.

'What the fuck Freud, no I don't.'

'De excrement is your jealousy flowing out, the people represent the penis you want to obtain.' Chew. Chew.

'Absolutely not.'

'Oh Amber, Amber, Amber.... Amber.... AMBER.'

Erin shakes me awake. 'Amber, sorry to wake you. I just got in from work and need to do my washing, but yours is still in the machine. Do you mind emptying it?'

I am incredibly groggy and hate her. She spoilt my dialogue with Freud for absolutely nothing of importance, for damp clothes, and just when I was about to verbally annihilate him.

'Just take it out and leave it on the side,' I reply.

'Ok,' Erin turns to leave, but then unfortunately changes her mind and continues to look at me and talk - 'have you been in bed all day, again?' Did she really have to add... 'again'?

'No, I went for lunch with Mother, then met Keith to give him my sick note and then I went shopping.'

'What did that cretin have to say?'

'Which one?'

Erin stares at me blankly. She is not in the mood for humour.

'Nothing really, I only met Keith to give him my sick note and then I left.'

'You guys didn't... you-know?' Erin hardly ever says the word 'sex'.

'Absolutely not. I told you never again.'

Erin seems surprised and smiles. 'You've done so well the last few months.'

Interlude about how I havent done so well the last few months

In reality, I said it before and I'll say it again, reality being the true source of all our pain on Earth, I haven't done well the last few months. I slept with Keith about five weeks ago. I was really drunk so it doesn't technically count. However, when I woke up the next morning, hungover and naked, my right thigh sticky with sperm that had trickled down from laying on my side, I looked over at him and realised he was an insanely horrible bastard. I watched his chest rise and fall. Each inhale seemed a proud declaration, 'I'm fantastic.' Each exhale a reinforcement of his sexual competency, 'I'm the best lay.' I wished his chest would stop moving. That he would stop breathing. That he would die.

'I'm going now, forever,' I said as I put on my clothes.

Keith was asleep and didn't care. If he was awake, he wouldn't have cared.

I took the scissors to my thighs when I got home. I just didn't know what to do about it.

'I'm going back to sleep, I'm really tired,' I say to Erin because my whole body feels like lead and her personality is lead.

'Ok,' she replies, 'how's your mother?'

'Same old. She had a fit when I told her I'm going to New York.'

'Why did you tell her that?' Erin sniggers.

'Because I am going. On Saturday, for a week.'

'You can't be serious,' Erin replies.

'Deadly.'

'But Amber,' she sighs and touches her forehead as if I am causing a headache or breakdown. 'When you're having a bad day, you can't even get out of bed. What if you get ill in New York, you haven't exactly been well lately? You'll be better off here where people can keep an eye on you.'

'I've already booked it.'

'Well couldn't you defer it until you're feeling a bit better?'

'No I'm going. I want to go.'

Erin shakes her head. 'Well, you know best Amber.'

I hate when Erin says this, and she says it a lot. Of course, I know best, who's better at knowing me, than me. I don't reply. She walks out of my room. Not giving any sort of shit about what she thinks, I go back to sleep.

I wake up at 11.32pm. I am safe to venture downstairs because Erin will be in bed. She goes to bed each night at 10.30pm, to fall asleep by 11pm, so she is fresh and rejuvenated when she wakes for work at 7am.

I am hungry and decide on a teenage feast: for the mouth – a crisp butty, and for the eyes - My So-Called Life. I enjoy teen dramas, despite hating my teenage years. To fondly reminisce about the romance of youth. That wonderful feeling of having your whole life in front of you. Of thinking that you can do whatever and be whoever you want to be. The excitement of not knowing, of nothing being set. Of having dreams that you know will materialise because you're special, and your life will be different to the people around you.

But life fucked me over. My mental health fucked me over. Nothing good could ever happen. It couldn't happen. My mind wouldn't let it. Welcome to the future: where dreams go to die. A reprise.

I text Jen: 'I'm rly sorry about the other night, I was out of order. I'm going to NYC on Sat, but we should catch up when I'm back. Love you xxx.'

I did love Jen. She was in my life at a time when I was happy. My drinking partner, my dancing wife, my sharer of clothes.

Jen replies straight away. 'Have fun. I'll see you sometime when you get back xx.'

Sometime. Sometime. Never time.

I wonder what Jen thinks of me now. In her adulting life does she look at me with total pity? The girl from college who never moved on. Who had so much potential but did nothing with it. The girl who insisted on being sad. On constantly breaking. On carrying pain around like a precious souvenir. Or is she resentful? Jealous that I am still single, without any real responsibilities and spend my leisure time drinking to oblivion and dancing with strangers? Does she wish she could be me, even for a night? Or is she in such a state of complete contentment – the good house, the good job, the good soon-to-be husband - that I disgust her? The fact that I'm all those 'steps' behind her. A glimpse of a past that she tries to forget.

It's closing time.

The lights go on in the club. I stand there squinting. Mascara gloop in the corner of my eyes. Lipstick smeared by the reckless slugging of shots. Hair sweating and messed. For a second, no one in the club moves. No one wants the fun to be over. Surely it can't be the end of the night. But it is.

It's closing time.

Everyone sobers up a little. They remember their real lives that must continue tomorrow. They put their drinks down and leave the club. But I don't go. The night can't be over. The club can't close so abruptly, so harsh and uncaring, without warning. I smuggle the bottle of lager under my dress and confidently but consciously saunter past the bouncers. They cannot see my stolen goods. They cannot confiscate my booze and waste my three pound and ninety-nine pence. I will bring the bottle out with me. It can say hello to the night. My chaperone so I am not alone.

It's closing time.

I stand outside hoping that THAT one person will come over to me, will save me. Perhaps a guy/girl will take an interest and we will go home together. Or the best friend I've always wanted will come over and we will talk until the sun rises. But nothing happens.

It's closing time.

Everyone gets in their taxis home, laughing with friends. As time moves forward the club's lights dim. The shutters are pulled down. The nightclub staff get in their cars and drive away. Everything is closed. Everything has finished. Fun has ended.

It's closing time.

The last few stragglers jump in their taxis. As the last vehicle moves away, a girl looks back at me wondering why I am still there alone. Surely, I am waiting for a friend, boyfriend or parent to pick me up. She looks me right in the eyes for a long intense moment, but then gets distracted by life.

Jen is that girl in the taxi. I am the girl alone in the night with an empty bottle in her hand. You see, I wasn't prepared to move on. I wasn't ready to leave and...

It's closing time.

My phone vibrates loudly. It is daytime. I am shocked out of sleep so abruptly that I answer without looking at who is calling.

'Hello.'

'Amber?

'Yes.'

'Hello this is Dr Johnson. Is this a good time to speak?'

'Yeah, I guess,' I reply, 'you just woke me up.'

'Up?' It's the afternoon.' I ignore the tone of disappointment and disbelief. 'Are you having sleep problems again?'

'No.'

I didn't want to tell her that only two months ago I had

such crippling insomnia that I thought I was losing my mind. Insomnia is like being dead, maybe worse. You view the world through a haze. It is like watching a mundane film whilst someone is blowing cigarette smoke in your face. Everything is blurry and stings. Like crying on the edge of some crazy cliff.

'Are you ok?' she asks.

'Yes.'

Dr Johnson sighs, 'Amber, I had your mother on the phone this morning, I gave her my number the last time I saw you in the event you felt...unwell again.'

'Yes.'

'She thinks you're struggling and wondered if we could perhaps meet for a session.... a catch-up, rather than a session.'

'But last time we met Dr Johnson,' I reply, fucked off , 'you said you couldn't help me anymore, that I must learn to help myself.'

'I didn't quite say that Amber,' Dr Johnson tries to hide the irritation in her voice with a professional syrupy tone. 'I said that you don't seem to want to change your behaviour. That you were stopping yourself from leading the life you could lead and that I couldn't help you unless you were willing to change. Remember we discussed reaching your full potential and trying to get over your irrational thoughts and delusions.'

'Mmmm.'

Delusional. Irrational. Impulsive. Depressed. Manic. Anxious. Paranoid. Disorder. Compulsive. Freak. Lunatic. Flake. Oddball. Schizo. Crazy. Kooky.   Nutjob. Loon. Cuckoo. Psycho. Mad. Insane. Deranged. Bonkers. Demented. Wacky. Lunatic. Unbalanced. Unhinged. Unstable. So 'un' it's scary.

'What are you thinking Amber? Mmmm isn't really an answer.'

'I don't know why Mother would contact you. I met her for lunch yesterday and everything was fine, my behaviour was spot on.'

'She said you've seemed well lately. But she believes that you're going to New York because of Holden.'

'Mmmm.'

'What are your thoughts on this Amber?' Dr Johnson asks.

'I don't see why I can't go on a holiday without everyone going berserk. People go on holiday - why shouldn't I?'

'Because it's New York Amber, remember what you used to say about meeting Holden there and living happily ever after?'

'Mmmm.'

'Amber, I'm getting the impression you don't want to talk to me. I'm trying to help you. I'm not an enemy.'

'I understand, but I'm just annoyed at all this labelling and paranoia. I'm trying to live my life by going on holiday, like most people do.'

'It's New York Amber,' Dr Johnson says curtly.

'I've always wanted to go.'

'I'm not saying you shouldn't go on holiday, in fact I think it's a great idea, just not there. I strongly believe this isn't a positive step in your recovery. Can you remember when I asked you to keep a thought journal, and every time you had an irrational thought, write it down, and then underneath try to rationalise it and address your behaviour. And you wrote the words Holden and Amber in New York Forever IDST, repeatedly... for ten pages.'

I laugh internally. At the time I had just watched The Shining and thought the above was a great pastiche. I was also gravely mentally ill. What you're seeing now is nothing folks!

'I was unwell then Dr Johnson,' I reply, 'I really was. I'm much better now.'

'Your Mother said she is proud of how well you were doing,' Dr Johnson says.

Mother forcing herself to say she is 'proud' of me, makes me shiver. An electric drill tickling at my core. I was everything she never wanted her daughter to be - plain, single, unsuccessful and an effort to communicate with.

'Your Mother confessed that she's getting tired Amber,' Dr Johnson continues, 'she doesn't know how to help you anymore... which is why she rang me.'

Mother always turns everything around to being about her. Her pain. Her struggle. I don't know if you're aware, but she had no choice but to work when that tosser left us.

'I am doing well,' I lie.

'Well, if you need me Amber, I'm a phone-call away. Please reconsider your decision to go to New York. I'm scared it will significantly set you back.'

'Ok thanks doctor,' I reply and hang up.

'If only you could just hang up on life' I say internally. I cannot melodramatically blurt this out as there is no one to hear me. Except my bedroom furniture - which don't hate me as much as the walls, but there is anger there, resentment.

I go downstairs into the kitchen. The kitchen is always happy to see me. I provide a bit of excitement from the usual dreariness of Erin, who does every kitchen chore meticulously and with little fun. When I do housework, I sing along to Bikini Kill and drink wine. Erin, however, has her phone on loudspeaker, talking to whoever is free to listen, and boring the kitchen with her mundanity. Cooking the tea whilst telling her mother about her walk to work. Putting in washing whilst telling Will what she'd eaten that day. Washing the pots whilst discussing soap storylines with her sister. Coincidentally – if I had to describe Erin as a household chore - I would choose the words – Washing. The. Pots. And I would say these words slowly and purposefully.

Erin has left a note on the fridge: 'gone 2 Whitby with Will, ring if need anything xxx.'

I immediately grab my mobile and ring her- 'Erin I need something. I don't know what I need, but I do.'

I don't really do this. It would be ridiculous and inappropriate. Given the circumstances. The circumstances being that Erin is furious with me and trying to have a nice day out to escape my insanity.

Whitby. What a beautiful and lovely place for Erin to go on her day off work. How happy she must be to escape from me via fish and fresh sea air. Go choke on a fish bone bitch. Finding a fish bone is the kind of catastrophe that would ruin Erin's day: I will ask 'have you had a nice day?' And she will say 'it was ok, until I found a bone in my cod.' She will expect sympathy which

I would find impossible to give. Our ideas of a bad day are so very different. She will ask how my day has been, just to be polite, and I will shrug and say, 'it was ok, until I found a hole in my soul.' She will grow quiet, and the conversation will end.

The day is luxuriously warm, so I sit in the garden. It is an uncomplicated green rectangle. We grew flowerbeds one year, but they died because we didn't care enough. We had hanging baskets outside the back door one year, but they died because we didn't care enough. Will mows the lawn for us every now and then, when the grass becomes knee high, because we don't care enough. I unfold the sun chair – it is old and shabby, borrowed from Erin's Grandad's garage, probably covered in spider AIDs, but we don't get new ones, because we don't care enough.

I laze back and take large sips of Erin's fruity ciders that will never get me drunk. A lame choice but I'd ran out of alcohol. I desperately want to escape. I can't afford coke – what with the cost of my holiday and the unnecessary stuff I'd bought yesterday. I could ring Keith and blackmail him, demand lots of money or I'd tell his wife he's been banging my tuppence off. But he'd tell her what – that a mentally ill girl from work who he'd slept with a few times 'couldn't get over him' and now wanted money for drugs. His word against mine. Men always seem to win in these situations. They are always believed and have the very best of excuses. I could go into my overdraft, live in the now and not care. To slip into the void of that delicious chemical taste which numbs my nose and mind and opens me up like an intricate piece of origami art.

Many writers have demons: Hunter S Thompson, Aldous Huxley, Tennessee Williams to name but a few. I will never create my Brave New World. My thoughts and addictions won't shut off and give me a chance. Am I too ill to create? My mind once crammed with ideas is now fucked and fuelled by vices and regret. Why did I get that office job and just give up? Why did I roll over and die? I never had to drink to excess and do drugs before I started a fulltime 'normal' job - when I had a purpose, a dream, something to look forward to. I should have told

Mother to go fuck herself and embraced who I really was. When did a steady pay check become more important than dreams, mundanity a plague of our time, the answers to happiness being social media likes and fake orgasms with strangers?

This could have been my life:

Cosmopolitan and ambitious Amber Elizabeth Grant lives the arty life of dreams as a writer in New York with her gorgeous beau. Amber, with nothing in her pocket but hope, took the chance and moved to New York where she worked her way up at 'Culture Vulture' magazine to become one of the greatest art journalists of our time. She has won international awards with her cutting, frank and funny insights into the art world. She has recently published her first book of poems, which has received critical acclaim and now she is writing her first screenplay with the help of her handsome writer fiancé. Recently engaged they are already planning their wedding and I'm sure it's only a matter of time before we hear the pitter patter of tiny artistic feet.

Mother would boast to her friends about her amazingly talented daughter. Dad would say he knew I was a special little genius when at the age of six I wrote this poem in his birthday card:

I love my daddy
He is not baddy
He hugs when I'm saddy
I love my daddy.

My parents would not consider my birth a mistake. They would not hate themselves for creating a nightmare-like combination of their genes.

My phone vibrates – it is Dad. Scary coincidence or the universe conspiring? Perhaps if I think about a darling bag of cocaine and visualise snorting the shit out of it, then the universe will deliver? My dealer will ring saying he has spare bags left over if I want some for free. Perhaps I need to write a poem about coke to get the universe on my side:

I love my coke
It ain't no joke
Better than a fanny poke
I love my coke.

My phone vibrates again – it is Mr Coke from Cokeland asking if I want free coke.

'Hello,' I answer.

'Hello Amber, how are you?' asks Dad.

'I'm good thanks.'

'I'm ringing cos I just had your mother on the phone, a delight as always.' He pauses, 'she is concerned and whingeing on about you going to New York. I think you should do what you want. I've been a couple of times and it's a fantastic city.'

I can imagine what Mother will say if I relay this conversation to her: 'oh yes, he can jet off to New York whenever he wants with HIS money. I had no choice but to work when that tosser left us, just to make ends meet so you didn't starve. The furthest we could ever afford was a weekend away at the Lake District.' Then she would probably end the conversation in a two-word insult such as 'selfish prick' or 'wanker man' or 'scum bucket.'

Mother talks shit: she received a good divorce pay out and Dad left us the house. We weren't living in a box. Mother didn't have to prostitute her body for a tenner. If she could even get a tenner. She'd probably chew the punters ear off complaining about Dad in between sucks and fucks: 'I had no choice but to work when that tosser left us...' Slurp. Dribble. Gyrate. The punters would not finish but slip Mam a tenner just to shut her up. They would leave the car, alleyway, wall, tree ... whatever glamourous location where illegal fornication occurs, thinking that they'll just bother their wife next time. Yes, sex with the wife was boring and after five kids her hole was as big as a four-by-four tyre, but she did make a smashing steak pie and could get the thickness of the gravy just right and she had good strong working arms to mash the potato to a smooth lump-less perfection. Save your money. Save your guilt. Fuck that wife.

Dad continues: 'in fact I could give you some pointers where to go. Where are you staying?'

'I'll probably just stay in a hostel or something, whatever I can afford,' I reply.

'You don't want to do that; I'll transfer some money. New York can be rough; I don't want to have to worry about you.'

'Ok thank you.'

'Will a grand be enough?'

'Oh my god really!' I shriek, thinking about all the drugs and alcohol I can buy.

'Just think of it as an early Birthday present,' he replies.

'Thank you.' A grand to make up for not spending any quality time with me my entire life.

'Your Mother is worried about you Amber; she said your... y'know... mental state... isn't too good.' Dad uses the term 'mental state' with great duress. As if my issues are a prominent and annoying scab on his knee. Should he pick at it? No. The blood may gush everywhere. He doesn't have a plaster. Nothing to clean it with. It could become infected. It could result in leg amputation. Worst case scenario – death. If he doesn't pick the god damn scab, it may eventually go away, or become fainter and less noticeable. To be honest he'd rather wear trousers forever, even in the bath than address that fucking scab.

'That's ridiculous,' I reply, 'you know she exaggerates for drama and pity.'

'I know Amber' ...Dad sighs again, 'but the other day I had a meeting in town right near your office, so I thought I'd pop in to say hello... and they told me you were off work, sick.'

'I've had a bit of flu, that's all. I didn't tell Mother because you know how she worries.'

'Worried! Your Mother is more than worried about you, after what happened last time. Amber, you must realise that you're the only person she has in her life' Dad sounds agitated, 'with your history she has every reason to be concerned. She said she couldn't take it if you had another…. (He pauses thinking of a tactful word) … episode, (yeah 'episode' will do dad, try to make it sound like I have epilepsy and not that I'm completely bonkers) you know how it affected her when she found you in the bathroom that time. Hell, I thought SHE was going to have a breakdown.'

Interlude about how Mother nearly had a breakdown because I tried to die.

My third from last suicide attempt was over some guy. I can't even recall his name. Isn't that awful. I had been talking to this guy online for a while, he was smart and made me laugh, we set up a date in Newcastle where he lived.

We met in a bar. You can tell if a guy fancies you practically straight away – if they do, they will try and touch you as quickly as possible- even if it's just a hand on the bottom of your back whilst you wait at the bar or a gentle brush-up on the way to the toilet so his cock can slyly skim your goods.

He smiled when he saw me, but the smile slowly began to fade. I wasn't good enough. I didn't live up to my profile pictures. He didn't give me a 'hello' hug or kiss on the cheek. He did not want to touch me. He did not want me to get the wrong idea.

We got a drink and sat at a table. His lack of enthusiasm and conversation made me nervous. I kept saying ridiculous things like: 'wow I love the grey walls in this place.' Grey is my least favourite colour – it's a shit washed-out version of black. I couldn't engage in any kind of dialog that was vaguely intelligent or stimulating. At one point I even commented on the cream shirt he was wearing: 'cream is a great colour – it's like a sad white.' He must have thought I was some sort of colour obsessed freak. In hindsight, the following comment was my finest: 'it's supposed to be drizzling later. I hope not, I hate drizzle. I'd rather we have a pour down and then it clears up and makes everything fresh. Drizzle makes you feel all soggy and

dirty as if someone is constantly spitting on you.' At this remark
he opened his eyes wide and sipped his drink. I said I needed the
toilet. I thought hitting my head against the cubicle door would
do me the world of good.

As I came back from the toilet, I saw him checking his watch.
As I sat down, he made an excuse that there was an emergency
at work. He apologised, but you could tell he didn't really give a
shit. I wanted to say that I hadn't travelled for an hour to have
one gin and tonic and go home. I said he should sack off work
and get drunk with me. He looked at me as if I was a leper. He
said he wasn't a big drinker. He said he would walk me to the
train station. I told him not to bother. It would only prolong
the agony for both of us, but I never said that, instead I smiled
sweetly and said that I hoped he didn't have to work too late on a
Saturday.

On the train journey home, I messaged him saying it was lovely
to finally meet and we should catch up again. It wasn't lovely.
I don't know why I sent the message. I guess I just have good
manners. He read it but didn't reply. I looked on Facebook. Some
of the younger girls from work were doing a pub crawl around
town. I didn't particularly like them, but I didn't hate them,
they were just young, giggly and stupid, the kind that watched
soap operas constantly as if it was research to understand life.
Over lunch they would endlessly talk about the characters as if
their existence really affected them, as if they were part of their
family. They were shocked that I rarely watched TV and gave me
gushing recommendations and regular story line updates as if
the nonsense they spoke about would convince me to watch this
marvel of television/life. Out of politeness they had previously
invited me to what they referred to as a 'cock crawl'. I'm sure you
can imagine what this is – going from bar to bar on the search
for da peen. At the time I refused and internally mocked their
invitation. I would now accept, lacking dignity, stimulated by
those sips of gin, and as I had nothing else to do.

They were in some god-awful bar. The type where girls
don't wear many clothes, and no one knows the real colour

of someone's skin or hair. The type where guys fasten the top button of their shirts and wear pointed shiny shoes. Their mothers had told them the importance of clean shoes: that this would find them a clean wife. Wife hahaha! These lads were after disappointing drunken foreplay leading to disappointing drunken sex. Mothers tear-wet tissues scrub soiled brogues.

I must have been exceptionally drunk AND exceptionally rich that night as I kept buying everyone rounds. Using it as some sort of bonding ritual, after all, everybody loves everybody when they're drunk, even more so if you're the one buying the drinks. I spent nearly three hundred quid. Well, that includes three bags of coke that I kept sneaking off to the toilet to sniff. The girls from work knew I liked a good drink, that was an accolade, a pat on the old muffin top - but a drug user, well they were scum and needed to be shot in rehab pronto before they snatched the purses from the wrinkled hands of old ladies exiting the bank with their fresh unspent pensions.

It was in about bar number six that I got groped by a groper. It was a squeeze of the boob. My left boob if you were having difficulty visualising the incident. I was so shit faced that I didn't care. He wasn't bad looking, so coked with confidence I went over and asked him if that was all he had. He seemed surprised at first but then laughed and stuck his tongue down my throat saying he would show me exactly what he had, all the time kneading my bum as if he was a premium masseuse. He asked if I wanted to go back to his and I said yes.

At his flat, in typical one-night stand fashion, he moved me into every conceivable (and inconceivable) sexual position. Each uncomfortable arrangement lasting approximately twenty seconds, including the obligatory young-guy-raised-on-internet-porn anal. When he was finished, as we women rarely finish, he went to the toilet. I'm guessing to clean his dick. We never used protection. Guys these days never seem to wear or carry condoms, well they certainly never ask if they should slip on the love-glove. Unwanted pregnancy or STI's are far from their minds. It will never happen to them, because they are young and indestructible. He came back in the room with a towel around his waist and said he had phoned me a taxi. He jumped on the bed and buried his face in the pillow. He mumbled that the taxi better be quick because he needed rest as he had footie practise at noon. Romance = dead.

Thirty minutes later, I was sat in bed in my pyjamas. I had a banging headache. I took some paracetamol, drank water and phoned my dealer for more stuff. Mother was snoring in the other room – oblivious.

An hour later and I had sniffed so much white that it burnt the inside of my nostrils. I sat there wired yet utterly devastated: a deadly combination. My comedown tomorrow would be horrific. Why couldn't I just be normal? Go out for a few mature drinks. I hated myself. I was more of a mess than I'd ever been. All the money I'd wasted- I could have saved up to buy a car or gone on a lovely holiday. But no, I spent it the only way I knew how: getting fucked. I needed a spiritual awakening of water, meditation and yoga, early nights and decent men. Tomorrow I would wake up filled with regret and promise to change my ways: I would not do this every weekend, I would not go to work bleary eyed and shattered on Monday, body and mind desperately trying to recover. I would say 'never again,' but by Wednesday I would forget all this and long for the weekend so I could get wrecked again. Then that cycle. Every weekend. Forever. The weekday abstinence leading to weekend debauchery. The let go. The yolo. The fear. Jen was right, it was ok at eighteen – not now.

Then a sort of paralysis came over me, an overbearing dread. I started to sweat and shake. I couldn't go on like this. I was a mess. A mistake. Broken and ashamed. Used and thrown away. I was nothing. I slit my wrists with a razor over the bathroom sink. I laid there on the floor, wanting and ready to die.

Mother said she awoke in the night and knew something was wrong: mother's intuition and all that. She found me. I remember seeing her blurred figure standing over me screaming, shaking me and shouting 'silly girl' again and again.

Then she must have phoned an ambulance.

I woke up the next day in hospital, my wrists covered in bandages. 'You silly girl,' she repeated as soon as I opened my eyes. Then she went on and on about the pain I had caused her and how I could always speak to her if I was having issues. I sincerely wished I hadn't bothered to try and commit suicide, or that I had in fact succeeded, because she then used it as a tool to control my every movement.

Mother 'had to' quit her job to look after me. She couldn't leave the house, couldn't trust me, she had to hide all sharp objects and keep the keys to the windows and doors hidden. I had spoilt her life and she loved it. I was a prisoner for months until my psychiatrist deemed me mentally well and medicated enough to leave the house for short periods of time. However, leaving the house was pointless because Mother kept ringing to ask where I was and how I was every five minutes. That's why I moved in with Erin.

'I'm worried about you Amber,' Dad continues, 'you cause people a lot of stress. We want you to get better. We feel sorry for you.'

I then decided to say something that I had wanted to say my entire life.

'I feel sorry for you and Mother...because you've never tried to get to know me. Not the real me. You don't know that I'm funny, or that I'm kind, or that I'm sensitive and smart. All I've ever been to you is a stranger. You both look at me as if I'm an alien. You have no connection to me. I feel sorry for you both. Why didn't you want to get to know me?'

There is a pause. A gulp.

'That's ridiculous Amber, not know you, you're my daughter,' Dad replies.

'You've never tried to get to know me.'

Silence.

'Anyway,' Dad heavy sighs. That's all I've ever been to him. A heavy sigh. A long exhale. His body pushing me out to make room for oxygen. 'I better go cos I'm picking up Charlie from that club he goes to.' He mumbles goodbye.

I do not feel better, for saying it. What did I expect Dad's response to be? That he would have some sort of epiphany and try and make up for all the years we'd lost. Or an apology for making me feel this way. No, my opinion of our relationship was 'ridiculous.' Our relationship was summed up in the brief silence that lingered before his goodbye. The things that can't be said.

Words lost in the rye.

PART TWO

CHAPTER SIX

Dad emailed to say that the money would be transferred into my bank account in the next 24 hours. He prefers to communicate via email rather than text as he doesn't like texting - he finds the shortening of words, and having to guess what it means, very stressful.

I want prosecco but I cannot be bothered to move or indeed leave the house to buy a much desired and needed bottle. Movement is an over-rated activity. The only alcoholic choice is Erin's juvenile bottles of fruity cider. I will drink them all. She will have little choice but to take yet another one for team Amber Fuck-Up. Go team AFU!

I can imagine Erin skipping to the fridge after some great victory/life event - i.e., a promotion, buying a new house, an actual orgasm. She will shout back to Will 'I'll get us some fruity ciders to celebrate.' But low and behold her tipples of triumph, only to be consumed at such momentous occasions, after all she isn't an animal (remember AMBERMAAAAALLL. Lol) are not there. She will screech and yell to Will 'Amber has drank them all.' She will not know how to channel her anger so she will slam the fridge door or get her own back by throwing my yoghurts in the bin or by calling me a 'silly cow.' Her rage will be very PG-13.

I decide to pack for my holiday: to make real conscious choices about what I need to take, rather than throw everything in the case an hour before I set off, as I usually did. It is a boring and unfulfilling act. All my 'necessities' crammed into a purple and white flowered pull-along case that Mother bought me years ago.

I then order a veggie pizza and read Sylvia Plath by candlelight. Loving life and chuffed that I am practising self-care instead of self-destruction, I have a lovely lavender oil bath. Water: the greatest of purifiers. I lay there in a state of baptismal pleasure. Washing away my old sins, my old life, my old beliefs. I focus on my future, the new me and my exciting holiday. For the first time in ages, I feel positive. I will go on this holiday, and it will change me. I will come back and get a new job; one I don't dread. Helping other people, working in the arts industry, or even just waitressing in a café, anything that doesn't consist of paper people and small talk. I will write again and forget my addictions and old ways of living. I will practise morning meditations and go for daily walks in the local park. I will take up a new hobby: life painting, yoga, aromatherapy. I will make new and wonderful friends who inspire me to be a better person. We will regularly go for lunch at quaint little eateries and discuss books, movies and politics. With a real passion for the art scene, we will hang out at local art galleries, attend gigs, plays and comedy nights. We will go to open mic events and read our poetry, applauding each other loudly without shame. I will grow.

Life always begins to make sense in the bath. I will show everyone that I am capable of happiness. 'I am not incapable of my own distress.' I will visualise success and contentedness and the universe will have little choice but to deliver. I will google positive memes and post them on Facebook and Instagram, so everyone knows that this girl is on the up. After this bath I will turn my life around.

Wearing fresh pyjamas and face serum applied I go downstairs to make a huge glass of water. The new me does not poison their body with alcohol. The new me is present and treats their body like a god damn temple.

As I chop up cucumber for my water, I hear the front door slam.

'Have you had a nice day?' I ask Erin as she comes into the kitchen.

'It was ok,' she replies, but sounds glum. 'Whitby was chocka with people, we went on a Friday thinking it would be quiet, but NO. We couldn't get in our usual fish restaurant because it was full, so we had to go to a different one and they didn't even do homemade tartare sauce, they only had those awful sachets. Then when we came outside after our meal, the sun had disappeared, and it was cloudy and cold. I hadn't taken a jacket because I assumed I wouldn't need one because it's been so hot lately. So, I was miserable, which made Will miserable … so … yeah, what was meant to be a beautiful day turned into a complete disaster.'

I would usually reply with some sarcastic comment. But the new me refrained.

'That's a real shame Erin, you guys deserved a lovely day out.'

Erin fills the kettle with water and switches it on.

'What have you been up to?' she asks.

'I've had a productive day,' I reply. 'I've read and had a nice bath, packed for my holiday. I feel absolutely amazing. I think this holiday is going to be the making of me, y'know.'

'Is that vodka you're drinking?' Erin asks.

'No, I'm all about the water now. I drank a couple of your fruity ciders earlier, but that was before, that was the old me. I feel so happy that I could dance around the house and go into a beautiful field and pick lots of flowers or something. I feel different and positive about everything.'

Erin puts a teabag into her cup. 'That's great Amber,' she heavy sighs as she pours the boiling water. 'But I've seen you like this before, you're on a high. We all know what happens next.'

'No this is different. I feel calm. Last time, yes, you're right, I was erratic and impulsive, but not this time.'

'Amber last time you jogged into town, gave one hundred pounds to a homeless guy, got your septum pierced, which you kept in for all of five hours, and then you spent over six hundred pounds on new clothes and accessories. You then messaged everyone you knew telling them how much you loved them and valued their support through your difficult times.'

'Yes, I know, but I was going through a bad time then. Now I know what I need to do, how to sort my life out.'

'Amber, last time you crashed and burned, and it wasn't nice to see,' Erin slowly stirs the teabag in her cup as if it is my brain, but instead of tea leaves from a bag, she is trying to drain the shit ideas from my mind. 'You wouldn't leave your bed and didn't speak to anyone for eight days, including me. What if that happens when you're in New York. You're not thinking straight.'

'I am.'

Erin flashes a worried patronising look. Just because she didn't get her home-made tartare sauce and should have considered the unpredictability of coastal weather and taken a jacket – doesn't mean she can come in here and burst my bubble by being a complete and utter sow.

'Erin, I think you all want me to be ill so you can make yourselves feel better,' I say calmly, 'you can give me a label and pat me on the head. You've all put me on a spectrum, we're here and Amber's there, so we must be well because she's so ill. You all use me to soothe your own needs and I'm sick of it.'

'Amber, what the fuck are you talking about,' Erin picks up her cup of tea and starts to walk into the lounge. If Erin swears you know she is about to explode. PG-13 to an 18 in five minutes. I sincerely apologise for the foul-mouthed motherfucker. 'After the day I've had,' Erin continues, 'I really can't be bothered with all of this. Just do what you want. Go to New York. Have a break down. I couldn't care less.'

I want to slap her viciously fast and hard across the face. To scream into her blemish free face, 'well lucky you miss perfect fucking mental health.' Erin and her vile simplistic life and cheery smile. What a complete vacuous cunt. How could I ever relate to her? Oh, Erin, I'll show you! And if I do have a breakdown, it will be glorious. I'll dance with the devil and enjoy it you stupid little bitch. One day my demons will become angels. Drizzle that on your fish and chips you ratchet Stradlater whore.

May the best woman truly live.

May the best woman live happily in the rye.

◆ ◆ ◆

The next day I get a taxi to the train station for the 11am train. I hate train stations because they're just full of 'goodbyes' and 'hellos' and not much else.

Erin was out with Will when I left, so I thankfully did not have to do fake pleasantry with that lacklustre whinge of a woman. Go choke on a salad crouton. Break your finger doing yoga. Get bullied in the workplace.

Train journeys make me anxious. I always worry about getting on the wrong train and ending up in Doncaster hating my life. I mean it's never clear if you're getting on the right train, the tannoys are always muffled, and there's never staff around to ask. You have little choice but to ask strangers, but then they look at you as if you're an idiot - 'I mean duh of course it's the train to wherever,' they really want to say, but instead reply with a – 'yes', 'no' or 'don't know' and then rush away. Everyone is always in a tremendous hurry at train stations. Their expressions and tones always convey annoyance. Their replies always fast and flustered. They make me want to throw myself in front of the train, preferably when it is going at a slow but lethal speed. Justification for being such a simpleton and general nuisance to the purposeful traveller.

Then there's always the concern that someone will sit next to you and instigate a conversation. So, you have to immediately slip on your headphones and play with your mobile. You must look both distracted and unsociable. If anyone comes near you for the duration of the journey you must pretend to be exceptionally busy. You must eat a ham sandwich and read about four magazines.

I find my reserved seat, on what I assume is the correct train. I put my suitcase in the above luggage carrier and then my handbag on the neighbouring seat: if I have to move it for an unwelcome stranger, I can act extremely inconvenienced (cold eyes, a smile that can be mistaken for a grimace, a quiet but audible sigh) and this will signify to the stranger that they should not engage in conversation.

I always avoid table seats as they usually appeal to families and people who enjoy socialising. I bore of families with their packed lunches and excessive trips to the toilet. That awful sweet smell of nappy poo that lingers for too long until harassed mammy notices. Card games that always get dropped on the floor.

I read the text that Mother had sent that morning. 'Amber, you must ring me every day, so I don't worry. If you change your mind, we can have a lovely day out to Harrogate and a girly shopping day instead. Love you xxx'

Unless it's shopping which involves the alcohol aisle at a large supermarket, then I'm not interested. I dread days out with Mother because it always consists of clothes shopping. Clothes and criticism. She politely forces me to try on awful clothes that she has picked saying she'll pay for them. If I chose clothes, she never offers to pay, as she purposefully dislikes them. She deems her taste to be superior to mine. Every time I try on clothes, I can feel Mother's eyes glaring at me in the mirror. She always looks me up and down as if seeing me for the first time. All the while bitterly thinking about the daughter she should have had and how this shopping trip should be such a fun mother and daughter bonding experience. But how can she connect with an alien? Why aren't I happy? Why don't we both laugh at funny anecdotes about work and friends and men? Why aren't we the best of pals? Mother has done her best and she is sick of trying. She loves me. She despises me.

Mother will eavesdrop on other mothers and daughters conversing in the changing rooms 'oh mum do you think this looks good'... 'oh darling you look beautiful'... 'I get it from you mummy.' The mother and daughter couple congratulate themselves for their genetic beauty and content lives and lovely floral dresses that fit their toned bodies so seamlessly. David Lloyd memberships well spent on these floating empty vessels. Now to girly afternoon tea so they can nibble (well not too much because it would be a waste of their mother-daughter gym membership) and chat their pretty little mouths off. Back home in time to dish out daddy's beef casserole that has been stewing to perfection all day in the slow cooker. You can't expect mummy to cook after a busy day of spending – daddy understands this, which is why they both love every inch of him so very, very, much.

◆ ◆ ◆

An hour later and I get off the train at York. Surprise! Come on now, as much as I'd love to go, there's no way I could ever afford New York, not with my debts and issues. You really thought? Aww you're too sweet.

I leave the train station, I don't look at anything or anyone, apart from the path below and my phone to use Google maps to find the hotel. I have to concentrate on how to manoeuvre around people with my pull-along suitcase without causing a disturbance. I do not want to be a disturbance.

The cobbled streets of York are busy as usual. A lot of students. Burger-and-pint deals galore. Chinese tourists and street performers. What the fuck am I going to do here for a week?

I go straight to the hotel. Tomend Hotel. It is a cheap hotel by the river. I wanted to get a swanky hotel with a hot tub in my room but decided not to spend all of dad's cash. I picked somewhere that looks a bit scruffy, because it suits who I am. Holden is right, money always ends up making you blue as hell.

I would like to say the hotel smelled like fifty million dead cigars, but it smelt of Febreze and leftover lunch. Roast chicken? I go to the reception desk to pay the rest of the hotel fee and collect my fob key. The usual shit is spoken to me regarding checkout instructions, use of the safety deposit box, and mealtimes. 'Sue' is the kind of person who speaks slowly as if she has a lot of time left in her life. She isn't patronising, but rather the kind of person who believes the rules of the hotel to be very important, so, she has to articulate them in an extremely slow and clear manner. If anyone disobeys these rules Sue can then say with conviction to the hotel manager that she had stated the rules thoroughly and she will know with all her heart that this is the complete truth. I need a piss, so I temporarily despise Sue and her precise articulation.

In the near future there won't be any Sue's. You'll just sign into a computer, and it will print out a list of hotel rules - actually, what am I thinking, we can't waste paper in this environmental Hades- you will have to scan the instructions onto your phone. Instead of a trusty door fob it will probably be one of those awful fingerprint security nuisances. Some shitty company will save £15,000 a year on Sue's wages, but Tesco will enjoy her. Stop. Supermarkets will surely get rid of all human workers. The self-scan service was the start of it - Grandma was right! Human interaction is so twentieth century. Since Covid-19 ordering goods on the internet has been the new norm – this way people can avoid others as much as possible. However, for those who don't like the idea of internet shopping - a typical response from the older generation as they 'can't see the goods' –then supermarkets will open one day a week. Self-scan only of course. Shopping will be a silent activity with no human contact, like a library, but this will replenish and satisfy the soul to a greater extent. Security guards will be robots who run after you with a hammer. I jest.

I go up to my hotel room, I asked for room twelve-twenty-two. My room is small but pleasant in a grubby way. At least there is a TV, which I turn on immediately. I go to the toilet and make a cup of tea using those awful little plastic cartons of milk. I take off my coat and get into bed. It is twelve forty-five in the afternoon.

I stay in bed all day and night watching inane TV. I feel blue as hell. Laying and staring. Thinking and observing. By 9pm I realise I am incredibly depressed. I can't move. I know I have to do something: but my body is fixed to the mattress. With great difficulty I text Mother saying I have arrived safely; you know before she rings the New York police.

'What are you doing on your first day in the Big Apple' Mother text back instantly.

I reply that I am going to see the Statue of Liberty and look around the shops. Mother text back 'fab' and a happy face, so obviously I have done well in my lie and indeed life. Mothers aren't too sharp about that stuff.

I then pull the covers over my head and go to sleep.

When I wake the next morning, I do not feel refreshed. It is ten twenty-one. Doom has entered overnight. All I can think about is dying, but instead of dying I make a cup of tea - as this is how us British deal with any sort of problem or issue. Been burgled – have a cup of tea, lost your wallet – have a cup of tea, gang raped - have a cup of tea, died – surely there will be a cup of tea waiting for you in heaven.

I pull open the curtain and look out of the window. I have a view of the river, but am not moved in the way I usually am by a waterscape. Pubs and bars are packed along the waterfront. There are boats and ducks and people. It looks like a warm but cloudy day. The sun only comes out when it feels like it.

Having had enough visual interaction with the world, I close the curtain and go back to bed. I get the book out of my bag and look at the cover. I remember the first time I read it. I was sixteen. It was straight after what happened, happened. There is always that one 'thing' that changes you. This is mine.

Interlude about the one thing that changed me

That morning, eighteen years ago, I had felt so happy. The start of my school holidays before college…my life ahead bright like a road full of streetlights. I was reading in the garden, listening to music and drinking tonic water as I began to read the book which I had heard so much about. It was the book Mark Chapman was reading when he shot John Lennon.

Everything felt magnificent. Magic was within me. For the last time. Then I got the phone call. I don't like to talk about it, but if you really want to hear about, y'know all that David Copperfield kind of crap, then I'll tell you. Then I never want to talk about it, not ever again. I'll start from the very beginning - as Julie Andrews seems to think that this is the way to go...

The winter before this I was walking to the local shop one Saturday afternoon, getting milk for Mother's constant consumption of tea. Back then I was the kind of girl who went to the shop to buy milk for her mother. It was cold and drizzling outside. En-route, I slipped on some wet leaves and landed harshly on my hands and knees, my hands were grazed and bleeding, my leggings torn.

I heard a voice behind me: 'are you ok?'

There he was. A green parka and scruffy dark blonde hair. My very own Evan Peters. He helped me to my feet and then we stared at each other. Drizzle can make some people look their very best.

'You're bleeding,' he said.

'I know,' I replied.

'You need to wash it,' he said, 'the gravel could get in and it could become infected. You don't want to get infected.'

'I know,' I replied.

'I live around the corner if you want to come and wash it.'

I didn't say that I only lived down the road and that we had a first aid kit.

'I don't want to trouble you,' I said purely because that's how British people reply to any sort of offer of assistance. I did want to trouble him, considerably so.

'No trouble,' he said, 'my mum is away this weekend, so she won't bother us.'

'Well...only if you don't mind?'

'Well, it is raining,' he said.

'Drizzling,' I added.

'Well come on then,' he said. He gestured for me to follow. I walked with him. 'I admire your trust,' he said and giggled, 'I could be a serial killer and have purposefully placed those sodden leaves for you to slip on. I could be Buffalo Bill or Ed Gein. People don't trust anyone these days, it's lovely. I bet you're lovely.'

I laughed.

'Are you unnaturally quiet or unnaturally nervous?' he asked.

'I have anxiety issues,' I replied. I couldn't believe I had just blurted this out to a complete stranger. I guess that was a sign - that I felt completely comfortable around him straight away.

'Oh really, me too, and depression, but I take meds.'

'Me too,' I replied.

'Society is fucked isn't it,' he said.

I smirked and nodded.

We went in his house, it was messy, tons of stuff everywhere.

'Forgive the state,' he said, 'my mum is a hoarder.'

He told me to sit down in any space I could find and then he left the room. He suddenly rushed in excitedly.

'Oh fuck, I forgot to say that my name is Josh.'

He laughed. I laughed.

'I'm Amber.'

He flicked his hand in the air dramatically and gestured to what I assumed was my hair:

'Your hair is wintry fire,

January embers,

My heart burns there too.'

'Ben Hanscom, IT,' I replied, instantly knowing the movie quote.

Josh smiled, 'we're going to get on.'

Josh then went into the kitchen and came back with two cups of tea and a wash basin to fix my hands and knees. He slowly washed off the blood and gravel with a flannel and then sat down next to me. He said he had some 'special' brownies if I wanted them, and I very much did. We ate them with our cuppas.

'You'll want to know all about me won't you,' he said, it wasn't a question.

Josh spent the next hour telling me all about himself. He had moved to Middlesbrough from Leeds seven months ago. His mum had had a mental breakdown after his dad was killed in a motorcycle accident. She began streaking round the streets and pinching stuff from shops, and after a stint in a mental health hospital (in the interim Josh went to live with his aunt in Sheffield) she was so embarrassed by her behaviour that they had to move. Middlesbrough seemed the obvious choice because nobody ever knows anybody who lives in Middlesbrough. Josh was seventeen, an only child, and 'taking time off life' until he figured out his 'calling'. He received benefits which he spent on weed. He liked to read books about philosophy; Nietzsche, Sartre, Descartes and said he would lend them to me. He watched horror films to death. He hated social media and most humans. He had one previous ex-girlfriend, but she turned out to be a fake cunt – his words not mine. His favourite band was The Smiths. His favourite day of the week was Tuesday because it was under rated and more depressing than Monday. He liked to watch documentaries about serial killers. He admired intelligence, integrity and creativity - qualities he felt I had.

Josh asked about me, so I told him that I was leaving school next year to go to college to study A-levels in English Literature, Media Studies and Art. I lived with my mother, who was a psychological drain and that I had a distant relationship with my dad, who I suspected secretly hated me, in fact I think they both did. I had never had a proper boyfriend but had had sex with two guys, but only because I was drunk, and it had seemed the thing to do. I said I wanted to be a writer or a journalist, but that journalism might not be suitable due to my inability to converse with others and the fact that I didn't really give a shit about what other people said or did.

I told him I used to read a lot but hadn't in the last few

months because I was too depressed. That nothing brought me enjoyment anymore except sleep. He said I should never stop reading. I told him I was fifteen, but he didn't care. I told him my favourite time of day was dusk, because anything can happen at dusk – and he agreed that it was the perfect time of day. I told him I was really into PJ Harvey and that David Lynch was the father I should have had. That I loved getting wasted and I loved the sea. These are the kinds of things you think it cool to talk about when you're fifteen.

Josh told me to close my eyes and wait there. I heard him faffing about upstairs and then he came down and sat close to me. He held something cold to my ear.

'Don't open your eyes,' he instructed.

I suddenly heard the gentle calming whoosh of the sea.

'Nature's lullaby,' he whispered in my other ear.

I opened my eyes. It was a seashell.

'You can hear the actual sea,' Josh said.

After everything happened the way it did and I was reminiscing about this time, as I am doing now, but then with such a melancholy it killed me, I googled why we can hear the sound of the sea in a shell. It's not the sea at all. The shell is merely reflecting sound, so what we actually hear are the noises around us resonating in the shell...say the noise from the TV, or the traffic outside, or our own blood flowing through our bodies. If you put a glass against your ear, it will near enough produce the same effect. So, one of the first things Josh ever told me was a great big lie.

Josh removed the cold object away from my ear and kissed me. It was the perfect time for a kiss. He was the kind of guy who had a knack for timing. That's something you're born with. It can't be taught like Maths. This led to sex; well not sex, we made love. He was the only guy I've ever made love to. Who knew it then at fifteen - you'd think it would be the first of many wonderful experiences, but I soon learned what men were really like and the major difference between sex and making love. The in-out-in-out new generation of fuck and run monsters, that cum on your tits like they're making art, who wiggle your clit in the name of sexual equality and send you dick pics that you never asked for. Not Josh.

After that first time, we snuggled on the sofa with his coat over us and watched daytime TV until we nodded off. I woke up in love. FYI Mother grounded me for two weeks for taking five hours to go to the local shop for milk and never actually bringing any home. She had been worried sick about me and had no choice but to drink milk-less tea! After that the wonderful times with Josh...the walks, the talks, the playlists we'd make for each other, the drunken picnics, the boxsets chill, the everything... everything we did was magic. We said the special words after only three weeks together. He made me feel normal. I was calm for the first time. It was us against the world. Our cocoon of weirdness. I'd sit in the garden reading T.S. Elliot aloud, him fiddling and twiddling my hair in his fingers. I felt breathless thinking...will this last forever, this feeling.

I can barely remember now what real love feels like: with an actual human and not a fictional character. They say that you've got to love yourself first to find love with or from another. But sometimes it's difficult to like, let alone love yourself. Especially when no one else does. When cupid has turned the whip on you. I've never been in love since Josh. I try to recall exactly how it felt, but it seems like another lifetime. If people don't love for a long time, can they forget how to? I try to conjure up the emotion, you know like if you think of a really delicious particularly juicy burger, or tomato for you vegans, and you can taste it, smell it...well you can't seem to do that with love. I just remember floating and believing I was safe. But that's all. For those of you who have been, or still are, completely in love, you will know exactly what I mean. For those who have never fallen - because 'fall' is the perfect word to describe the entire experience, a special kind of fall, well, all I can say is that it's bloody great and I pray with all my heart that you feel it one day. Everyone deserves to feel real love at some point in their life.

Interlude about the one thing that changed me ...cont.

Love: we were in this state for ten months. We decided to both get jobs, his fulltime and mine part time whilst I was at college, so we could get a cheap little flat together and turn it into an arty, flower, crystal, cushioned, candled, book shelved, coffee brewing, cake cooking, love dome. I took ten thousand pounds from my grandparents' inheritance (I got more when I turned twenty-five, which for your information I spent on dresses and drugs) and put it in a joint account under Josh' name – this was for our deposit. It was all very wonderful, honestly. I wasn't even acting like a fuck up cos I had no reason to.

So that day, when what happened, happened, I'd been to the library to get a few classics to read before starting College. I hadn't seen Josh in five days because he had been to visit his aunt in Sheffield. Then he phoned me.

'Hey,' Josh said.

'Hey you,' I answered.

'What are you doing?' he asked.

'Just chilling in the garden.' It had only been five days, but five days when you're in love is a long time. It was a Friday, and he was due back on the Sunday. I missed him terribly.

'What are you doing?' I asked.

'Not much,' he answered, which was an unusually short reply for him because he talked a lot. Too much sometimes.

'The weather's been so beautiful this week,' I said, 'I was thinking we could go for a beach picnic when you get back.'

There was hesitation.

'I've been talking to my aunt, and we've both agreed it would be best if I stayed here for a while. There are more job opportunities for me down here.'

My stomach turned to lead. My heart pulsed against my teeth.

'Ok,' I said slowly, 'that's fine, do you want me to look at college courses down there?'

'No, you've already got a place in Boro,' he answered.

'I don't mind,' I said, 'as long as we're together.'

'No, I think it's best if you stay there.'

I was going to cry. My voice started to shake.

'That's fine,' I said, trying to be appear unphased, 'I suppose we can take it in turns visiting every weekend. I've not been to Sheffield; it will be fun.'

'I just…' Josh sighed, 'we're both so young, maybe we should just enjoy our lives.' I didn't know what to say. Josh continued: 'long distance relationships never work, and you'll be going to college soon. I don't want to be baggage.'

'Baggage!' I exclaimed in a squeal of pain, 'of course not, you make me happy, we can make it work.'

He sighed. 'It won't work Amber. I've given this a lot of thought; we're young and need to enjoy our lives and not be tied down.'

'Maybe you just need time to think,' I said crying and not caring anymore that he could tell I was crying.

'Please don't get upset,' he said, 'this is for the best, one day you will thank me.'

'Why don't I come visit you and we can talk about this properly.'

'No Amber,' he said curtly, 'you need to calm down.'

'But I love you. I thought we were in love.'

'Amber, you're young, you don't know what love is.'

'You're only two years older than me.'

'Yes, but I'm very emotionally mature and worldly. I'm not saying you're not…' Josh paused, 'we're just different, we're at different points in our lives. This isn't what I want anymore.'

'It's what you wanted five days ago,' I replied.

'Let's not do this. Let's not end things like this' Josh said, 'I'll ring you when you calm down, give you some space. I need to go now.'

'But…' I said but he had hung up.

Josh had hung up our relationship. It had ended. We had ended.

I went to bed and cried for hours. I didn't have any proper girl friends to come over and console me, no sleepovers and ice cream, no hugs or kisses, no one to call him a bastard to. By the time Mother came home from work I was all cried out. I was in bed watching TV. When she said my eyes looked puffy, I said it was hay fever. I couldn't bear to speak to her about it. She would just bitterly say that that's what men were like and that I was stupid to expect anything less. She would then go on about my dad and that she had no choice but to work when that tosser left us. She wasn't the Mother I needed. She has never been the mother for me.

Mother said she was going out to the pub quiz with Lesley. She asked me to hoover and wash the pots as I had, 'clearly just sat on my arse all day'. When she was gone, I ignored her cunt-ness and instead switched on my lamp and began to read my new book. I needed to occupy my mind. I needed to escape. To disappear.

I never came back.

The book came to life in my mind's eye, soothing and comforting. I read the entire book that night. When I had finished, I felt like a different person, as if I had been freed from a cocoon. Holden understood. Holden could never hurt me.

I never heard from Josh again.

Well, that's a slight lie, I warned you that I lie. I messaged Josh about five months later when I realised my weekend job (which I had whilst studying at college) at a shoe shop would not pay for my constant alcohol and weed and occasionally cocaine consumption. I asked if he could return my inheritance money now that we weren't going to move in together. He ignored my text. He then ignored all ten of them. I emailed him. He didn't reply. One night I got wrecked and rang him. He didn't answer so I kept ringing all night until he did. He kept changing the subject. He said I was money hungry. That I had changed. I never got a real answer. I never got the money.

I just sank. I never loved a real human again. But I didn't need Josh anymore. I didn't need anyone anymore. I had someone to save me. I had my Holden.

I had my Catcher in the Rye.

CHAPTER SEVEN

Safe in my hotel bed, I read the book from beginning to end – like I had done after what happened, happened. Afterwards, I debate doing something, anything, but I just can't. The constant drip of life, slowing and then stopping. I text Mother saying that the Statue of Liberty was wonderful and that I have been shopping all day and bought a hat from Bloomingdales. This will make her extremely happy. Shopping is like a lover to my mother, as she can't hold down any real romantic relationships because of her personality.

She replies: 'so glad you're having a good time, take lots of pics xxx'

I eat a rich tea biscuit - a little 'comfort' extra, courtesy of the hotel. The biscuit is as dry and tasteless as the décor. Do you get chocolate covered Hobnobs in the Hilton? I am starving but unable to do anything about it. Eating food requires movement – the physical exertion of hand-food-mouth. It also means some form of human contact: which I absolutely cannot endure. I do not want to hear a knock at my door or thank a stranger. I definitely do not want to smile. I had put the 'do not disturb' sign on my door days ago to avoid any sort of interaction with people.

I have an intense, perhaps irrational, fear/dislike of maids … and window cleaners.

Interlude about scary maids and window cleaners

Maids (called Cleaning Attendants nowadays) have slightly ruined all my holidays for the following reasons. Firstly, they get over-excited when they observe the 'room empty' (or words to that effect) sign on the door. They always knock once and then rush in the room without waiting for a reply. Then they are all blushes and apologies when they see the room is occupied and that the newly embarrassed occupant has merely forgotten to flip the sign. You tell them, as you rub sleep out of your eye and try to remember where the fuck you are, that you won't be long. But the pressure is too much, and you quickly dress and go for a breakfast you aren't hungry for, or a walk around the block just to pass time. Just so Maria can make your bed and give you clean towels. Neither of which matter to you.

Secondly, they tend to make a complete racket outside your door, hectically fiddling with sprays and sachets, jealous of your leisure. So you have little option but to get up.

Thirdly, when you leave the room, they are ALWAYS cleaning a few doors down. All smiles and hellos, but their eyes glisten with irritation for you ruining their routine, they will now have to back track to clean your room. They think we are all spoilt. Spoilt and ungrateful. Why can't we all be up and out of our rooms by 7am so they can do their job. Geez you'd think we were on holiday!

And window cleaners- well that doesn't need an explanation. Who doesn't fear/dislike window cleaners?

I decide that rather than feed my hunger I will sleep.

Tomorrow I will leave my room.

When I wake the next morning, I do not want to do anything. I do not want to be around people. I do not want to live. I know I sound like a broken record and you're tiring of my melancholy – but I can't help the way I feel, so just fuck off, or carry on reading if you'd like to indulge me. Also, why we're here -there's nothing indulgent about depression. When people say, 'I haven't the time to indulge in my depression – I'm too busy.' Fuck off cunt. Your issues WILL catch up with you. If you have real depression, then you will not be able to function. Go indulge in suicide you numpty.

I feel like stepping in front of a bus or throwing myself into the river Ouse. I want to Virginia Woolf my holiday away: to fill the pockets in my jacket with rocks and slowly walk into the water, 'to look life in the face, always to look life in the face and to know it for what it is. At last, to know it, to love it for what it is, and then, put it away.' Oh, to put life away. I've tried it dear and it's not for me. Like Auntie Kim's homemade marmalade. It just doesn't do it for me. It doesn't hit the hole in my tastebuds or soul. I shan't spread it on my toast. I appreciate you letting me try it. But I shall put it in the bin.

After tossing and turning the idea over a cup of tea, I decide to continue with life. Even if just for a few days/weeks out of pure grim curiosity. Then I will commit – what's the term Mother uses to describe my behaviour – 'complete selfishness,' yes, I will complete my very last act of selfishness. How will Mother ever go on after my passing? A week of remorse and then… oh let me see; a grief filled shopping spree, a needed Mediterranean cruise, a return to her shitty retired-and-bored classes so she can lap up the excessive and continuous condolences. Mother will resume to being her usual cunting self: she only needs me alive to make her a martyr.

I get out of bed and shower and dress. I put on makeup and do my hair. Actions are forced and hated. I bravely leave the hotel room. Avoiding all maids. I take the lift down to the hotel lobby all the while deciding if I should have breakfast in the hotel restaurant or eat out in a sweet little café. You can never find a place nice and peaceful, because there aren't any.

I decide to eat in the hotel. This will get me used to being around humans and if it is all too much for me, I can run upstairs back to the safety of my bed. Despite it being breakfast time, the hotel restaurant smells of leftover cottage pie.

There are a lot of older people in the restaurant. I wonder if they are on a coach trip. Old people love coach trips; it's like their heroin. Had a bad day- book a coach trip. Ethel died – book a coach trip. Can't be arsed washing the pots for a few days -book a coach trip.

I love old people; I always get on well with them. I mean real oldies in their eighties and nineties. Every wrinkle tells a story. Have they lived through the hardship of war? Have they lost lots of loved ones? What is their general experience of life? Are they glad they'd made it this far? Are they scared of death? Do they hope to die soon? Did they once get fucked on the regular? You'd think they'd all be terribly depressed being closer to death, but they never seem to be. Depression and anxiety are the sickness of modern society. Our brains are over-worked with the constant bombardment and over-cramming of everything. Life is making us ill. Or maybe something has happened to our brains - some scientists believe that our serotonin levels are decreasing over time. In twenty years will everyone walk around silently consumed by severe depression, the light from their mobiles lighting up their frowns and wet eyes. I joke, but who knows and who cares.

You'd think the Coronavirus would've made us realise the value of being alive. The importance of slowing down to enjoy every moment. But it didn't. Some say life is a beautiful gift, but people are ungrateful, they treat it like a recyclable Christmas present. Before Covid I believed I had to go through something awful to appreciate life – a great war, or something shit like cancer. Then I would be happy. But I'm not. I've lived through a pandemic, and I feel nothing (great merchandise slogan opportunity-print it on a t-shirt- treat yourself!). I've watched the horrific documentaries about those that have died or suffered as a consequence of the virus – sure it makes me sad, but afterwards I feel empty. Everything is nothing all the time. In the greater scheme of the universe, for one person to exist means absolutely nothing. So, it means nothing if I feel nothing. From nothing, into nothing.

Like Holden, I order bacon, eggs, toast, an orange juice and coffee.

There are about twelve people in the restaurant: the types whose days are punctuated by bread. Toast in the morning.

Sandwich at lunch. Bread and butter with their dinner. Toast for supper. I don't have anything in common with them. I mean I enjoy a bit of bread - who doesn't, but you can tell we are very different. I absolutely do not want to talk to them or accidentally make eye contact. I often wish I didn't have to see humans. But if I poke my eyes out, I will never again see a sunset, beautiful beach, or majestic forest. I could recall these glories from memory, but then I could also recall humans, so what would be the bloody point. Deafness would be preferred: that way I can see things of splendour, but I won't have to hear idiots speak... but then I can't listen to music, which always brings me such joy.

I eat my breakfast all the while contemplating which of the two senses I would prefer to lose. A roomful of people buttering toast always makes me introspective.

On the way out of the hotel I pick up a tourist information leaflet to find out what there is to do in this marvellous city. The day is plump and ripe. There are clouds blanketing the sky. No way out. I'm glad that I have got out of bed: that I haven't wasted my holiday in the same way I have wasted my life. That I would experience new and wonderful things alone and free. Isn't it wonderful to not be tied down by anyone or anything? To roam the streets without a plan? I try to make myself believe this.

I won't give a step-by-step recollection of what I did that day because it's tedious and what's the point, you can visit yourself. I began at the cathedral, then went to the Viking Centre, the National Railway Museum and then roamed the city walls. I did this at my own pace and finished around eight.

I am proud of myself for staying out the entire day, for not giving up and returning to the hotel even though my body and mind were tired. To conclude, the day has been fine. 'Fine' the very blandest of words, the less attractive twin of 'nice.'

I don't take any photos because I don't want to remember anything. I haven't really taken in any information because my mind is fried. I just move my legs and look. The silent voyeur. The un-bothered tourist. The happiness diffuser. I vaguely remember the blurred faces of strangers as their eyes slip to and then away from mine. A collage of various smiles, smirks, grimaces and frowns. Eyes that reveal an array of emotions. Constant snapshots in my mind, running continuously until I feel defeated. I wonder what people think about me as they walk past. Why didn't I have friends or a partner? Why am I alone? What's wrong with me? What's more toxic and damaged – my looks or personality? Or do they not notice me. A psychologist once said that I am paranoid. That everyone is getting on with their lives and never give me a second thought. But if this is true then why do I notice them? Some people must notice. Some people must wonder about me. We're not born to walk around and not notice a god damn thing.

You would not remember a tree that you walk past every day on your way to work. There are after all many trees and the mind has too much information crammed into it to remember a simple tree. But one day as you pass there are two men from the council who are about to chop it down for health and safety reasons. You suddenly realise that you will miss that tree and the way it makes you feel (it's been there since you started your job- safe and secure, beautiful at times, the white blossoms of spring, the fiery tones of autumn, the stark hug-reaching branches of winter) and you want the tree to stay. But you would then have to take time out of your busy day to phone the council and you can't be bothered. So, you let the tree get chopped down. You never see that lovely tree again. At first you notice it's disappearance, but within a week you've forgotten about it. You're glad you didn't make time to stop its destruction, because it doesn't really matter. No, it doesn't matter at all. The tree and I are both unremarkable. Taking time out to help won't stop our destruction. Our being alive won't make much of a difference. Continue as before.

I go to a food van and ask for a hotdog laden with onions, mustard and tomato sauce. I am a bother to the hotdog seller (who looks like a Stephen, Mark or Chris) who is tidying away and about go home before, conspiracy theorists on the internet may suggest, I mysteriously appear. Stephen-Mark-Chris has his eye on the last hotdog for his Cockapoo (cannibalism?) and has just binned the last of the fried onions. He begrudgingly opens a sealed bag and throws a handful of the transparent worms onto the griddle. As the onions sizzle and spit, Stephen-Mark-Chris makes a great show of making sure I know he has finished for the day and his tiring task of flipping. He takes off his apron, hairnet and hat. Technically he shouldn't do this as he is still working and I'm sure the York Food Standards Agency will not approve. Stephen-Mark-Chris removes his mobile from the back pocket of his jeans and after a few rings and heavy sighs he, perhaps pretending, leaves a voice message: 'Hi babe, I'm finished now, desperate to come home. Just got my last customer. Can you put the tea on for half past? You will need to give Roger a tin of Chappie, no lovely treats for him tonight, someone's just eaten the last dog. See you soon love.'

Two minutes later and a hotdog is pushed into my hands. I am given a few seconds to add condiments, but at the very last drop of mustard, as soon as the bottle is upright, Stephen-Mark-Chris whisks them underneath the counter, rushes out the word 'goodnight,' sounding more like 'ga-na,' and pulls down the hatch. It is so theatrical – as if he is auditioning for RADA and asked to: 'act like a harassed hot dog seller who wants to go home asap,' that I laugh out loud. I sit down on a nearby bench and eat the meaty (well whatever is in it) buggar. I'm sorry that Roger has to eat actual dog food and apologies for the exertion of Stephen-Mark-Chris. I really hope he gets the part of harassed and knackered hot-dog seller. Every artist deserves to thrive at least once in their life.

I go to Sainsburys and buy a bottle of red wine- the five-pound type. I take it to my hotel room and pour a glass, which I then drink in a bubble bath. Slitting one's wrists in the bath seems like a beautiful way to go. The razor neatly cutting your skin. Pressing down until reaching bone. The thick red blood diffusing in the water - now pink and impure. To be found floating in your own life source.

I think about suicide a lot. It's more like a morbid obsession rather than wanting to commit the act. Even when I think 'I want to die,' I don't think I actually do. Sometimes I'd be driving (when I used to drive before I told the psychiatrist what I'm about to tell you, and he told Mother, and she took my car away 'for my own good') and thoughts would just pop into my head - put your foot down and crash into that wall, that tree, that house. It was just thoughts. You can't control thoughts. They just float up and disappear, like bubbles. I tried to tell Mother this, but she wouldn't listen – a thought meant I could possibly do it. Thoughts and actions are completely different things, but no one would listen to me. I would have gotten away with it too, if it wasn't for that meddling shrink. Now I must use public transport - a menace to both the soul and immune system.

I wrap myself in a towel and move the vomity-looking desk chair to the hotel window. I open the window (it's on a latch – don't worry, I shan't jump) to try and create a shit version of a balcony, that is inside, so not resembling a balcony at all. I sit there and drink another glass of wine. Words and conversations alone.

I take the phone out from my bag. I have avoided it all day. There are a few missed calls from Mother, one from dad, and five texts. The first text is from Erin 'hope you're having an amazing time, keep safe xxx. I reply. You see, if you reply, people don't bother you so much. 'Having a great time, its fab here xxx'

I have three texts from Mother, 'haven't heard from you, have tried to ring you several times, please ring back, very worried.' That was at ten twenty-five this morning. The next text said: 'Amber you need to ring me I'm worried sick, love you.' That was at five minues past three. The next text said: 'Why are you doing this to me, I feel ill with worry, I don't deserve this.' That was at four minutes past eight - a recent concern. I text back, 'sorry the day was overcast so I couldn't get a proper signal, having a wonderful time, don't worry. Look what I saw today, can't talk on the phone cos I have a sore throat.' I sent her a Google picture of the Empire State Building.

There is an email from Dad: 'Your mother has text, she's

worried about you, please ring her back. Hope you are having a lovely time. The money should be in your bank now.' I reply: 'thanks dad, I have contacted Mother, so all is well, having a fab time, thanks for the money.'

With the money in the bank, I order a bottle of champagne from room service. However, as I guzzle the second glass, I begin to hate myself (shock horror!). What am I doing? Getting drunk on expensive alcohol that tastes awful. Then what – I'll make a fool of myself. Dancing around the hotel room. Crashing into walls. Spilling fizz. Messaging guys on dating sites. Regretting tomorrow today. Looking through old Facebook photos. Crying. No good would come of it – and I'd had such a semi-successful day.

I put on my pyjamas and get into bed. There is nothing on TV, so I decide to rent a film for three pound and ninety nine pence – expensive - but hey I'm on holiday! I pick The Great Gatsby, the Baz Luhrman version because I long to see prosperity and decadence, obsession and pain – flappers and silks and gold and naughtiness. Jay is a beacon of romantic idealism: a dream to odd girls like me. He is obsessed with the past, with a time when he was happy, and believes this can be replicated. That life can get better. That happiness can exist again. Can a man really be like that?

I sincerely hope that my life thus far has been a harsh preparation, a test, so that when love eventually comes my way, if it does, then I will fully appreciate it and be completely ready to succumb. Being broken, to be emotionally cracked as it were, is the only way for light to get through. Without cracks there is only light or darkness – both are unremarkable on their own – but if the darkness has cracks, light escapes, jumps in or out, however you look at it. When light pushes through the cracks it becomes patterned magic – a work of art. Am I being cracked into a work of art? Is the universe preparing me so that a Jay or Holden can enter my life? In my tipsiness I have clearly turned into Carrie from Sex and the City – asking ridiculous half-rhetorical questions that no one needs or wants an answer to.

I decide to go to sleep. Underneath my lids is a kaleidoscope of visions and colours. The universe is ready. I just need my light to flow through the cracks. It is my time. Afterall, I have been waiting a long time, so patiently in the rye.

I sleep soundly and wake a few minutes past ten. The restaurant finishes serving breakfast at half past and as it takes about twenty minutes to do my makeup and fifteen to do my hair, then I will undoubtedly miss this. Given the aged ambience yesterday, then this is probably a good thing. It also means that instead of rushing, I can saunter around York until I find a quaint Parisian style café. Here I will eat fresh croissants, drink strong lively espresso, and peak out occasionally from my book to watch the world go by.

I step outside the hotel and see that the day is indescribably gorgeous, the sun strong and high. It smiles down and winkingly gives me an extra zap of vitamin D. The universe is on my side, and I am thankful. I feel amazing.

I search the cobbled streets for a good ten minutes but can't find a Parisian Café and all the Costa's and Starbucks are busy with laptop people. I have to make do with a McDonalds. I order a cappuccino and double cheeseburger. When will McDonalds do the world a favour and serve the breakfast menu all day. I don't mind waiting a bit longer for them to prepare a fresh sausage patty. Joy should not be cut off at eleven every morning.

McDonalds is hectic. I find a high stool in front of the windows which overlooks the street. You know those ridiculously uncomfortable seats where you have to watch your balance, so you don't fall, whilst simultaneously making sure your thighs and buttocks aren't sweaty, so you don't slide off.

Burger eaten; I start to read the book with a cappuccino. I know I just finished reading the book the other day, but I like to pick it up and read random passages. I always discover something new, and it always makes me happy. When I flick through and land on a passage- I consider it my horoscope for the day – nothing in life is coincidental.

A gang of about ten chavvy lads enter McDonalds. They are all wearing black T-shirts with white writing on the front saying, 'Keep Calm We're on Dave's Stag Do.' There is a fat hairless nuisance of a man dressed in a large nappy, a white frilly baby's bonnet and a huge dummy around his neck. Dave.

They are loud, lairing and awful. Shouting about lining their stomachs with 'fucking beef' before they, 'get on it big-boy Dave style.' I try to ignore their ranting and read the book – difficult given their volume.

One of them enters my space, smelling of beer and hair product.

'Eeya love,' he says. 'Eeya love,' he repeats and then a dirt-filled nail prods my book. I have little choice but to look up. He is of average height, skinny and heavily tattooed, short black hair with a non-descript face as unremarkable as a wall, although some walls are exceptionally more remarkable than the face before me. Wall Man.

'My mate Dave's a baby and wondered if he could suck your titties,' Wall Man laughs.

'No sorry,' I reply. I smile politely so I don't seem stuck up. I look back down at my book.

'Please,' Wall Man continues, 'he just wants some milk.'

'Well, he's in McDonalds why doesn't he get a milkshake,' I reply curtly. I still smile, even though he disgusts me to my very core. Two of his mates have now joined the 'conversation' and start to sing 'my milkshake brings all the boys to the yard,' whilst stroking their nipples through their tops.

'I know but you've got such lovely titties,' says Wall Man, 'and he only wants a little suck.'

'Sorry no,' I reply, 'why don't you ask someone else.'

'Well, what about a kiss?' He asks and then shouts over to Dave who is stuffing a BigMac into his mouth, 'Dave come here, this lass will give you a kiss.'

'I definitely won't,' I reply.

Dave waddles over in his nappy.

'You what mate?' he asks Wall Man, ketchup smeared down his chin.

'This lass said she'd tongue you for a bite of your BigMac...or did she say cock I can't remember.' Wall Man laughs raucously. The rest of Dave's crew are at the counter unaware of what is happening.

I shake my head, 'I didn't say that.'

'Aww howay,' says Wall Man, 'just a kiss. He's only a free man for another nine days.'

'No,' I say firmly and look around for security or protection from the staff or customers. Everyone is engrossed in what they are doing – flipping, pulling, cleaning, eating, drinking, queueing, picking, holding, dunking, talking, laughing, listening, thinking.

'What about a kiss on the cheek then, be a good sport? asks Wall Man.

Dave takes a step forward.

'Listen,' I shout, 'this is assault. I'm just trying to drink my coffee and read in peace. Any more of this and I'll phone the police. This will be on CCTV, so they'll catch you all.'

Wall Man and Dave laugh.

'There's no need to be a stuck-up little bitch now is there?' says Wall Man. 'Come on Dave mate.' He puts his arm around Dave, 'let's go to the pub, she's an ugly cunt anyway, probably likes the flange.'

They laugh and walk outside.

I sit there in shock as tears well in my eyes. I only wanted to have breakfast in peace. Just time to myself without stress or upset. I feel violated: my positive mood torn away. I know they are a pack of knobheads, but they make me sad: sad that men like them exist, and millions of the hounds at that. I am exasperated that there's nothing I can do about it. The fragility of the male ego, that rejection, even if you are rejecting their friend, is considered a slur to the male species. Wall Man wanted me to feel lucky that he had given me attention, then when I had rebuked it, it surely wasn't for the fact that he and his mates were charmless unattractive Neanderthals…but of course I was the one who was a stuck-up bitch and an ugly cunt of a stuck-up bitch at that, who loves the flange. Even though the insult is empty, the words sting.

How can art and poetry exist on the same planet as those men. If you look up the word 'lovely' they are the antonym. I can't bear to read. Or to think. I put the book in my bag. I look in my compact mirror. Am I indeed an ugly cunt like he suggested? I wipe away the watery mascara gunk from the corner of my eye. I apply lipstick. Do I appear vulnerable? Maybe they can sense my oddness; that I deserve to be bullied as the 'other.' It's all schoolyard fun and games, all shit and bullying giggles until the weird girl throws herself off a cliff. Just a bit of McDonalds craic with the lads until the little loon jumps headfirst from the high stool and purposefully lands on her skull. 'Little Nathan don't dip your fries in that. It ain't ketchup.'

My nerves are on edge – the only solution is a good stiff drink. I walk to a pub a few doors down. I want to destroy myself, lose control, let the alcohol take over my body and brain. To be a complete mess. I don't want to speak to anyone: I can perhaps muster a simple grunt, a gesture to what I want, or preferably use an app service to order. In this day and age, we shouldn't have to verbally communicate. You should be allowed to ignore people. I mean isn't this (ironically) the whole point of mobile phones.

I order a straight whiskey and down it: a warm and pleasant hug. Today's plan is complete obliteration. Afterall, the future is uncertain. I order two gin and tonics and sit in the corner. Being alone in a pub/bar always makes me anxious and paranoid. I assume people are watching and wondering about me. When I am not joined by an unpunctual companion, they will titter and question why a woman would go to a pub or bar to drink alone. Why not just drink a bottle of wine at home? They will pity me and think I am pathetic. That there is something wrong with me.

Some people enjoy their own company. I must admit, I prefer it to being in the company of about ninety-five percent of the people I know. Well maybe one hundred percent, as I can't even think of a five percent whose company I can endure for any length of time. However, I can't help but feel sad when I see an old man sitting in the pub by himself, staring into his pint. Or a little old lady by herself in a coffee shop, who is desperately trying to catch somebody's eye to start conversation. People avoid them because they are 'busy' – when a chat, however small and trivial, will make their day, an acknowledgement that they are still alive, that they still matter. I once mentioned this to Erin, but she scoffed and said that 'people like that' were having the time of their lives: that the old man was probably escaping his nagging wife of fifty years and that the little old lady probably lived in a residential home knitting jumpers for grandchildren who never came to visit. She said I overthought everything and that we would all be lonely one day.

Is this true? Do we all get a quota of loneliness in our lifetime? If you are young and have a full and happy life surrounded by friends, family, noise and fun; is it then your turn to experience loneliness at some point? Does this then mean that I have already endured my quota of loneliness and unhappiness and a content and crowded life awaits me? Or are some people lonely all their life? I'm being Carrie Bradshaw again, sorry.

If I wasn't lonely, maybe I wouldn't drink. But I am lonely, and drink is the only real friend I have. I hope to get alcohol poisoning. I want what makes me happy to consume and perhaps kill me. Alcohol and love have so much in common. Having said the most emo sentence of all time, I celebrate by going to the bar and downing a Jager bomb. I feel slightly tipsy. Once I start drinking I can't, nay won't stop, so I decide to eat something substantial to line my stomach.

I leave the pub and turn left onto the main street and head towards the market. It is full of overpriced shit that middle class wankers buy by the recycled cloth carrier bag full. The think-they're-a-bit-quirky-and-earthy types, who try to balance their karma by giving money to the local community, those in need and the planet – that is on a weekend, during the week they fellate Mr Capitalism in the back of their Mercedes. The types who buy organic fennel, kumquat and satsuma squeezed handmade soap and Fairtrade vegan dark chocolate handmade truffles with fillings such as 'lavender rose' and 'salted caramel infused essence of parfait farts' ... the kind who shop at Waitrose and have children called Jasper and Conran and regularly holiday in Italy whilst the rest of us fuck off to Benidorm or Butlins to give blowies to waiters who aren't really called Pedro.

I opt to buy another hot dog- you know one of those great German frankfurter motherfuckers topped with greasy onions, mustard, ketchup and anything else on offer. What would Freud make of all this sausage eating?

'Amber it meanz you envy da penis. You must eeeet it, consume the phallic symbol to feel complete, you feel as if something is missing in your life, ya?'

'Yeah, a hotdog in my mouth because I'm starving. Fuck of Freud.'

All the nearby benches are occupied by students, tourist's and the resting-between-benches elderly. I decide to be completely uncouth and sit on the kerb whilst I eat. It is pleasing to know that people will have to walk around me and not over me as they usually do. I splay out my legs and enjoy being a major tripping hazard.

Hotdog eaten; I am due my next pub. I walk through the market stalls stopping occasionally to internally snort at the produce. I mean 'fresh ginger, cucumber and lemongrass jam. A hundred percent natural fruit, no additives or pips.' What's wrong with a hundred percent sugary un-fresh strawberry jam with ten hundred additives and a billion annoying pips? Why can't Piers and Portia spread that on their toast?

I am just thinking about the last time I ate strawberry jam... when I spot a hat stall. One must always buy a hat on holiday-it's a rule and not really a holiday until this purchase is made.

There are the usual - straw hats, caps with touristy captions, head scarfs and funny hats – like cat shaped hats and horse shaped hats, you know for the fool in the flock. At the back there is a half-price sale on winter hats – woollen hats with bobbles in a variety of colours and patterns. It is as I venture closer that I see it. I was always meant to see it. The red hunting hat with the long peak. Holden's hat. I move towards it slowly as if under a spell 'touch the thimble, touch it I say,' but in this Disney classic Maleficent uses the word 'hat' instead of 'thimble.'

It is like two lovers walking towards each other from opposite sides of the room. Every obstacle invisible. The prize being love. Except the hat doesn't move. I just progress towards it creepily. The hats all nudge each other. The coral and white striped straw hat titters, 'little weirdo is going to pounce.' The green frog-head hat with the purple pom-pom whispers, 'urgh who would want to buy that red hunting beast, who even wears that kind of gross shit.' The black and white 'I Love York' cap says, 'they deserve each other, borkies.' But I don't listen. I am in love. Will the hats have to buy a hat for the wedding?

I pick up the hat. It is warm from the heat of the sun, like holding a newly removed heart. I put it on my head. I hate to state the obvious, but that's what I did. It fit perfectly, as if replacing said heart back into the body. Everything is together like it's meant to be. I look in the small round mirror placed above the hat stand.

'It look good. Meant for you,' says a voice behind me with an Eastern European accent. It is the stall owner- a young lady in a purple flowing dress, with dark hair and dark eyes and undoubtedly with a plethora of dark stories which she only reveals in a dimly lit candle and cushioned environment for twenty pounds. 'It is fate,' she says and nods her head.

I look at my reflection in the mirror. Did this lady, perhaps gypsy, perhaps a fortune teller, perhaps such a stereotype that she is a figment of my imagination, is she trying to tell me something, is this hat fate, would this hat, Holden's hat, change my life?

'The hat will bring you right man,' she smiles as if reading my mind.

'How much?'

'Fifteen,' the lady says, 'but for you ten pounds.'

'Thank you so much,' I hand her the hat and then a ten-pound note from my purse.

I don't know why I hand her the hat because she gives it straight back.

'You want a bag madam?' she asks.

'No thanks. I'm going to wear it.'

'It make you happy,' she says, 'good day madam.'

'You too,' I say and walk away wearing my hat of fate.

I go to the nearest bar and head straight to the toilet so I can view myself. I couldn't do this in front of the hat stall lady because you can't really fuck about doing a range of expressions and poses with someone watching. You've just got to look quickly in the mirror, a fleeting glance so you don't appear vain and self-centred. But in private I can be as narcissistic as I desire. I turn the long peak to the back of my head, as Holden did, and reapply my lipstick. I am cooking on gas.

I go to the bar. It is two for one cocktails, so I get two raspberry mojitos. I sit down in the loneliest place possible and get out the book. I am just starting chapter twelve. It's the part where Holden is in the taxi and asks the driver, Horwitz, if he knows where the ducks go in winter, the ones on the lagoon in Central Park. Horwitz explains what happens to the fish but can't say what happens to the ducks. Holden never finds the answer that he so desperately seeks.

I finish both mojitos and slurp on the ice and mint at the bottom of the glass, making a ridiculous noise trying to suck out the last dregs. You see, there is a special place in hell for people who waste alcohol.

Now on to the next pub or bar. I am a little tipsy, enough to trip over a sticking-up cobble. It is a little trip though – just a fall forward and not a full-on floor affair, not the kind of fall that makes you die inside. I look at my watch; it is only quarter past four. I need to slow down and sip my drinks. I go into the next bar and order a bottle of toffee-apple cider. I snuggle up in the corner and watch the TV placed above the pool table. Sky News on repeat. I watch it with vague interest; I'm not nonchalant about current affairs, on the contrary, but the news is always pretty much the same. There will be some sort of war or terrorist attack, a celebrity will have died or done something stupid, a natural disaster will have occurred, a criminal or serial killer will be on the loose, there will be an update about the repercussions of Covid-19... and there is always a chance of rain. It doesn't matter what day you watch the news - I could come in the pub tomorrow, or next week, next month, or even next year and the news will practically be the same.

But alack - I have wasted an hour. One bottle of cider whilst watching a thousand tales of woe. I decide to go to the cinema. If you sit at the back, it's an excellent way to people-watch. The harassed mothers with too many kids. The teenage boys trying to cop their first feel of a tit. The bored couples on date night trying to keep the romance alive when it had already died a death when Game of Thrones finished. Then there is always that person by themselves that you look at and wonder – what is their story. That person will now be me. 'Tonight, Matthew, I'm going to be... Freak Single Girl Alone at the Movies'. Audience applauds. Matthew grins ridiculously, his eyes slim to slits as I disappear backstage. A moment later the doors open, mist fills the stage, and there I am on the maroon velveteen chair, eating a tiny tub of over-priced Haagen Daaz, looking up, looking up always, as the audience applauds in a stale rehearsed manner.

On another note, I love ice cream. What genius thought of freezing milk and adding whatever shit they do, to make it taste so good. I imagine it was a hearty Italian gentleman, in the days when everything was black and white. Antonio is his name, and he has a large black moustache:

Interlude about the genius creation of icecream

Antonio wakes one morning and goes into the kitchen. His wife

Giulia is there eating loaf after loaf of bread, the kitchen stinks of freshly squeezed oranges. 'Where iz di milk?' asks Antonio (for the sake of this tale he is kindly speaking English in a strong Italian accent, but in reality, he only knows a handful of words in our un-poetic tongue). He looks into the fridge and moves the recently picked grapevine tomatoes, fresh oregano and bowl of mozzarella. Antonio cannot find the milk.

'It not there?' questions Giulia (for the sake of this tale she is kindly speaking English in a strong Italian accent, but in reality, she only knows a handful of words in our un-poetic tongue). She has long black hair tied on the top of her head in a loose bun and is wearing a floral button up dress, her magnificent cleavage poking over the top like fresh focaccia rising from the tin.

'Nor' he says sharply,' and I needa cappuccino after drinking all ze red wine last night which was tree bottles for ten lire in Morrisonia.'

'I don't know where it eez,' she replies, 'just have da orange.'

'No,' Antonio replies curtly, outraged by the suggestion.

'Well, the milk was there last night,' says Giulia.

'Maybe the cow came back for it,' says Antonio stupidly, thinking he is funny.

Giulia is not allowed to say anything funny, or anything that appears to contradict Antonio.

'Check everywhere,' says Giulia, 'it can't just disappear.'

Antonio meticulously checks the fridge. Then the cupboards. Then not knowing where else to look, he checks the freezer.

'Here it is,' says Antonio, pulling it out. He laughs, 'I must have put it in here when I was drunk.'

But oh, it would not have been funny if Giulia had committed this silly act. She would have been beaten.

Antonio takes a swig from the bottle.

'Stupid bastard,' says Giulia, forgetting herself.

Antonio is about to grab Giulia and pull her down by her bun until it touches the kitchen floor, and she screams apologies amidst tears. But he stops. He licks his lips.

'Mmmm,' he says, 'it's icy and creamy, delicious, I wish milk was always like this.'

Ding. Ding.

'Giulia, let's make eet like this forever, we sell it to people, we be poor no more.'

'You and your silly ideas Antonio,' says Giulia, 'first it was putting pulped tomato and mozzarella on bread ...now this!'

'What shall I call it, this new delicious creation?' Antonio asks.

'Oh, I don't know,' Giulia replies, 'something simple so it can easily be translated into languages for distribution all over the world and become a staple of the American diet.' She thinks for a few moments and then says ... 'ice cream'

Ding. Ding. Ding. Ding. Ding. Ding.

FYI the bread with pulped tomato and mozzarella never took off. Americans especially hate it.

Of course, the above story is a work of my imagination, a complete lie, and full of stereotypes that may appear unkind and not politically correct. The icy treat which is ice-cream has been around long before you and I were born. In Persia 400 BC the Persians chilled rosewater and vermicelli (you can find vermicelli in any hipster market just head for the sign, Posh Pasta for Cunts). In China 200 BC the Chinese ate frozen milk and rice. In Greece 5 BC the Grecians ate snow mixed with honey and fruit. Basically, it goes on and on throughout history with bloody sorbets and frozen yoghurts and what not, until hey presto - Ben and Jerrys.

I scoff my tiny tub of pralines and cream, whist watching some blockbuster action film where the plot can be summed up in a simple sentence. I care nothing for the characters. What do people get from watching these types of movies? It's just fighting and guns and cars until it all mingles together, and I can't make sense of what is happening. Kill-kill, bang-bang, car-car, fight-fight, snog-snog, fight-fight, car-car, bang-bang, kill-kill. Don't see it if you don't want to puke all over yourself.

The cinema is quiet. The only people there are a group

of seventeen-year-old student types. They giggle irreverently, not really watching the film- what from talking and toileting and snacking and drinking and thinking about fucking. They don't annoy me though as I just enjoy the actual experience of cinema: the fact that everyone is together, watching a film, like a beautiful cult. Then coming out of the cinema in a crowd, into the light and thinking, oh I'm so glad to see your face instead of the back of your head, because we may be strangers, but we've just shared hours of our lives together. The same film was watched by all: yet each person brought an entirely different perspective and would have a completely different opinion about it. I want to invite the students for drinks so we can discuss the film. I don't, because I will appear insane.

Instead, I will use Dad's money to go for a well-earned cocktail and discuss the film with myself. The review won't take long – probably lasting all of four words 'well that was shit.' I go to *Vodka Revolution* and order a Cherry Boulevardier: I fancy buying a packet of cigarettes so I can smoke on the balcony which overlooks the river. I stopped smoking last year. I don't give a shit about the damage to my health, as I'm sure you will have figured out by now that I hate being alive, but I would rather spend the money on alcohol and drugs. I think the right person (not a cumbersome chav) smoking a cigarette, looks very French and film noir fantastic, especially if they have a faraway look in their eye. But cigarettes stink and kill- so you must always be honest about the life you want to lead kids.

The drink is delicious. I then order a Butterfly Effect – as it sounds scrumptious and I want to see if it tastes as sad and lovely as the film. A waiter comes to my table to take my empty glass away. He is whistling happily. He has quite a lot of sex appeal – out of my league – a shorter, less desirable, specs-wearing version of Zac Effron.

'You're a terrific whistler,' I say as he places my glass on the tray.

He looks at me sharply as if just realising I am there. I am not stereotypically pretty, so he looks down and starts to wipe the table, then he places the dishcloth over his shoulder. He does not bother to instigate a conversation as I'm not up to his level of physical attractiveness.

'Where you whistling Little Shirley Beans?' I ask.

'Thank you,' he replies and smiles, ignoring the question as he has absolutely no idea what I am on about.

Maybe he is shy not arrogant? Not disgusted by my lacking looks, but merely coy and unconfident around women. Then he does a rather bizarre and awkward macho-wannabe-action - he aggressively grabs the dishcloth, flips it in the air and catches it in his other hand. It's as if he is shaking a cocktail, but with a white and blue striped linen cloth and not a delicious plethora of alcohol and mixers. Arrogant. Is he the kind of guy who is going to flirt with me for a bit of practise? You know like a friendly game of football. No harm done. Or is he just after a fuck and might do me the honour of entering my body after he has finished work?

He winks, presumably trying to be seductive, then walks away. You elusive man of mystery and cloth throwing skills! Winkers are always wankers.

I then have a two-minute fantasy about having sex with him in the nearby toilets. As he bangs me animalistically doggy-style over the sink, he winks at himself in the mirror, thinking - if he can cause all this mischief with a dishcloth, what damage could he do with a full-size family towel. In the reflection I see a singular bead of sweat running down his forehead. It will soon be dripping into his winking eye. This will cause him to blink uncontrollably as he tries to dispel the salty intruder. It will be embarrassing and awful for both of us. So, in reality, reality being the true source of pain on this earth, it's for the best that he doesn't fancy me or want to hook up.

My eyes follow Cloth Man around the bar. He wipes over menus, fills up containers of napkins and then flirts with a blonde waitress. Ah one of those - only has eyes for the blondes. Eyes on the golden prize. You can tell she isn't interested – she is after the handsome muscled black guy making cocktails. In the hierarchy of attractiveness specky Zac Effron falls short. That must be a real blow for his self- esteem. Snort.

I leave and go to the next bar – *Pitcher and Piano*. I sincerely hope a piano is not playing, but the pitcher bit sounds spot on. Piano music: not only does it sound depressing no matter what song is being played, but you can tell that most pianists hate their lives. This hate comes from pain and this pain comes from ego. They always consider themselves too talented and accomplished to be music teachers because they are 'artists.' So, to pay the bills until they make it big, they have to play Adele covers to women drinking prosecco. Someday, hopefully, one of the prosecco-guzzling women will be a record producer who demands they immediately sign a million-pound record deal. But until then … 'there's a fire, starting in my heart,' … go on our Lisa and Kath sing your hearts out, you can hit them notes, Adele was only from Tottenham.'

I sit on a table overlooking the river and drink an elderflower cosmopolitan. I look around to see if there is anyone I fancy. The lighting is dark and complimentary, so I can possibly pull someone more attractive than myself. I can punch way up high into the sky, where the pigs fly. There is no one.

I scroll through Facebook. I then text Mother to say what a fantastic time I was having and that I had 'been all the way to the top of the Empire State Building today, and gosh was it high.' Mother replies straight away 'I'm ill with a cold, in bed. My immune system is low due to stress.' The 'stress' she refers to is that I have disobeyed her and gone away, because if it was caused by something or someone else, I would have undoubtedly been told about it in excruciating detail.

I down my drink. Mother is the kind of person who makes me want to down any drink or liquid that I have to hand – be it milk, lemonade, wine or bleach. As if I need something cold or hot to consume and occupy me for thirty seconds, time needed to compose myself and think of a tactful reply to whatever nasty or uncalled-for comment she has undoubtedly said.

I begin to feel down. I desperately want some coke. I kick myself for not bringing any with me from my dealer at home.

146

After a few drinks it's inevitable - my nose gets thirsty. I text my dealer and ask if he knows anyone who sells in York. I am tempted to ask him to drive here, but he will only travel this far for about a grand's worth- which I don't think my body can muster. He always takes a while to reply as he is generally stoned. I get a gin and tonic for old times sakes and order some halloumi fries. About thirty-five minutes later all I get is a: 'no sorry mate.'

I scan my brain to think of anyone I know who lives nearby. There is a snotty girl, Shona, who I went to university with: she used to follow me about because neither of us had friends and I was too polite to tell her to fuck off. I message her on WhatsApp. She would never do drugs. But there is the slimmest chance that she may know someone who does. When you desperately want a fix - slim chances are pounced on and ridden until exhaustion. It is nine thirty, so there is a good chance she won't respond as it's past her weekday bedtime.

'Hey Shona, not seen you in ages, how are you lovely? I'm in your hometown for the next few days and I know you said to make contact if I was ever here. Just seeing if you're free sometime. Currently sat in the Pitcher and Piano enjoying some cocktails.' I add five kisses and some emojis that connote excitement and love.

Shona is on me like a hungry dog. 'Hi Amber, I'm actually at a tapas bar right near you with some work buds, come join xxx.'

Fucking hell Shona, tapas on a school night, whatever next? You're about to enter a dark downward spiral: returning home late and catching up on Netflix shows – hitting snooze on the alarm button until you haven't time to make a packed lunch for work. You will have to resort to a shop-bought sandwich - a one hundred day-old barely chicken, barely tikka, barely edible sandwich.

The idea of hanging out with Shona and her work buds- probably Next suited clones who listen to Coldplay and drink herbal tea, makes me want to die. Shona, however, is my only hope for a fix – for this I will sing Viva la Vida naked, standing on top of a table, stomping on leftover patatas bravas with my bare feet.

'Wow Shona that sounds awesome, I'd love to join you for some tasty vino, thanks so xxx.'

Please note the odiously fake way I speak to people like Shona.

'Fab honey, hurry we're probably staying for another hour max with it being work tomorrow, we're in Las Pahamas in Goodramgate, you know it?'

'Yes, I adore the tapas there, see you in 5 xxx'

Shona is the kind of person who frequents tapas bars just so she can say the words: 'tapas bar.' I have never been to Las Pahamas and have no idea where it is. I'm the most terrific liar you ever saw in your life. I google-mapped it - a seven-minute walk. I down my gin and stand up. I wobble with boozy in the brain.

I sway semi-content in the rye.

CHAPTER EIGHT

I easily find the tapas bar. As I go inside, I immediately see Shona and her annoying muck-brown bouncing bob. She has never changed her hairstyle since the age of three – her hair always springs up and down, nauseatingly, you always feel like telling it to calm the fuck down. She is laughing with a wine glass in her hand.

'Amber sweetie,' Shona exclaims when she sees me. She waves me over, then stands and gives me a hug. She is wearing a plain, grey, tight fitting shift dress with matching kitten heels. 'You look amazing,' she squeals, 'have you lost weight.' Well Shona when you sniff naughty powders at every opportunity it does kill your appetite somewhat. 'Yoga, right?' she asks and pulls a chair from an empty table next to her.

I laugh internally – for a joke I once checked myself in on Facebook saying I was attending a local yoga class – 'this amazing time of the week again.' No way would I stretch my body to bits for so-called fun with a bunch of vegan aquaholic skeletons. On a Tuesday night it's two for one on Dominos …would I really be doing anything else? Apart from getting wrecked, but even I have the occasional night off to indulge my passion for carb-ridden meal deals, ok so I lie, I usually enjoy a pack of tinnies with my meat feast.

'Life changing,' I lie, 'Shona, I can't even remember life before yoga.'

Am I speaking differently? Have I immediately altered my voice to fit in with Shona and her middle-class vocal norms?

Shona laughs. She gestures to the people around the table, there are two women and a man. 'Amber- this is Florence, Alex and

Sam.'

Florence is small, roller-skater skinny with a square squashed face and an auburn blunt fringe, the rest of her hair is tied back in a ponytail, she wears a leopard print blazer with a red shirt underneath.

Alex is a bit older (say forty-five) and has brown shoulder length hair with a few crimson lowlights near the front, no makeup, and wears a floral blouse and long skirt – by her sense in fashion I'm guessing she works in admin or finance.

Sam looks in his early twenties – handsome but with a hoity toity mouth, all pursed together like a tight little bum hole, which I'm guessing matches his entry hole of choice. He wears a cream shirt and tie immaculately and has a face that looks like it has recently been washed.

'Nice to meet you all,' I say in the most chipper and friendly way possible.

'Amber and I went to Uni together,' says Shona giggling.

Shona is now an English Literature lecturer at York University; according to Facebook her specialisms are Renaissance Literature and all that Shakespearean stuff.

'Many moons ago,' she continues, 'gosh it feels like forever.'

I laugh forcefully.

'We all work together,' Shona continues addressing the group, 'Florence is a fellow academic, Alex is our assistant and Sam here is starting his first teaching job next term. The poor lamb. He's gay.' She blushes and shakes her head, 'I don't mean he's a poor lamb for being gay, I mean for starting a career in teaching. I just thought you should know he's gay.'

What so I don't try and tongue him over prosciutto and calamari? Everyone laughs, except Sam, he just looks hoity.

'So, what are you up to now Amber, you don't state your occupational status on Facebook?' Shona asks.

Yeah, so stuck up cunts like you can't judge me for not earning over fifty grand a year. I decide to lie: to say something that will completely rile her.

'I don't really post on Facebook these days, but I've actually retired to be a full-time wife…you know I married Spencer right.'

Shona stops laughing. Her grin becomes restrictive. Jealousy is the restriction.

'No, I didn't see anything on Facebook,' she replies.

'I never posted about it. Spencer wanted to keep it quiet, he's that type. We got married in the Maldives last year and have just bought a beautiful house in Wynyard. I'm in the process of meeting with the interior design team to decorate. Spencer owns an Accountancy firm in London, so he's only back at the weekends, but thankfully he trusts my tastes,' I laugh and lie.

'Wow, an accountant in London,' says Shona slowly, her eyes flicker.

'Yeah, Spencer really doesn't want me to work, well we don't need the money, but after the house is finished and the extension for the sauna room is complete, which he absolutely insists on building to help with his sinus issues,' I roll my eyes as if having a husband who insists on building a sauna room is a real ball ache. 'Then we're trying for a family straight away. He wants me to be at home to look after our family and instruct the staff.'

I laugh again. Have I gone too far with my lies?

'I didn't realise you were married,' says Shona, 'you don't wear your ring?'

She gestures to my empty fingers as if to expose that my words are indeed empty.

'Well, that's a touchy subject,' I look distressed, 'I lost my ring scuba diving in the Galapagos a few weeks ago. It was Spencer who noticed over dinner, cos he always makes a joke that every time the diamond hits the light, it blinds him. It must have slipped off my finger in the turquoise waters – perhaps with all the weight I've lost from doing yoga.'

'Oh dear,' says Shona.

'Was it insured?' asks Alex, a stickler for policies and procedures.

'I'm afraid not. Spencer is in the process of getting it re-made. He bought it when he was on a business trip in Switzerland so it's taking its time to arrive. I feel naked without it.'

Everyone looks at me with admiration. Is this what respect feels like?

'Oh dear,' says Alex.

Florence shakes her head. Sam toits his hoit and then he hoits his toit.

'Are any of you guys married?' I ask, having the upper hand. I guessed that none of them have a love interest or as much as a Tinder flirt. Except Sam, I bet he likes to 'talk' to leather daddies on Grindr.

'I know you're not Shona,' I say rubbing in the salt with a dash of vinegar.

Shona looks gutted. I recognise the 'what the fuck is wrong with me,' tension in her posture, the 'why haven't I found the one' glance at the floor, the 'how come everyone is happy, except me' unnecessary touch of the hair. I must switch tactics and be nice to her if I have to ask for a favour shortly. It's fabulous fun, but it has to stop.

'Shona is only single' I say, 'because she can be as picky as she wants, I mean look at her....and that brain.' I shake my head with faux bewilderment as if Shona has so many amazing qualities that my head is going to explode thinking about them all. Shona laughs, she loves it. She shrugs her shoulders as if believing she is actually single because she is too much of a good thing. Not because she is a boring, stuck up, personality-less nerd with an irksome hair do.

'I can't believe you're married,' Shona repeats, 'I thought you'd always be the wild one, partying forever and bed-hopping from man to man.'

I laugh at the truth, I exhale the lie, 'we all change Shona.'

'I thought that we were the only ones our age not married with kids...but now it's just me.' Shona says and looks sad.

'Don't say that' Alex says, 'you're amazing. There's no rush.'

I feel bad. If only they knew my real and dire vice-ridden, lonely, excessive existence.

'You'll meet your prince Shona,' I say, 'I thought I'd never meet mine, but Spencer and I just clicked, and it was a world wind romance. That's what will happen to you, I have no doubt.'

'I hope so,' she says meekly, 'It's just so difficult to meet people these days, it's not like in our parent's generation.'

I nod with conviction.

'Especially with a job like mine,' Shona continues.

'There's nothing wrong with your bob,' I reply, 'the vintage look is very 'in' at the moment.'

'I said job,' Shona corrects. She strokes the ends of her hair, as if it has suddenly dawned on her how fucking horrific it is. I howl inside, because my mistake, my GENUINE mistake, is hilarious.

'That's what I meant.' I answer. Not really knowing how to answer, but knowing I have to answer.

'I guess I'm married to my work,' Shona continues, 'it's my life passion... I guess Renaissance Literature is my husband.'

I nearly choke on my own spit. I cough instead.

'I think I'll get a drink,' I say.

'Here have this,' Alex says and shoves a glass of red wine under my nose, 'I've already had one glass and I've got work tomorrow.'

I am sat with people who know their limit. If only I was bestowed with this maturity and self-restraint.

'Thank you,' I say and snatch the glass from Alex's hand. Shona looks at me with a suspicious glint in her eye. Perhaps I should have been more unenthusiastic when accepting the wine. Free wine though. So... I act all demure and say to Alex, 'only if you're sure, I just hate waste, but I shouldn't really.'

'Are you still a big drinker Amber?' Shona asks. 'You'll have to stop that if you're trying for a family?'

Come on then. Let it out bitch. If we're going to fight – let's have you.

'Not much anymore,' I reply.

'You drank a lot tonight' Shona says it as a statement rather than a question.

'Not much,' I reply, 'this is only my second glass, but because I hardly drink anymore, when I do, it goes straight to my head. I'll be regretting this second glass in the morning.'

They all laugh and groan in understanding. I feel part of the un-fun crew.

'When Amber was at Uni,' Shona says, (what the fuck is she going to reveal ...the time I was hungover in a lecture and puked all over her copy of Great Expectations ... the time I wanked off a really geeky guy in a student pub so he would write my essay on White Noise that was due the next day... the time I wrote a poem so disturbing the tutor sat me down and asked if I needed counselling...the list goes on) ... 'she had the worst taste in men. Always one for the bad boys, you know – the druggies, the drinkers, the addicts, tattoos and piercings, no job, on benefits for life...what did you call them Amber... 'free thinkers' the ones that 'could not be controlled by the system.' Shona laughs, 'that's why it's so unbelievable that now you're married to an accountant with a house in Wynyard. Gosh you couldn't get any more clean-cut. I bet your mother is over the moon, she was always so worried about you.'

I gulp down red grapey hate for Shona.

'Mother IS over the moon,' I say brightly.

'I mean you and her never got on, did you?' she laughs, 'hence why you call her 'mother' instead of 'mum' or 'mummy.'

They all laugh, well half laugh, because Shona has never big on banter. The reason I call Mother 'mother' is because she hates the term 'mam' – she says it sounds far too mammary-like and common. I'm sure she secretly would have loved it if I'd called her 'mum' or 'mummy' like the other pigtail-wearing girls at nursery; but it felt too intimate and sweet. 'Mother' is un-bonding and fits the wintriness of our relationship.

'You said you hated her,' Shona says taking it too far.

Awkward glances. That's the problem, people always think somethings all true. Some days I do hate my mother and some days I love her: but most days my feelings are completely neutral.

I shake my head and laugh, 'wasn't I a horrid teenager.' Then I lie. 'It's strange to think I was ever like that, now we're simply best friends.'

'You were always so harsh on her,' Shona laughs …mockingly and cruel. 'Remember when you laid in the middle of the road until she gave you twenty pounds…probably for a bottle of vodka.'

Her friends exchange more awkward glances, thinking I'm some sort of reprobate. I want to kick Shona's teeth in. There was a legitimate reason why I laid in the road, not that miss simple life would know or understand. Shona heard this story from her mum, who knows a woman down the street who witnessed the laying. One-sided stories are never true stories.

Interlude about lying on the road for twenty pounds

A year or so after Josh dumped me, I developed an eating disorder. I didn't know what to do about everything and found a beautiful control in not eating – the hunger pangs, the lovely bones. Mother would not let me go to the local eating disorder clinic, because a cleaner from the hotel she worked at, also cleaned there. You know, Madge, the 6 til 10-er who likes to spread gossip about bulimics and is shit at polishing brass doorknobs (according to Mother). Mother was quarrelling with me about not eating my dinner and how absolutely awful it was for her. Not only to cook a meal and see it uneaten- but to see her daughter wasting away. I didn't say anything. What could I say? After a few attempts of her trying to make me eat corned beef pie, 'oh come on Amber, it's your favourite, it's grandma's recipe…what would her and grandad think of this behaviour, why they'd turn in their graves at the person you've become.' Mother is a shit person. I was going to argue that I couldn't help it – but I had said this many times before and it didn't seem to make a difference. Mother felt my not eating was a direct attack at her. Maybe it was. I once read that eating disorders were linked to unstable and unhealthy relationships between mothers and daughters.

'You don't care, do you?' she shrieked, 'you might as well go and lie in the road, that way you will die quicker, and I won't have to see you fading away.'

Mother rushed over and grabbed my plate. She went into the kitchen and furiously scraped the pie into the bin – slapping the metal against porcelain, hoping for a split or scratch so she would have something else to complain about. She switched on the taps full blast and slammed the dishes and pans into the sink.

Mother was right. I calmly left the table, walked down the hallway and out the front door. I was only wearing an oversized Pixies T-shirt. FYI. I laid on the road and looked up at the sky. I waited. I was not hit by a car but my mother's unearthly scream. Maybe I had been killed and this was hell – having to hear my mother scream for all eternity. There was a sharp pain in my side. Mother had kicked me.

'Get up right now,' she aggressively whispered...you know the way Mothers do when you're in immense trouble, as if only you can hear the anger-hiss and everyone else is oblivious to it. She leaned over and grabbed my arms. 'Get up right now,' she repeated, 'you're showing me up, get up before a car comes or anyone sees you.' She was more bothered about what the neighbours would think than if I was hit by a car.

Mother held on tightly to my arms and tried to pull me back inside. Like I was a heavy garbage bag, but instead of dragging the rubbish out to be disposed of, she was dragging it back in her home, so the neighbours didn't see the junk from her loins. I dug my toes and arse into the ground, Mother Earth save me, hug me and let me be one with you. I hoped I could somehow stick to the asphalt. If not, it would be my ass-faults – see what I did there. Ding, ding.

'Get up right now Amber or you're going to be in more shit that you can handle.' Mother kicked me again, but I did not move. 'Get up and I'll give you twenty quid.'

Mother would eventually pull me back into the house. My body was too weak- it was days since I'd eaten that damn calorific oat cracker - I could not resist her forceful tugging for much longer. So, I stood up. Twenty quid was twenty quid.

'Get off my arms then' I said wriggling free.

I fled into the house. Leaving Mother to do a full sweep of the street. Not knowing the whole dreadful fiasco had been witnessed by the nosey neighbour three doors down who then told the entire street and of course Shona's mum.

I got my twenty quid and a slap across the face. And yes, I did buy things I shouldn't have bought with the money. I don't like to talk about it, if you want to know the truth.

Is that the clucking of tongues? Did they cluck? Clucky, clucky, clucky, here clucky clucky cluck. Suck a fucky fucky fuck.

I shake my head, 'crazy young 'uns, hey,' I say in a scoffing manner and move my arm in the air as if swatting away my past like an aggravating fly. I laugh knowing the perfect revenge story.

'Shona, remember the time you gave a blowjob in the guy's toilet of Blaise's? And you were wasted and gagged and vomited all over the guy's dick and he made you lick it off because there wasn't any toilet paper.'

'Oh gross,' Alex exclaims.

Sam looks disgusted. He squirms in his seat – clenching his groin. Florence shakes her head and frowns, not knowing what to say.

'That wasn't me,' Shona says jaw wide open, like on that fateful night. 'Are you sure you didn't dream it Amber? You know what that imagination of yours is like.'

Shona gulps as if reliving the moment: she must destroy the lingering liquids, the evidence. I am enjoying myself and want to go on, but remember I need to ask Shona a favour. I raise my eyebrows and fake bewilderment/puzzlement.

'Oh really,' I say, 'well your memory has always been spot on. Maybe it was Iris.'

'I most certainly think so Amber,' Shona says firmly 'what do you take me for?'

A toilet cock sucking vomit guzzler.

'You're one of the most decent girls I know,' I say, 'sorry, now I come to think of it, I'm sure it was Iris.'

The story causes a whisper of amusement. Wee chortles of glee will be heard when they remember the story tomorrow over Renaissance texts. 'Is this a vomit covered cock I see before me, the foreskin towards my mouth.'

'It WAS Shona' I want to scream. Now let's all stick lots of spikey shards of laughter and mean comments into her until she bleeds to death. Drown the vomiting witch, burn the fellating slut.

Shona did slurp vomit off a penis. I had sex with said penis, about a year later and he told me about it afterwards when we were lying in bed. Tom told me - not his penis, but he may as well just be a penis because his name really doesn't matter. Oooo dear patriarchy, doesn't it hurt when the tables are turned! Ok let's be fair and call him Penis Tom, best of both worlds, I'm all about equality.

'She actually licked the sick off your cock?' I asked in utter disbelief.

'Yeah, and I was only joking,' said Penis Tom, 'I said, shit there's no toilet paper, you better lick it off...thinking she'd tell me to go fuck myself, but she didn't...she slurped that shit up, maybe she thought it was the right thing to do.'

'Yeah like it was cock sucking decorum or something.'

Penis Tom laughed, 'you're so funny Amber.'

I never saw him again. I wasn't that funny. I wasn't dateable or girlfriend material funny. But then again, neither was Penis Tom.

Shona smiles, 'apology accepted Amber.' She finishes the tiny drop of wine left in her glass, 'anyway I must go to the ladies before the taxi home.'

Sam looks at his watch, 'yeah I suppose we should make a move.'

Shona stands up. This is my chance.

'I'll come with you,' I say, 'I need the toilet.'

'Me too,' says stupid shitty Florence and stands up.

Now bosom buddies, the three of us walk to the toilet, shooting off small talk all the while about how we've had a hot summer and other stuff-you-might-say-to-the-cashier-as-you-bag-your-groceries-in-Asda type talk. Obviously not in Lidl or Aldi – there you can barely get out a hello before your items are thrown at you and then you're dirty looked to swipe your contactless and shift away asap. With the groceries in your arms, sweating and harassed, receipt between your teeth, to stand by the doorway trying to bag everything, all the while wondering if anyone has ever committed stress related suicide because of a supermarket.

We go in separate cubicles to wee. I hate to state the obvious, but that's what we did. I wipe and flush, winning the race. Followed by Florence and then Shona. We wash our hands in silence as if we have already spoken enough. At this rate we were all going to leave the toilet together, all get a taxi together, all say goodbye together, all scissor in bed together…and to hell with my need for narcotics.

Shona concentrates on the drying of her hands. Washing and drying is an act she very much enjoys. She is a hygiene stickler. Every particle of water must be destroyed. Death to every germ.

I undo the back of my necklace and let it fall to the floor.

'Oh hell,' I say as I pick it up.

'Gosh I hope it's not broken,' says Shona.

'No, the catch is a bit lose.'

I try to do the catch at the back of my neck, but I can't, because you see, I don't want to.

I groan, 'oh I'm all fingers and thumbs, Shona will you help me please.'

'No problem,' she replies.

I shoot Florence a look to say: 'well fuck off then dear.'

My eyes must be wonderful actors because Florence takes the hint.

'I'll wait outside,' she says.

'The Oscar goes to… Amber Elizabeth Grant's right eye for her performance in The Toilet in Las Pahamas.' The left eye looks at the right eye, fuming, but trying to appear pleased, clapping its lashes.

I hand Shona the necklace and turn around so she can fasten it. 'You're so kind,' I say grovelling, 'actually I need to ask you another favour, but it's a bit embarrassing.'

'What?' she asks fiddling with the clatch.

'Well, it's just so embarrassing,' I say. I look at her reflection in the bathroom mirror. 'Do you know anyone around here who sells sniff?'

Shona looks up, a vague expression on her face, her eyes meeting mine in the mirror. I try to gauge her reaction to see if drugs are something she entertains or if she is against it.

'You know... cocaine,' I whisper.

I want Shona to burst into a high five and exclaim jubilantly: 'baby girl I thought you'd never ask,' and then rush me into a toilet cubicle to eagerly shove key after key up my nose. She will hand me a free bag of Whitey Mighty as a goodbye present because she has missed me so. She will then give me the contact details of her dealer, who buys first-rate stuff, and tell him that 'Shozza' has passed on his number and to remind him it's half price for first time buyers.

In reality....reality being the true source of our pain on this earth, Shona stares. She quickly finishes tying my necklace. She steps back. I turn around and we face each another. Thumbs toying with our holsters.

'Cocaine,' she asks screwing up her face, 'but...but why?'

'Oh y'know,' I say, 'I only do it on holiday. It's just to let my hair down, have some fun.'

'But Amber, you're married,' Shona's tone conveys utter disbelief.

You'd think I'd asked for smack. And married?... Does she really think that marriage can save you? Is she holding onto that dream – a dream forced on us girls from nearly every movie, book and song we have been made to digest since birth? Of being saved, of finding 'the one.' Surely, when you get to our age – in your mid-thirties, and you have been lied to, cheated on, accepted kisses from people with empty eyes, words and hearts, with unemotive embraces that crave one thing – it's then that you die inside because you realise - it's all a fucking lie. So why not drink the prosecco until you feel numb and snort lines until your nose burns. You deserve it. Queen, you fucking deserve it. You know that one day you will save yourself. You will make it – whatever 'it' may be. When you're ready you will get back on your feet, wiser and better – stronger, perhaps even a little cruel. It's got to be a journey or it's all pointless. It's a special kind of journey. A special kind of fall.

'Spencer does it now and again too, for fun,' I reply.

'You want to do drugs by yourself...and then what?' Shona looks disgusted.

A change of tact is needed, more lies are needed. 'Oh, sorry no, I've given you the wrong impression. I came to York with my friend, she's meeting me soon, she had to go back to the hotel because she has a headache. I'll be honest Shona, she's the one who wants it, not me. I said I'd try and get her some, she said it helps her headaches.'

Shona stares at me.

'I just thought you might know someone; I know you don't do it,' I continue.

'Amber, I think you need to get some new friends,' Shona replies.

'You're probably right,' I say, 'she's not usually like this, she's just going through a very painful divorce'.

'Well drugs won't make things better and it certainly won't cure her headache' Shona replies.

I facially fake concern, 'I know I've told her.'

'I'm very anti-drugs,' says Shona.

How do you respond to a killjoy statement like that? I'm so pro drugs I could just eat and sniff and smoke the lovelies all day. Everything should be legal.

'That rubbish is bad for you,' continues Shona, 'it's poison for your system. I can't believe you've asked me to be honest, you know my Auntie Pauline overdosed.'

I didn't know. 'Sorry, I didn't know,' I reply.

Shona seems cross, 'everyone knows about Auntie Pauline – it was the only scandal my family has ever had.'

'So, you don't know anyone?' I ask impatiently, not giving a shit about black sheep Auntie Pauline.

Shona looks at me blankly. 'Anyway, I better go. My friends are waiting,' she says the word 'friends' in bold, as if I am no longer a friend.

'Ok,' I reply.

Shona turns to leave. She is just about to open the door, but I need a definitive answer. My lust for coke is intense. I cannot cope without it up my nose.

'Do your friends know anyone who deals?' I ask.

Shona pauses but doesn't turn around: she doesn't want to see my miscreant mush. 'I really hope your 'friend' gets the help she needs, or she's going to ruin her life.' She again says the word 'friend' like it is in bold. Then she walks through the door and disappears.

I look in the mirror. I really do need help. What am I thinking with all the lies? All Shona has to do is ask someone who knows me to discover the truth. Fuck she only has to ask her mum. I'm not married, not even close. No glorious large house in Wynyard, definitely no sauna. No man has ever even loved me.

I want to bash my head against the mirror. I can't bear to look at myself. I re-apply my lipstick. I stay in the toilet for five minutes waiting for Shona and her friends (not in bold) to leave. I go back to the table and down all the dregs of alcohol that they've left. I look around the restaurant to see if any of the staff or patrons look a bit dodgy – as if they like a little sniff or a quick injection to make their lives more tolerable. Not that you have to be tatty looking to do drugs: statistically the majority of people who take cocaine are affluent – you know the bankers and wankers and business pigs. Perhaps not all the time, but you know the weekend party users, the 'work-hard, play-hard' toilet cubicle abusers, the let's snort lines off a sex worker's vagina losers. They can shovel it up like paradise because they can afford the tremendous price of the love-sugar. Plus, they have private healthcare to sort them out if things become a bit pear shaped.

But not us plebeians - we will fucking die and deserve it.

Everyone in the restaurant looks clean cut. Middle-class students and retired couples. Or are they? The shadows from the candlelight turn them into obscene distorted monsters. They sit smirking in the shadows like film noir villains. All waiting for my demise over manzanilla sherry's. As one of the waiters passes, I raise my arm schoolgirl-style and ask if the group has paid the bill. I try to ask the question in a casual manner to imply that it's fine if they haven't paid cos y'know I have it, y'know the money, y'know the mean green, y'know, yes y'know waiter man. He says yes. Imagine they hadn't paid. Yes, you can pay the bill Amber since you have this rich pretend husband and a rich pretend life. Pay cos you've ruined our night. Pay cos you're a lying cocaine slut.

I walk outside with a stale smile – trying to appear regular. The night is colder. As the breeze hits me, I realise I am wasted. I decide to find my way to *The Evil Eye* so I can pick cocktails from their superb range and lie on the beds - they have actual beds upstairs - cool and comfy. It's always a busy place because it's too damn cool for its own good. It is the cocktail bar equivalent of an Indie band who haven't quite made it yet but been rated in the Local Gig section of NME as having plenty of potential and being the next big band to sell out. Although judging by the veil wearing gaggling hens and football and beer ready types who frequent the place, especially on a Saturday, then perhaps it has already done so.

A young homeless man sits in the doorway of a charity shop. He has long brown dreads tied in a blue ribbon (like a charming courtier in the Palace of Versailles -but with a modern urban scruffy vibe) and is dressed in a million layers. I reach into my purse and put my spare change into his bowl.

'Thanks sweetheart,' he says.

There's nothing more annoying or tut-worthy than when someone refers to you as sweetheart and they're younger than you. Like nor. Dear sir, please rewind to the last words you uttered and change it to something more fitting and less patronising. Just say thanks. I could have a real hang up with the term 'sweetheart.' Like maybe a rapist called me sweetheart when he violently pummelled me. Or perhaps I have a complex about my heart being sweet because it is considerably bitter. Or perhaps I have a heart defect and this slight-of-hand comment could cause floods of tears. He is quite literally an insensitive beggar!

'Actually,' I bend down near him, you know like you're supposed to do when you talk to children, so they don't feel intimidated, 'I know this is a long shot, but do you know anyone around here who sells coke?'

I use the term 'long shot', so he doesn't think I presume he is into drugs just because he lives on the streets. That until proven otherwise I consider him a man of drug innocence. I of course assume that he knows all drug dealers in a ten-mile radius. It's like asking a paedophile the family swim times at their local leisure centre, or playtimes at the local primary school.

'Is it for you?' he asks in a soft well-spoken voice. He speaks slowly: I cannot tell if he is terrifically bored or terrifically tired.

'Yeah, I have the money.'

He shifts on his bony bum – as if deciding whether he can trust me and that he will let his bum bones decide by giving them a little shuffle. Right cheek comes up trumps– yeah give her a chance.

'You're not with the police or owt are you,' he laughs.

Why do all druggies /drug dealers ask this? Like if you aren't a druggie and/or drug dealer and drugs do not occur in your life in some form, then surely you would repel back in disgust and indignantly reply 'no way.' Then perhaps perform a sign of the cross in a gesture of holiness and lack of soul corruption, not reply with: 'are you with the police?' If I was a bobby then I would know straight away that this person is a diddler and take them inside and in usual police fashion, get them done and then nick their stash to use and/or sell at my own convenience.

'I'm fucking wrecked, do I look like a police officer?' I reply.

We both laugh. He has pure blue Jesus eyes. Is this my

saviour? Under his dreads and beards (I suspect he had beards everywhere) is an attractive man who has undoubtedly endured awful life events, resulting in him being homeless. I'm sure it's the alcohol talking ...but I would like to have sex with him. Maybe I could suggest bath or shower sex so I can get in there first with the soap and sponge, give him a good scrub, and lather his genitalia before any sort of penetration occurs into any sort of orifice. But first...

'Listen you sort me out and I'll buy you a bag.'

'For real?' he asks.

'Yeah honestly, I will do anything for coke right now, you'll be doing me the biggest favour.'

He thinks for a moment. A very brief moment. In fact, I doubt he is thinking at all – just giving the impression of thinking. I had him immediately in the bag at 'bag'.

'Ok,' he says. He looks into his massive rucksack and brings out an I-phone. An I-phone – whatever next! Will a butler appear from a chauffeur driven Bentley holding a silver tray with a bouquet of over-spilling white bags? He presses a button and then hands over the phone. 'Talk to this guy, he's called Richie, say that Morris gave you his number and just ask for what you need.'

The homeless guy is called Morris – lol.

'You know how much it is?' I ask.

'Fifty quid a bag, but it's great stuff.'

Fifty quid a bag – jeez Toto let's go back to Kansas. The dealers back home sold three bags for a hundred.

'Hi, is that Richie?' I ask when someone picks up.

'Yeah' says a posh Yorkshire accent.

'Hi, my name is Faith Cavendish, I'm using Morris' phone, he said I could contact you for some coke.'

'Yeah sweetheart, how much?'

'Four bags please.'

Why not eh... I'm on holiday! It will last me. It will get used. And Daddy has transferred me all that money. He'd want his daughter, who he's emotionally neglected since birth, to fill the void somehow.

'You got the cash on you?' asks Richie.

'Yeah.'

'Ok where about do you want me to drop off.'

'I'm stood in Barnardo's doorstop; you know the one near the main street.'

'Ok two streets down, there's a road that cars can access, there's a butcher's and then an alleyway, go down there and it will take you to the back of the shops, I'll be there in fifteen minutes. I have a white Beatle; Morris will show you where to go if you give him a line...he'll do anything for a line.' Richie laughs and says bye.

Anything for a line – and he's me offering him a bloody bag!

I inform Morris where we have to meet Richie. He says it's just around the corner, so we can set off in 5 minutes. Morris moves his rucksack so I can sit down next to him. I hope he doesn't rape me or beat me or nick my money.

What can I talk to Morris about? Work - nope. Family - nope. Friends – nope. The security and comfort of living in a home with central heating and regular meals - nope. Let's resort to a subject that us British excel at!

'It's getting colder,' I say.

'Aye,' he replies, 'according to the weather report, we're in for a cold winter.'

'They say that every year,' I sneer, 'coldest winter, hottest summer, load of shite. Y'know what they'll say next... 'most leafy Autumn'...'most springy spring.' Meteorologists are up there with politicians in my book.'

'I hope it's not going to be a cold one,' he says, ignoring my drunken over-exaggeration, 'last year was rough.'

I want to ignore his grim reality, which I can't really relate to, but feel I must comment in some way.

'So, if you don't mind me asking, how come you're...y'know... in this position? You don't have to answer if it's too personal.'

I sound like my dad whenever he asks about my mental health. 'Amber, oh, err, mmm, well.' Pause. Exhale. Shuffle. Sniff.

'How come you...y'know...erm...have a problem.' Dad will then gesture up to imply that the problem is in my head. Pause. Shuffle. Sniff. Hands shoved into pockets as they had already done too much... they had indicated up - up referring to the demented and tormented brain of his daughter. Dad must avoid eye contact at all costs. The mouth can lie. Eyes cannot. Shuffle. Pause. Exhale. 'Not that it matters.' Shuffle. Sniff. Then dad will quickly change the subject because he does not want to know the answer – the answer that matters greatly.

'I always wondered the same thing about people like me when I was in your position,' Morris shrugs as if it's all a very light-hearted affair, 'I lost my job...then not long after that, my house. Then lots of awful things happened so I had no choice but to live on the street. People are closer to being homeless than you realise.'

'You had no family or friends to take you in?' I ask.

'None I'd like to live with. I was never really close to anyone and I didn't want to burden anyone with my problems. I sold everything I had and bought a camper van. Thought I'd wander around the country and live off the land.'

'So, you're not actually homeless?'

'I am in a sense, I don't have a conventional home, you know luxuries like en-suite bathrooms and a king size bed. Just a lovely little campervan.'

'Why do you sit here and not in your campervan?' I was going to insert the word 'lovely' before campervan but thought it would sound as sarcastic as I meant it.

'On a busy day here, I can make quite a bit of money and save up for the next place I travel to. Petrol costs money, food costs money. I've been here for about ten weeks and enjoying it so far. It's a really historic and a chill place, plus its packed full of tourists and rich people,' Morris laughs.

'Where is your van?'

'It's in a forest area, about a thirty-minute walk from here. I can usually hitch a lift there and back if I can't be bothered walking. It's a sweet life, living in nature, feeling free, not being tied down to a job and responsibilities, not caring what others think. Losing my job was the greatest thing that's ever happened to me.'

I laugh, 'it sounds wonderful, I'm actually jealous.'

'Do it, don't be a slave to the system. It isn't worth it.'

'Do the other homeless people know that you're not really homeless?' I ask.

He shrugs, 'well they might think it's strange that they never see me in the shelters or soup kitchens ...but I don't think they've caught on. I eat pretty well to be honest, if it's a particularly good week I can even afford a few restaurant meals.'

Morris the massive not really homeless phoney.

'Let's go and get the drugs,' I say and stand. I very much need drugs to deal with Morris and my life.

'Remember life is as easy as you want it to be, only you are stopping you,' Morris says but I have already stopped listening to him.

I am not going to take life lessons from a phoney. Life isn't easy. People are actually homeless and starving and dying. Morris is so smug in his freedom, too smug, a smugness that only comes with having money – without getting too Orwell on y'all.

I imagine Morris saying to his upper-middle class CEO father – 'No I won't live in our holiday home in Cornwall, I want to make it on my own father.' In three years from now, the prodigal son will return to his father's arms – all braided and campervanned out – it was great whilst it lasted, but nothing lasts these days. Morris will cut and shave away the years of freedom, hop in a designer suit and sit next to his father at the next board meeting. His father will proudly proclaim that his son had 'made it for years on his own and as a reward he will now be the new Assistant Director.' Applause. Perhaps even a thankyou speech by Morris. But Margaret - Morris' father's long-suffering secretary/PA will barely tap her palms together, for she knows Morris' history of money squandering – that he has on numerous occasions lost everything to drugs, gambling and women that were so wild – lord they took it all! That Morris had to run away and lay low for a while, before his father disinherited him.

I hate Morris a little - whilst simultaneously wanting to use him for intercourse. I often have these mixed feelings about arseholes.

Interlude about our dreamy camper van life

Our camper van will be rainbow themed. My hair long, thick and flowing. My skin peaceful and glowing. Morris will go 'to work' for the day and I will stay in the campervan making it even more rainbow-y. I will spend my days reading books, philosophising, playing with my chakras and peaceful shit like that. I will wash our clothes in the nearby river, coming back with pails of water to prepare our vegan stews made fresh each day for when he comes home from a hard day's begging. As I carry the pails my cleavage will look simply marvellous in a hippy milkmaid get up, perhaps with some sort of plait or flowers in my hair. Incense will constantly be on the burn. Candles and cushions erratically spread. We will sit around a campfire toasting vegan marshmallows, the moon and stars ready to light our nightly love making. I will ride him like a Wiccan goddess, pulling at his grimy dreads as if they are reigns.

One-night, mid-ride, I feel a little wriggle under my forefinger. My eyes fling open and I see an insect poking out from his brown wiry mane. As I peer closer, I can see flies and worms and spiders, the lot, dozens of them lit up by the moon. All squirming for attention, eating and playing and copulating. It is like a black and white horror film – a new Cronenberg masterpiece without the tech. Perhaps the tech bit comes later.

Freud why can't my sex fantasies be normal?

'It iz becauze you envy za penis. Da insects are da men in your life. The way...'

I am suddenly pushed out of my day (technically night) dream.

'Watch out for that dog shit' Morris shouts, 'you were miles away.'

There it is: brown mountain. Ain't no denying.

'People never notice anything,' I reply.

I follow Morris down an alleyway besides the butchers. I feel dangerous, but am then grabbed by a sudden fear - what am I doing? This guy could be part of a sex trafficking gang – I might never make it back home, instead I'll be drugged and transported to some unknown place where I will be fucked from pillar to post. Morris could be acting, being all free spirited and camper-van-y when in fact his life is financed through tourist pootang.

The white beetle is there as we exit the alleyway.

'Now bud,' Morris shouts. He immediately adopts a deep voice and swaggers to the car. I'm assuming this greeting is aimed at the inhabitants of the car and not the actual car – as this could suggest that Morris sought relationships with inanimate objects and perhaps has intimacy issues.

Morris leans on the car window; they do some sort of ridiculous thug handshake. Vomit at everything a man is.

'How's life treating you mate?' asks Richie. I can't see Richie's face because he has black-out windows. I am later glad for this delay.

'Real good bud, real good, no complaints,' says Morris.

'Except the fact you're a homeless motherfucker,' Richie laughs.

'Sweet for me bud, life's easy breezy,' Morris laughs.

Morris gestures for me to come forward.

'Is it still two hundred for four bud?' asks Morris.

I come closer so I can see Richie. He is not attractive. Imagine 'Craterface' from the movie Grease but with a black moustache and black bushy hair.

'Hi sweetheart,' he says.

I get the money from my purse and then we do that sly hand thing, where you turn your hand and discreetly exchange money for drugs. I drop the bags in my bag: they shine like heaven.

'What's with the hat?' Richie asks.

I had forgotten about my Holden hat. Surprisingly this is the first comment I've received about it. If I was back home, I would probably be in intensive care by now for wearing anything as unique. Hatless in a coma. I know, I know, it's serious. My, my, my, my, my, my baby, goodbye.

'This is a people shooting hat,' I reply, but then add quickly, 'I bought it because my head is cold.'

'What in this weather!' Richie exclaims.

'I'm getting over a nasty ear infection.'

'Where are you from?' asks Richie.

'Durham' -once you start lying it's difficult to stop.

'I thought you sounded more Northern,' Richie replies.

I don't know how to answer that.

'Thanks,' I say gesturing towards the illegal deposits in my bag.

'Anytime,' says Richie. 'I'll let you get on mate,' he says to Morris, 'you'll have begging to do.'

They both laugh and do a weird hand-shake goodbye. Morris bangs the edge of the car window once, then twice, like some symbolic goodbye ritual.

'Later bud,' he says as Richie winds up his window. Well not wound, you know pressed the button for it to go up.

'Soooo' Morris says looking at me.

'Thanks very much. You're a life saver. Do you fancy going somewhere to crush this up and have a few lines?' I ask.

'I better be getting back,' he says, 'If you don't mind, I'll take my bag and head off. My missus will be waiting; she has to be up early tomorrow to teach yoga.'

Missus Morris Yoga Phoney.

'Ok, no problem,' I reply and hand him a bag. Why does a lump rise in my throat?

There is an actual problem with this. I am the problem. I wanted to befriend and maybe even shag a homeless, my apologies, campervan man. Just to make me feel better for a short period of time. To cure a loneliness which alcohol and drugs can't touch. Can't he see it in my eyes? Couldn't he hug me and say that everything is going to be ok? I want to hide between his shoulder blades. Bury in the concave part of his back. I want to wet his clothes with my tears. To have some miniscule effect on his life- even if it is just the tiny hindrance of having to dry his tear-stained top. In that very act of inconvenience, he will think of me for all of five seconds and that will be good enough. But no, he will go home to his 'missus' and they will do lines of coke and he will passionately pull off his tear-stained top so they can have the coke-fuelled sex that we were meant to have. The next day when he picks up the top, the tears will be dry. As if I never existed.

'Thanks so much and I hope you have a great night,' Morris says walking backwards.

'You too,' I say and produce a fake sickly-sweet smile that over the years I have practised to perfection.

Morris waves and walks down the back street. I turn and walk down the alley. Tears gush. I crush a bag against the wall and do two lines on my hand-mirror using a tightly wound fiver. Pick me up. Hold me up. Lipstick re-applied. Rub the gums and forget. I broke the garage windows once. I stumble to *The Evil Eye*.

To lie in the rye.

CHAPTER NINE

I haven't time in my life to keep going to the bar, so I buy two cocktails. Not wanting to be bothered by humans, I sit in the outside terrace where it is quiet, apart from the occasional smoker. The night is now too cold to be enjoyed by beer garden enthusiasts and general knobheads who think that because it's summer then they must sit outside at every opportunity as it will somehow make their lives better.

I take out the book. I am too high and keep reading the same sentence again and again until it becomes a little melody in my head. Did you know that if you speak his name aloud – Holden - it makes you pucker your lips as if to bestow a kiss. Kissing. Slowly. Intimately. Forgetting. Easing. Fiction is so much more real than reality. The words become fuzzy all raining into one. I down one of my drinks, put the book back in my bag and go inside. I don't want to sit downstairs because I don't want to be seen by the bar staff. Alone and gurning. A lovely girl, nonetheless.

I go upstairs, spilling my drink. To my utter delight one of the beds is unoccupied. There is a sign saying that to stop the spread of Covid can you please sanitize your hands as much as possible. A large bottle of hand sanitizer is attached to every bed – a sign underneath reads: 'Use me. Don't' be a jerk.' A new and relatable life motto.

I put my drink down on the table and climb on to the bed. On the bed opposite is a couple: repugnant student types who might appear on University Challenge. Kooky knitwear and organised files.

'Hey,' I say to them, 'can you watch my drink whilst I go to the toilet...I need this bed, my sanity depends on it.'

'Yeah sure,' the girl replies. They look apprehensive.

I smile shit eatingly and stomp off. When I have coke, it makes me really confident, so much so that I'm in people's faces, spoiling their personal space, slurring and chewing my inner mouth off. I go to the toilet, which is inconveniently downstairs, and snort another two lines. The beat-beat of my heart. Kissing. Licking. Secrets told. Petals stroked on stomach. Who wants flowers when you're dead? Nobody.

I go back upstairs and onto the bed. My drink is still there – the geeky beauts.

'Thank you,' I shout over.

'No problem,' says the girl smiling. I can tell the guy has no option but to keep silent as his girlfriend seems the controlling type that doesn't like him talking to girls. She squeezes his hand tightly and quickly starts a conversation so I can't cut in.

I take a sip of my cocktail and get the book out of the bag. The words spit at me. I am jittery and alive- as if I've been zapped with electricity, warm and present, alert and bright.

The couple smile at me as they leave. It is just after eleven. I look around the room and realise I am alone. How long have I been here? A barman comes upstairs to collect the empty glasses.

'What time is this place open til?' I ask.

'Twelve on a weekday,' he replies.

'Where's good to go afterwards?'

'Mmm' he thinks about it, 'the best and busiest nights are on the weekend- but there's Popworld which is a cheesy pop night if you like that sort of thing.'

'I like anywhere,' I reply, 'and I like anyone. I'm that kind of person'.

My words run into each other; I don't even know what I'm saying. Lie after lie - I hate everywhere and everyone. He smiles, embarrassed for me. Then after one last wipe of a table and a check around for empty glasses, he goes back downstairs.

I text Erin, 'hey hun, how's things?'

She replies: 'Great here, how's things in New York, what time is it there and how's the weather?'

It is past her weekday bedtime, so I'm slightly surprised by this rebellion! When I'm away how the tame sane little cat will play. Then again, she probably cuddles her phone in bed, like a teddy, to wake her up at any notification however insignificant. Sleep is not important when she has to keep up to date with fake social media acquaintances. Erin is the kind of girl who lives with her phone in her hand, nothing is ever seen or experienced first-hand, always through her phone. At a concert - raise arm in the air and film gig. At a dinner with friends - text your other friends. Watching a film at the cinema - oh better check every little thing on social media. Life in simulacrum isn't a real life, hopefully one day she and millions of others will understand this.

I have no idea what the time difference is in New York or what the weather is like, and I can't be bothered to look on google- so I don't reply. I pick up the book and continue reading. It is the scene with the escort.

I hear the hard thuds and creaks of someone coming up the wooden stairs. I assume it is the bar man telling me to go downstairs. That way they can keep an eye on the silly drunk girl. Then throw me out at the chime of 12.

A guy appears – pale with light brown hair. He looks at me. I pretend to read; hoping he'll go away. Praying he isn't one of a group, following him with their cocktails, giggles and lack of silence.

'Have you seen my friends?' he asks.

I look up, having little choice.

'The couple?' I ask.

'Oh god no,' he scoffs, 'who in their right mind hangs out with a couple. Couples are awful company.'

'I only remember the couple,' I reply, 'there were others here, but they're a nondescript blur.'

'Were my friends ever here though?' he asks, clearly drunk.

'I don't know,' I reply.

'Well, if you don't know and I don't know, who will know?' he asks.

'You could describe them to the bar staff downstairs, they might have seen them.'

'No,' he replies, 'that's not the answer. I've already asked them, and they weren't helpful.'

'Ring your friends,' I suggest.

'I've lost my mobile.'

'You can ring them off mine if you like?'

'I don't know any of their numbers…do you know them?'

I shake my head. He comes closer and sits on the edge of the bed. He is wearing a Dave's stag do t-shirt. I am immediately repulsed, although I don't recognise him from the gang of pricks I'd met earlier in McDonalds. That awful encounter seems so long ago now. Sometimes a day can last forever.

'Are you staying at a hotel?' I ask.

He nods.

'They've probably gone back there,' I say.

'I don't know the name of the hotel.'

'You don't?'

'No I didn't think it was important.'

'Do you have a door key swipe thing?'

'No, the other guy has that.'

'Do you know where the hotel is…like roughly, that would be a start?'

'No,' he replies, 'honestly, I wasn't that bothered where I was, I just wanted to get drunk.'

'Well if you go outside and listen, you'll probably hear them, if I remember rightly your friends are quite loud.'

He has pale blue eyes, fair skin and is good looking in a James McAvoy kind of way.

He pulls a confused face, 'were you with the stag do?'

'No, I unfortunately ran into your friends earlier in McDonalds. Lovely, aren't they?' I say sarcastically.

'I hate them,' he pulls a face, 'I only came on this trip for something to do. I went to school with Dave, and I couldn't stand him then. He's one of those friends who you don't like but can't seem to part with. Do you know what I mean? I knew as soon as I got on that minibus that I had made a major mistake. As soon as they started to talk about football and titties, I should have taken my own life. Or at least I should have jumped out the vehicle and said I couldn't go because I had gout or syphilis or both gout and syphilis.'

'Gout and syphilis!' I laugh.

'Yeah,' he replies, 'you can't go on a stag do with that combination – it would be worse than having head lice with a chest infection or piles and a sprained right wrist.'

I laugh, 'what are you on about?'

'What would be your worst illness combination?' he asks.

'I've never really thought about it.'

'Well think about it now, it's extremely important,' he replies.

'Erm…I'd hate to have crabs and a migraine. That would be horrific.'

He laughs. 'That's the very definition of a nightmare. What's your name?' he asks.

'Amber'

'Tree shit.'

'Pardon?'

'That's what amber is…tree resin. Were your parents into tree shit?' he asks seriously. What peculiar creature sits before me?

'I don't think that was a hobby of theirs,' I answer.

'Did they meet looking at tree shit and were so aroused they immediately had to copulate and have a daughter called Amber?'

'Maybe,' I joke.

'I'm kidding. It's a beautiful name.'

'Thanks, what's yours?' I ask.

'Lewis'

'I'm too drunk to think of any sarcastic or slightly humorous response to that,' I reply.

Lewis smirks, 'that's fine… when you think of one just throw it my way and I'll see if I can take it.' He reaches for my drink. 'Can

I have a sip please? I'm parched.'

'Sure,' I reply because it doesn't seem I have a choice.

'What the fuck is it?' he asks taking a sip.

'Some lemony mixture – I got it because I liked the name. I like cocktails with cool names. It's the only way to pick them these days, because there are so many.'

'The only way,' he says and takes another sip. 'Bitterly beautiful.'

'Just like the girl who bought it,' I say and laugh. 'Not that I think I'm beautiful, or particularly bitter. In fact, if I was a drink, I'd probably be something boring like orange squash, but the type where there isn't enough squash, so it's just diluted watery shit with a vague taste of orange.'

Lewis shakes his head, 'don't ever compare yourself to over-diluted juice. If we're playing around with orange-based drinks, you'd be a Buck's Fizz.'

Lewis takes another sip of the cocktail and looks around.

'Where are your friends? At the bar?' he asks.

'No, I'm by myself. My friends are in my head.' I reply, not feeling the need to lie.

Lewis lays back in the bed, getting comfy. 'You have your book there,' he says gesturing to the book which is page down spread on the bed, 'you're never really alone if you have a book. What are you reading?'

I pick up the book and show him the front cover.

'It's my fave,' I say and quickly put it in my bag as if I have already revealed too much of myself.

'So why are you here by yourself then, what's your story?' Lewis asks again.

'One body, a thousand flies,' I reply.

Lewis stares at me intently.

'I think we both need another drink before I go into that,' I say. I go into my bag to get my purse.

'Here I'll get it, what do you want?' Lewis asks.

I can't remember a time that a guy has bought me a drink with what seemed like a genuine intent. The kind of guys I usually meet are all 'next time' promises. Next time I'll take us out for a meal, next time I'll pay for our night out, next time I'll buy the booze and drugs. Or the complete opposite – the guy who insists on buying the drinks, the drugs, the taxis, the pizza - so you then feel you must hand over your vagina as some sort of fair exchange.

'Surprise me,' I reply. Lewis smiles and goes downstairs. I wait, feeling warm inside.

Lewis is quite a long time. But time can be strange when you're wrecked – it either goes extremely fast – a whole night can seem like ten minutes, or extremely slow, and ten minutes can seem like an entire night. This feels like the latter. Has he found his 'friends' and ventured off? Has he sobered up, come to his senses at the bar, and legged it? Has he found a pretty girl and decided to take his chance with her, her being the obvious choice? I am the constant romantic fool.

Creaks on the stairs. Has Lewis instructed one of the bar staff to tell me he has left? Let me guess- some emergency. A friend in need. A family member rushed to hospital. He suddenly felt ill. We've all done it – well actually I haven't because I can't hurt people like that, it's a repulsive way to treat others.

It's Lewis. He heavy sighs, 'sorry, I needed a pee and then it took me ages to pick a cocktail that I thought would suit you.' He hands me my drink. It is layered - black and white with a red frothy top. 'It's called The Black Lodge...I guessed you'd be a Twin Peaks fan.'

'Obsessed,' I reply.

'I knew it,' Lewis sits down on the bed. 'Do you have any drugs?'

'Just coke.'

'Can we get as fucked up as possible and hate our lives tomorrow?' Lewis asks.

'That's basically how I spend my life,' I reply.

'Let's have some here now, there's no cameras.'

I get the coke out of my bag and we each have a couple of keys. Then we talk. Shooting the crap. We discuss everything and nothing at all and everything in between. Between love and hate, life and death. I don't want to discuss what was said because it's special and belongs to us.

The bar man tells us to finish off our drinks as they closed ten minutes ago. He had forgotten we were there.

'Time hey,' Lewis shrugs in a sad way, 'the man-made beast that grinds us down.'

We finish our drinks. We float down the stairs. We float outside. We float up the street. We float to Popworld. We float coke up our noses. We float in and out of conversation. In short, we did float. Is this real? Had I been drugged by Morris, and this is all a dream before I wake to a sex trafficking life of needles and multiple forced penetrations? Julee Cruise falls off stage mid ballad. Dorothy Gale dies in the tornado -she lands on Toto and crushes him to death. Scarlett O'Hara marries Ashley Wilkes.

Lewis and I are both ridiculously wrecked. It is usual at this point for the guy to turn all slobbery and gropey, but not Lewis. When we dance together, nothing romantic or sexual happens. No kisses or squeezes. Perhaps he isn't interested in me in that way. Although our gaze always lingers longer than it should.

We have both enjoyed a great night and don't want it to end. When it is closing time, we linger until the staff are annoyed.

'I won't be able to sleep,' says Lewis as we walk up the steps to the exit, 'let's go for a walk before we go back.'

My feet must be moving forward, but the action isn't conscious.

'Let's walk by the river, it will be lovely' he suggests. The night seems warmer.

We pass the bright lights of the takeaways, the yells and laughter, the taxi honks and glass shattering, the snogs and goodbyes, the garlic and meat, greasy fingers rubbed on taxi seats. Mind popping-ness surrounds us. I hope so much that this is something. Us. But then that pang, that resentment, that hate. The knowing what can happen. How I will feel if, or when, things didn't turn out. Yet I can't stop walking, hoping. What if. My heartbeat asks. What if. What if. What if. And then. If what. If what. If what.

Nothing will happen. Just another heartbreak. Don't risk it.

Ditch him. Lewis can be your last nice memory before the end. It's time to end. Let the people in your life get on with their lives without the constant worry of you. Everyone is tired by you. You are tired by you. Just rest. It's time. Jump in the river. Never resurface. The long, beautiful sleep.

I frequently fantasize about stabbing myself with a large sharp knife. To ease it into my heart or to slowly lower my body onto the blade. That soothing surge like a bullet breaking water, prying into my organs, a wanted visitor- 'hello little one, we have been waiting for you.' The end of the blade will tickle, not hurt. The release, that crimson spurt.

'What are you thinking about?' Lewis asks.

'About different ways to commit suicide,' I blurt out, then immediately regret the confession. Lewis will realise I am unstable: he will suddenly and conveniently remember the location of his hotel. He will leave me alone by the river to get on with it. I will be right.

Lewis doesn't look bothered, 'I'd slit my wrists in a bathtub. That way the blood diffuses in the water... like a sad song.'

'That's a beautiful way to go,' I reply.

Lewis takes a sharp left and we go down the steps to the river. I follow this strange man who is strange like me. I am about half in love by the time we reach a bench to sit down. We talk a little more about different ways to commit suicide. When our ideas dry up, Lewis steers the conversation.

'I want to ask you three questions,' Lewis said, 'you have to answer them truthfully and then you can ask me three questions and I have to answer them truthfully. The questions can be as personal as you like, but we have to answer properly.'

'Ok,' I reply.

'But first,' he says, 'do you have any more coke?'

'Don't you think it's a little late to be having it now, we will be awake forever,' I reply.

'Do you have plans tomorrow?' Lewis asks.

'No.'

'Well let's just enjoy now then,' he replies.

Lewis has a way, not manipulative, but of making me see things differently. I don't have any plans tomorrow. Why not live in the moment. That's what it says in the self-help books. Carpe Diem. I don't think it means – enjoy lots of cocaine with a hot guy, but all written text is open to interpretation. We do a few keys.

'Question number one,' Lewis says, 'what are you most scared of?'

Sigh, then release. 'Of wasting my whole life being unhappy. Of never finding happiness or not knowing what would make me happy. Of never feeling happy, even once.'

'Good answer' he replies.

'But you can't judge me by any of my answers' I say. I hope Lewis does not internally wince at my depressed melodramatic replies. Although he also seems a bit hammy and intense, so perhaps he won't mind. And if I never see him again and this is a one-night thing then it won't matter anyway.

'I'd never judge,' he exclaims with faux shock. 'Number two, what's the most important thing, person, whatever, in your life?'

'*Catcher in the Rye*,' I reply. 'I first read it when I was at my worst. It gives me hope. It makes me feel normal. That there are people out there like me, who aren't phonies. It's a huge comfort blanket. Like having whiskey on the rocks – it fires me up whilst simultaneously cooling me down. I love it. I love what Holden stands for. I know it sounds silly to most people.'

'It's not silly,' Lewis replies. He sits still like a chalk body outline at a criminal investigation. 'Yes, it's an object and not a person or a belief- but it's more than just paper, it's words, words that obviously mean a lot to you. It defines who you are and when you read it you've added to its life. You created it in your mind. Author and reader, the most beautiful of relationships.'

'We're getting so deep,' I laugh.

'Unapologetically deep,' he replies, 'this is better than small talk, chit chat. Even if after tonight we never see each other again, I will always remember this conversation I'm having here with you now...and it isn't the alcohol and coke talking.'

Does Lewis mean it? My heart inhales: my head exhales. Can he see I am worn down by life? Can he see what I am? Or is he using my vulnerabilities for one night of fun? Fun then run. Fuck then chuck. Fornication then deportation. Do the nasty then get out fasty. Down and dirty then blow your brains out like Kurty. You get the drift.

'Third question,' Lewis says, 'what are your best and worse qualities.'

'Worst,' I reply, 'wow there's a lot. Erm …I'm an idealist. I over think. I read too much. I love too much. I feel too much. I have severe depression. I judge unfairly. I bite my nails. I have no self-control. I abuse my body and mind constantly with alcohol and drugs. I believe people. I am weak, I…'

'I'm going to stop you there,' Lewis cut in, 'because I need to tell you off for talking a load of shit. Idealism… over-thinking… feelings, surely, they're good qualities.'

I shrug.

'Ok, well what are your good qualities?' Lewis asks.

'I'm good at reading and I'm a genuine person most of the time.' I stop. What else is good about me?

'Well, you are what you tell yourself,' he replies, 'it's up to you what that may be.'

Breathe.

'So, what are my questions?' Lewis asks.

'I can't think of any,' I lie. My mind whirs with ideas. But how can I ever say them without sounding needy or psychotic. Do you really like me? Can this be something? Have you got lots of girls on the go? Have you ever been in love? Do you feel…this? But instead, I say… 'I'll just ask you the questions you asked me, that's fair. So, what scares you most?'

'Life,' Lewis replies, 'it's an obvious answer. Of just being alive and wasting it all on the mundane.' He looks at me, 'Next.'

'What's the most important thing to you?'

'Myself,' he replies, 'I'm important to me. Next.

'You said no one word answers.'

'My answer is concise and says everything that's important. So …next.'

'Ok, what are your best and worst qualities?' I ask.

'My best qualities are also my worst qualities – like self-assurance and confidence, they are both an asset and barrier. I also don't care what people think about me, which has its positives and negatives.'

There is silence, Lewis does not expound is answer, so I say, 'in one way I don't care what people think about me. I've always been my own person, with my own interests. But at the same time, I'm crippled by how I think others might judge me, you know, that I have a life of drugs, alcohol, bad decisions, weaknesses and that's all there is and all there will ever be. There's more to me though. I know it. This isn't my story, it's a journey, a fall. A special kind of fall.'

'You're using these vessels to escape yourself and your issues,' Lewis replies, 'that's a weakness. You need to sit down and truly experience your feelings. To grow you need to turn the table on your 'negative' experiences and make them positive …realise it's made you who you are and then… let it go.'

'It's not as easy as that,' I reply.

'It is,' Lewis says.

'You should be a counsellor,' I suggest.

Lewis stands up and gestures for me to do the same. We move to the railing surrounding the river and leant against it. The moon echoes in the water. I look up. Every star tells me about its existence. Confirms its presence and whispers 'believe.' Glittering fossils. In a black tomb, in bloom.

'Did you know that every single year the moon is moving away from the Earth at a miniscule rate,' Lewis says matter-of-factly. 'About eighty-five million years ago the moon was only about thirty-five feet away from the Earth's surface. Even the moon thinks human's suck: it backs away slowly.'

The moon: love begins there.

I can't hold it in, I have to say it out loud, 'the moon: love begins there.'

'Wrong' Lewis replies.

Then a warm hand pulls down my chin and his lips meet

mine. This is the way the world ends, not with a bang but a kiss. I'm dizzy, one hand on the railing, but then both in his hair, on his neck. The stars hide. I can't make sense. We kiss for a century. Kisses can be a lot of things: soft, teasing, hard, sensual, animalistic, forced, loving, comforting. I thought I had experienced every kind of kiss- but not like this, this kiss was none of these things and yet all of them at once. We stop. Lewis smiles. I think I am smiling.

'The moon isn't a person though,' he says and grabs my hands, 'let's go back.'

'Where are you going to go?' I ask.

'Would you mind if I stay with you?' he asks.

'No of course not,' I reply.

So let it begin. The final act. I want him to go away. If he leaves now, he will be a perfect memory. If he stays, he will become another failure, another rejection, another blade. This is probably all a game. The lay game. Perhaps I am a dare - his stag-do buddies wait around the corner giggling into their beer froth. Perhaps they saw me go into *The Evil Eye* and spurred Lewis on to try and spunk in my stuck-up frigid ugly nerd cave.

I can't fall in love again, how could I ever prepare for the aftermath. Love is like a terminal illness. The doctors don't know how long you have left, but that you will die at some point in the future, so you're just trying to make the most of the time you have, knowing it could all be over at any moment. Sometimes a cure is found, or your body reacts positively to treatment, and you can live for some time, but you're always in fear that the illness may return, that happiness will end - that love is temporary. However, you need to free your heart and feel true love or life is pointless. Cliché as it may be, it is better to live a life of 'oh well's' than 'what ifs.'

'When we get back, we can watch a film,' Lewis says, 'we'll be up all night anyway with all this coke. I'll let you choose what we watch.'

I nod and okay the idea. He holds my hand, and we start to walk to the hotel. What if - says the stars. What if - says the breeze.

What if. If what.

I have to google the hotel on my phone, my bearings are shot. We hold the illuminated phone in front of us. Our guide. We giggle when we can't understand which way to go and get lost for about ten minutes.

We eventually find the hotel. The bright lights in the hotel lobby reveal our darkest secrets of booze and drugs – pupils like drops of mud, skin embroidered with sweat.

When we get to the room Lewis asks if he can sleep in his underpants. I say I don't mind. I say I need the toilet. After a night on the lash (lash lol) I usually scrub off my makeup and wear my most comfy pyjamas. But not tonight. I look in the mirror and wipe off my make-up, not all of it, just enough to try and look naturally attractive – you know as if I was born with curly thick eyelashes and a faint black line round my eyes. I look in my bag – have a quick key for confidence and then apply concealer, lip gloss and a touch of shimmer eyeshadow. I stick toothpaste in my mouth, I don't brush my teeth because I don't want Lewis to hear and think I am doing so in preparation for snogs leading to sex.

I have a wee and then rub liquid soap all over my vagina, so it doesn't smell. If he then goes down on me – which I don't want him to, but boys will be boys but also accountable for their actions, then I will smell like ...what does it say on the bottle, honeysuckle with a hint of rose, rather than sweaty ham with a hint of mackerel. Afterall, I have been dancing all night. I don't wipe my vagina with toilet paper as it sometimes gets stuck on the flaps and that's the very last thing I want to spoil tonight. I'm sorry for the above information, but it's the honest to God truth! I flush and go into the bedroom.

Lewis lies in bed, he has the duvet over his legs, his bare chest on show. He has a pleasant body, not fat, not muscly, not skinny – an average body with a sufficient sprinkling of brown chest hair. He has switched on the TV and is flipping through the channels.

'What do you want to watch?' he asks and flicks about. 'There's Film Four playing *Predator* and ...let's have a look, there's TCM and a film called *Cat on a Hot Tin Roof,* it's been on five minutes.'

'OMG Tennessee. We have to watch it,' I reply with glee.

Lewis smiles and gets cosy in bed. He never asks who Tennessee is, so he either knows, which makes him perfect, or he is pretending to know, which makes him less perfect, but at least he is trying to impress/amuse me.

What should I wear? I don't have any sexy nightwear, just my nightie - a baggy black t-shirt with the words 'Despair' in blood red writing.

'Ere Lewis, wanna fuck a goth mate?' I ask. I don't really. Lol.

I do the whole putting my t-shirt over my clothes and then distorting my body into weird shapes to coyly remove my bra and dress underneath. I get into bed next to him.

'This is better than a cinema date,' Lewis says, 'at the cinema you're only seeing a white screen with the images projected on to it- this is more authentic.'

I don't really know what he means TBH. We both lapse into comfortable silence, the colours of the screen dancing on our faces – making us part of the story and the luscious dialogue between Maggie and Brick. I wait for him to get bored. The younger generation often dislike old films. Perhaps it's the lack of CGI, violence and sex. Perhaps it's because the actors are dead, and this reminds them of their own limited time on earth. Perhaps I'm just looking too much into things as usual. No doubt the real reason young uns don't like old films is they think it will make them uncool. You see it is very important that people know what you are watching or eating at all times, so you must post it on social media, especially if it is deemed 'in' or will make others envious. A dozen likes or get the fuck out of this life. Imagine seeing these statuses:

Facebook status: 'Claire Smith is watching *The Third Man.*'

Claire's comment: 'getting me film noir on, go on Orson pet.'

Facebook status: 'Dan Timpson is watching *It's a Wonderful Life.*'

Dan's comment: 'just settling down to watch this after the Boro match, fucking smashed – #ChristmasExistentialism'.

Facebook status: Louise Jones is watching *Breakfast at Tiffany's.*

Louise's comment: 'pots done, kids in bed, vino out, go on Holly shag him lass.'

Interlude about bad taste and ear wax

I was dating a guy a few years ago and it was a rainy Sunday afternoon in late November. I suggested that we eat sweets, get cosy and watch a good old black and white film. By the look on his face, you'd think I'd suggested going around the streets of Middlesbrough and conducting rampant paedophilic abuse at any child who crossed our path. That was our last date. I didn't like his negative and unattractive reaction to the proposal of watching a black and white film. And more importantly I didn't like the build-up of gross orange wax that he always had in his ears.

Lewis does not get bored watching *Cat on a Hot Tin Roof.* He watches the film to the bitter end and doesn't speak once. This is a quality I find really attractive – I mean, I don't mind people saying the odd comment during a film, but anything more than this is unbearable and annoying. When you think of the amount of time, expense and passion it takes to create a film, it's disrespectful to not give it your complete attention.

As the end credits come on screen Lewis let out a big sigh. 'That was fab.'

'You really enjoyed it?' I ask.

'Yeah, how could you not,' he replies as he fluffs his pillow. 'I'm knackered now, can you be little spoon please.'

Lewis closes his eyes and gets in big spoon position. I turn my back to him and cosy back until I firmly slot into the alcove of his body.

'I hope you don't mind if we don't have sex,' he says quietly, 'I'm absolutely wrecked, plus... I really like you.'

'That's fine' I reply. I mean, how do you reply to that? I can feel his warm breath against the back of my neck, his warm groin area against my bum. I could easily have had sex with him. In the past it was the only way I could determine if a guy liked me.

But this wasn't like that, was it? There was more to us than that. My previous 'relationships,' if you could even call them that, have never lasted long, because sex simplified things. It made it on their terms, animalistic, a need cured without spiritual connection, a physical act without emotion.

Is Sex for the Simple? A book by A.E. Grant. The back cover will simply show a penis going into a vagina and the blurb will say - 'Is sex for the simple? Is coitus for clods? Is p in the v for the d to e graders? How's your father or let's not take the gene pool any farther? Is rumpty pumpty for the numpty numpty? Is dicking for dullards? Is knobbing for nincompoops? Is copulation for those with intellectual constipation? Is dipping the wick for the thick? ....

Lewis interrupts sleepily, 'I know you're still awake and over-pondering everything (if only he knew the ridiculously stupid nonsense playing in my head!) but please don't think I don't want to have sex with you. I think you're fab...but timing is everything and I want things to be as perfect as possible...and I'm just really tired.'

Lewis starts to snore softly. I close my eyes.

I have a recurring dream of a faceless man: in fact, that's the incorrect way to describe him as he does not have a face or body or present himself in any physical form, he is merely a feeling. We love each other in an all-consuming way. We are at peace.

I doubt this feeling can ever be real because love is complicated, and we are all flawed individuals who fear love because it confuses us. It's like my favourite lines from a song I adore, famously sung by Dinah Washington, called Mad About the Boy, which was written by Noel Coward FYI:

'Will it ever cloy
this odd diversity of misery and joy.'

That line perfectly encapsulates love: it's both misery and joy. And a million feelings within this spectrum. You know joy will lead to misery, and if you're lucky joy will return, but then so will the misery. You can never really appreciate joy because you're waiting for misery to rear its ugly unwanted head. Misery always seems inevitable.

Yet when I am with the faceless man, I know there will never be misery, when I as with him, I feel safe. Safe with my faceless man.

I turn around and look at Lewis. He has turned over since our initial spooning. I stare at the back of his head for a long time – you know the way a serial killer might do before they hit their prey with a hammer. Love me - I whisper repeatedly – a chant - as if casting a spell. Universe give him to me, but not if it will cause too much pain. If nothing comes of this, then at least we have had a lovely night. We have shared stories and memories. A kiss. The moonlight. A bed. Tennessee. I should be happy with this, but I'm not. I want more.

'Lewis don't let me disappear,' I whisper.

Lewis suddenly turns around to face me. I immediately close my eyes. I breathe slightly heavier to imply I am sleeping. What an actress! Maybe I should jump up and proudly exclaim, 'Lewis I'm not really asleep, I bet you didn't know you were in a bed with an actress. Last night my right eye won an Oscar for its performance in The Toilet at Las Pahamas' and now my 'breathing technique to suggest deep sleep' in The Bed at the Hotel Tomend, has won Best Performance of Sleep.'

'I just want to thank everyone who has helped me get here to receive this very highest of honours. My inspirations are those who I have seen asleep, be it in real life or on TV. When I was a little girl, I watched these people carefully and copied their every action, now I am over the moon to be able to share my rendition with you all and to win this prestigious accolade. I want to also thank God, because he created sleep and also Deepsleep beds who are my sponsor. Have you folks tried their new delicious Deepsleep bed spray, just a spritz on the pillow and the delicious lavender, chamomile and 'grandma's little

secret summit' aroma gets to work straight away to give you the most relaxing and deep sleep of your life. It can also be used as a fly spray, so great for those sweaty summer months.'

I count to five and then open my eyes. Lewis is staring at me.

'Hi,' he says.

'Hi,' I reply, 'I feel like roadkill.'

'I better be going,' Lewis says, 'add me on Facebook and I'll message you sometime.' Lewis climbs out of bed and pulls on his clothes.

Or does he say?

'Fuck me, who are you? Where am I?' I go to reply but Lewis jumps out of bed and rushes on his clothes, avoiding eye contact. Is this how Medusa felt? Without the spooning. No wonder her snakes hissed ever so loudly.

Or does he say...

'Why don't you have a nice hot bath whilst I go get us a Maccies breakfast?' Lewis climbs out of bed and pulls on his clothes.

Or does he say...

'What?' I ask.

'I said you should have a bath whilst I go get us some breakfast, it'll make you feel better.'

What mischief is this.

'What would you like?' Lewis asks. He goes into the bathroom and turns on the taps. He re-enters the room. 'I put bubble bath in, cos what psychopath has a bath without bubbles. What do you want for breakfast?'

'A sausage and egg McMuffin and a coffee please.'

'Ok I'm going to have run cos I have ten minutes before breakfast finishes,' Lewis scrambles to put on his shoes, 'when will this magnificent franchise address the elephant in the fast-food universe and serve breakfast all day.'

'I think that every day,' I reply.

Lewis turns towards the door, but then runs over and kisses me on the cheek. 'Enjoy your bath. I'll take the fob-thing, so you don't have to get out to open the door.'

Then Lewis is gone. I get out of bed and move slowly to the bathroom. Dazed. Coming down. T-shirt off. I step into the bath. The bubbles smell of cucumber cleanliness. I splash water on my face. Reborn.

Maybe this is all a lie and Lewis is the most awful person who has ever lived. He has run me a bath and promised food but has no intention of coming back. He is giving Mrs Schmidt the time. I will grow wrinkled and sad in the bath. The bubbles will disappear. The hot water will turn cold. I will wait forever - an aquatic Miss Havisham. I will never see him again. I will Ophelia myself away without crow-flowers, nettles, daisies and the like. Bathe in the rye. Float in the rye.

Drown in the rye.

Stop. Don't start a new chapter here. Yes, it's going to be a mighty long chapter but so what?

Lewis is getting breakfast and has run you a bath because he is a kind man who likes you. It is difficult to accept kindness when it's something you have rarely received, but some men are decent, kind, and genuine; for example, please insert the name of a good man you know ....

I begin to relax – in a hypnagogic state of consciousness. Falling in love is a special kind of fall. It is like stepping off an unseen kerb. That happy relief when your foot finds the ground and you realise that you're safe, no broken bones. Or the opposite of this: the excruciating pain when you fall hard and hurt/break your foot. So next time you walk outside. you are cautious, you do not let your legs reach out too far or walk too fast. You spend the rest of your life looking for kerbs that may or may not be there. But despite the bruises and sprains, your foot will fix. Bones will fix. Hearts can't fix. Which is why next time you find yourself falling in love, you extend your heart out gently before placing it down next to another's, because you can't risk another fall, last time you survived it, but this time it could be fatal.

Tears creep into my mouth. It's just the comedown, I tell myself. Tomorrow you will be fine. The hotel door opens. I splash water on my face to disguise my tears.

'Hey' Lewis shouts, 'do you want me to bring your breakfast in there.'

The sound of hungry fingers tearing paper. I uncork the plug. It's always sad to see the water disappear.

'No, I'm coming out now,' I reply.

The idea of Lewis seeing me naked in the bath fills me with overwhelming anxiety. We aren't wrecked now. Even if I strategically placed the bubbles over my rude bits, what if he catches a glimpse of the flesh, the nipple, thigh or pubic mound? Pubic mound lol. He will think my body grotesque, he will drown me and/or vomit in the nearby sink.

I step out of the bath and immediately pull the towel around me. I dry myself and pull on my t-shirt. I look in the mirror and run my fingers through my wet hair, using my digits as a brush. I'd forgotten to bring in my makeup bag. I don't feel safe. The fresh air will have cleared his mind. Lewis will see me as I really am. All the flaws and imperfections. The great monster reveal in the horror movie.

I have nowhere to go, nowhere to hide. If the bathroom had a window, I would fling my body through it. I could dash my head off the pot sink until I knock myself out- that way when Lewis runs in to see what the noise is, and I am ugly, it will be because my face is covered in blood and bruises, not just because it's my face. This act however could potentially lead to brain damage -which in one way would be a blessing because I will forget everything and lead a simple life. I would quite like someone to feed me, clean me and tuck me into bed at night. I look forward to the day I am finally incarcerated in a mental hospital. To sit back and do nothing. To not think, just exist. How free it is to be insane. The only real way to escape the rat race. One is not born a rat. Out of a rat to be a rat. If you are insane, you are not a rat. Then I considered Lewis' shocked face as he rushes into the bathroom hearing the thud of my skull against pot. I can't do that to him. What if he actually likes me? We will never get to the cheeky Nando's stage. Also, if I start fucking about splitting my face open, the McDonalds breakfast will get cold. A McMuffin isn't created to be ignored.

I go into the bedroom. I need to get this over and done with – if Lewis is going to run out screaming, then so be it. He has put the food on the table next to the window and pulled out a chair ready for me to sit in. He sits in the opposite chair.

'What do you fancy doing today?' Lewis asks as I sit down.

I try to avoid eye contact. If I can't see him, then maybe he can't see me.

'The day after the night before, I usually just lay in bed all day hating myself,' I reply.

'That won't help,' Lewis says tucking into his muffin, 'we should go out and explore.'

'You don't have to,' I say, 'I mean, wouldn't you rather try and find your friends?'

'Absolutely not,' he replies, 'I'll let the bastards stew, they shouldn't have left me.'

'But wouldn't you rather spend time with them?' I ask and then realise how lame I sound. According to studies men like confident women who are self-assured and comfortable in their own skin. Ironic given they are the ones who cause women to struggle with these positive character traits. Or do us women cause this, do we do it to ourselves, who knows? I like to blame patriarchy for everything.

Lewis laughs, 'I can see them anytime. Or not. I get a better conversation from a wall. They're off home this morning anyway, the coach was picking them up at 9.00am. I choose you.'

I choose you. I choose you.

People choose things throughout their life: a sport, a hobby, a religion, a genre of music or film they particularly enjoy...but a person, an actual human being. Yes, I like this person, I will choose it even for its flaws and imperfections and I will try and forget these in order to not drive myself insane. Lewis chose me.

'How will you get home?' I ask, trying to act cool even though. HE CHOSE ME.

'I'll get the train back when I'm ready. Now I'm not completely intoxicated I have a rough idea where the hotel is. Hopefully, they've left my bag there.'

I nod and sip my coffee. HE CHOSE ME.

'After breakfast let's get ready and go out and do something,' Lewis says.

I feel as disappointed as a child who has received socks for Christmas. I hoped Lewis was a lazy hangover sort of guy. I want to spend the day drowning in remorse for our previous night's sins. To just lie in bed and discuss life...perhaps occasionally breaking free from our cocoon of pretention for coffee breaks and snacks and what would hopefully be meaningful and enjoyable sexual intercourse. I mean what is there to do outside? I do not want to cope with the humans today. Surely the point of finding someone special is so you don't have to bother with anyone ever again.

Lewis talks about a nearby art gallery that we can visit. He then talks about his views on art whilst I eat my McMuffin. I give the odd nod and guttural mmm. We have dissimilar tastes and ideas. He is old school. I am future school. Yet last night everything seemed so perfect. Our beliefs. Our dancing. Our kiss. Have I overlooked who he really is? Was I just drunk and lonely and grasping at some kind of bond? Different tastes in art, probably in music and films too.

'What do you do for a living?' I blurt out, interrupting his ridiculous discourse on how modern art is rubbish.

'Just tele-sales,' he replies, 'but I'm in a band. I told you about them last night.'

Lewis had told me about his band last night: they were called *The Wide Bit of the Funnel*. On the way to Popworld Lewis had stuck his phone to my ear to listen to their music. I moved my head up and down as if enjoying the beat and said they sounded 'very cool.' They sounded mediocre and trite - generic background Indie music with an asthmatic fake-Cockney

Frontman who sounded as if he had just run from the tube station for an audition in EastEnders. I remember one lyric that stood out as it was particularly bad and unfortunately repeated throughout the song 'you're like a wall, but not very tall.' What does that even mean? I want Lewis to be my Bob Dylan, my Leonard Cohen, my Jack White. But no. At the time I had faked being impressed and said what a creative person he must be. I don't know if Lewis is creative, but judging by the awful music, apparently not. I was saying that just so he'd like me. According to studies, men like to be complimented by women and to be asked questions. The questions must be carefully selected, one wouldn't want to appear intrusive or insensitive. Women must then listen to their answers intently and appear enthralled by everything that comes out of their mouths. For a relationship to work men must constantly feel superior and appreciated.

'Oh yes I remember now' I reply.

My come down is chronic: there is zero happiness in my body or mind. Less so after being reminded about The Wide Bit of the Funnel. Why aren't I happy? Sat opposite a guy who appears genuine and kind. I feel nothing. Is it because he's not Holden? I'm never usually fussy – I've previously shagged guys just for having stubble. My body is never lonely, just my soul.

Lewis pulls a face, 'I like the guys in the band, but their tastes in music are different to mine. I'd really like to go in a different direction. I like something raw with a bit more meaning – like The Smiths, Nirvana, Radiohead, that sort of thing. The difficulty is we've been in the band together for years, it would be hard to cut loose, but I've started writing a solo album.' He shrugs, 'it's early days, but I'm happy with how it's going. If, or should I say when, I get to know you better, I'll let you hear it. I guess it's so personal to me, I've never let anyone hear my music because it's like exposing my soul.'

'I'd love to listen to it,' I say, perking up at this excellent news. Oh, how the fallen have risen. 'You're a goddam prince.' I tell him and mean it. He is a goddam prince.

One sentence, one conversation, can completely change your

mind about someone. He isn't some laddie indie boy. He doesn't get wrecked on Bud and throw his arms around his friends, pogo jumping to Mr Brightside and then throwing up donner meat at the side of his bed at 4am and desperately trying to wank off his pilly willy. To be fair, I have done all of the above.

I stare into his eyes. Love me - my soul screams, my mouth smiles. Lewis stands up and sits on the bed. Isn't he interested in me? Shouldn't we be making love all over this small slightly claustrophobic hotel room? Shouldn't we be excreting so many bodily fluids that we'd blush when we run into housekeeping? Shouldn't I be begging him to give my genitals a break? Has Lewis realised I'm not great: that I'm not girlfriend material? When would my forever stay in the friend zone be confirmed by Lewis? Maybe tomorrow or a cheeky 'how are you mate?' text in a few weeks' time. He will laugh about our silly star lit snog 'eee remember when we pashed off when we were both wrecked.' It will break my heart. He kissed me on the cheek this morning. Mothers kiss their children on the cheek. You kiss unwelcome relatives on the cheek. Judas kissed Jesus on the cheek. If a man is interested in a woman, would he only kiss her on the cheek?

'I'll just watch some shit whilst you get ready,' Lewis says.

I stand up with my coffee.

'Hey I forgot something,' Lewis says. Lewis searches his coat pockets. 'Last night you said you loved these.' He hands me a small bag. Inside is sticky brown goddess, no not an affectionately executed shit, give your brain a bath...it is a delicious gooey caramel topped doughnut from Greggs. Almost every time somebody gives me a present, it ends up making me sad. I take out the doughnut and begin to lick the caramel.

Lewis smiles 'you're lovely.' He takes my head between his hands and kisses my chin. 'You missed a bit,' he giggles and licks off the caramel. He gestures to the bathroom as if to say, 'hurry up get ready.'

I grab my pull-along suitcase and go into the bathroom. I sit on the toilet and scoff the doughnut. Is this love? Eating a doughnut bought for you by your special someone whilst urinating in a hotel bathroom. Was this it. It.

I bring a piece of toilet paper to my mouth to hide my smile and wipe away the sticky icing. It becomes a lace handkerchief, delicately veiling my blush as I giggle femininely like a twentieth century's vicar's daughter being introduced to a handsome soldier visiting the parish.

I get ready in a hurry, throwing makeup on lasciviously and pinning my hair back in a loose bun. I wobble my head until some of the hair escapes absolutely on purpose, wanting to look like French film star. I put on a flowered shirt dress, then brush my teeth before applying red lipstick. I am unconquerable.

Lewis looks up when I enter the room, 'you look pretty.'

I smile and grab my bag, ensuring I have everything in it before we leave. I fold the red hunting hat and put it at the bottom …just in case. We walk down the hotel corridor, the eyes of nosey maids upon us. Do they know I have booked a room for one? Will I get reprimanded by the hotel manager for having a guest? Sue will ensure she is present at the bollocking, all the time wishing she had enough confidence to deal with any kind of confrontation instead of having to rely on the hotel manager. Sue states that she had clearly told me the rules. I had not complied, and now I must pay. Sue's clit will throb.

Outside, the sun is too bright. I am anxious it will make me look ugly. It has ruined everything. We walk over the bridge. Lewis doesn't try to hold my hand. We don't talk. He does not glance my way. Am I a night-time only gal? Unacceptable by day. We walk past girls who are beautiful. Does Lewis wish he was with them? The cool dude wants an Alexa Chung but got an Egg Foo Yung? I feel sick. A lilac hue.

'Why don't we go to the pub?' I suggest.

I want to get stinking drunk: this will make me feel better. I am better looking when I am drunk. After a few drinks, conversation will flow. He will like me again. I can pretend to not be me.

'Why do you want to go to the pub?' Lewis asks. He walks ahead of me and turns around, walking backwards, smiling. He has a way of walking that cannot be imitated: like a spatially unaware phallic alien. I want him so bad. To be my final fail.

'Just so we can sit and chill with a pint,' I answer.

'Ok if that's what you want,' he smiles a series of questions.

The first pub we arrive at, he takes my hand, and we walk inside.

'What do you want?' Lewis asks when we reach the bar.

'Depends on if we're having a drink or getting drunk?'

'Just a drink, but I will warn you, drinking often leads to getting drunk...alcohol's funny like that.'

Lewis tells me to go and find a nice seat by the window so we can stare at the world going by and judge and comment accordingly. He brings over two pints. Unfortunately, only one is for me. I am thirsty and down a third. Lewis looks out of the window. Does he hate me? I can't think of anything to say. I am too sober.

'Where's your cute red hat today?' he asks.

'It's too warm,' I say and shrug, 'thought I'd try out a new look. I've put it in my bag in case I decide to shoot someone later.'

I can't forget about Holden and the reasons behind the hat, the reasons behind me. I am he. He is me. The only constant. The river. The trees. The birds. The bees. Lewis can hurt me. It doesn't matter. None of it matters. I look at Lewis and feel smug – hate me, fuck me, use me, cut me, hurt me, kill me. Do it, do it now or not at all. It doesn't matter, I have Holden.

'I wish I'd brought my camera,' Lewis says, 'it would be good to catch them all, all these people going about their day. Look at us in comparison, momentarily out of the rat race... we have nothing to do, nowhere to be. Just us here, existing in the now, sipping a pint. Well, I'm sipping, you're downing yours.' He laughs, 'how come you drink so fast?'

'You do photography?' I ask. A necessary change of conversation.

'Not since art college, way back when. I did my final on flies: I photographed flies.'

Don't do this to me. He must stop.

'Why don't you just use the camera on your phone?' I ask.

'That's for the selfie generation, it's not art.'

I want to tell him that I don't consider photography true 'art.' It's just lighting and setting. It isn't heart and soul. That isn't to say that a photo cannot be beautiful or arouse feelings, on the contrary. But that's all it is and will ever be. Taking a photo can never capture the real emotion present in the artist or subject.

I take a gigantic swig of my lager.

'So why do you drink so fast?' Lewis asks again.

'Because when I'm drunk, I'm awake.' I tell him straight.

'You're not really awake,' he replies, 'you're asleep, you're escaping. What are you escaping from?'

I might commit suicide later. If this is the last conversation I am to have with a human being, it might as well be the truth. At least then we will have had something of nothing. Ossenburger I am ready for thee.

I tell him about my un-happy childhood. The years and years of damage and self-abuse. Cutting. Burning. Scratching. Starving. Drinking. Drugging. Fucking. Most people only half-listen when you are talking about yourself: they wait for the tiniest gap in the conversation, that second when you reclaim your breath, so they can but in and talk about themselves. We live in the 'Me' society – everyone's problems are bigger, their emotions more genuine, their experiences more fucked up. That's why people go to therapy – to speak with minimal interruption. A therapist listens because they are getting paid to listen; paid to be selfless. People enjoy therapy because they get a chance to really speak. Therapists have become people's God's, their saviours, and merely because they don't stop the flow of speech. They let people outpour so that that person can continue with a life filled with interruptions. But who listens to the therapist? The therapist's therapist? But then who listens to the therapist's therapist's therapist...does this go on for infinity until the grand therapist, counsellor, psychologist, whatever, is stood there talking to God or the Great Eye of the Universe or whatever you believe in. But then who would they speak to? Or are they happy to hear the troubles of every single person on the planet because someone has to take one for team human.

I don't go into detail about my love life or about the love of my life that I found in a book. How can someone understand that?

When I finish, I take a big swig of my beer, 'that's the general gist. I could go on, but my throat is getting sore.'

Lewis looks at me intensely. In the most intense way, I've ever been looked at.

'I don't want to be this way,' I say. I feel the grey lump form inside. 'I want to be happy. That's all I've ever dreamed of. I just can't stop…the drinking, the drugs and everything else. I'm broken and I can't be fixed. I'm in this self-destructive cycle. I want to stop.'

'Stop right now. I can help you. No more of this shit,' Lewis says and pushes my beer glass off the table. It smashes on the floor.

'Sorry it was an accident,' he shouts towards the bar.

Lewis grabs my hand and drags me to my feet. He begins to run, holding my hand, pulling me behind him. Out of the pub, up the street, over the bridge and down the steps to the river, near where we had been the night before.

'Shout it out,' Lewis says holding both my hands and facing me. 'Shout it out to the river. Shout 'fuck you, life.' And then just let it go. Start anew.'

I look around. There are boats on the river and people walking their dogs on the riverside path.

'Don't give a shit about who's around, you care far too much about what people think. Do it now. Grab the railing with both hands and shout it out to the river. The river doesn't care it's just flowing past. It will carry the weight of your words far out to the sea and away from here.'

Lewis lets go of my hands cautiously as if I'm a small child on a bike whose stabilizers have just been removed. Ride or fall? I hold on tight to the railings.

'Fuck you, life,' I shout meekly.

'No louder,' he says, 'even if children are listening. You can't save them Amber; everyone eventually comes out of the rye and grows up.'

I grip the rails tighter and scream the words as if exorcising a demon.

'FUCK. YOU. LIFE.'

'Don't you feel better?' Lewis laughs and then kisses me.

'Woooooohooooo' we hear shouts and wolf-whistles.

We turn to see a tour boat float past. On it are students giggling and making rude gestures. We laugh. He puts his arm around me.

'Well do you blame me,' Lewis shouts, 'look at her, she's beautiful.' He hugs me close to his chest. 'Well, you are you know, even though you don't think so' he kisses the top of my head.

Lewis grabs my hand, and we start to run again, 'I'm going to run the unhappiness out of you,' he says excitedly. He drags me up the steps and along the streets. People look at us – but I don't care. We run into the marketplace – into the smell of onions and life. There are a group of youths (aged about ten to fourteen) street dancing – the crowds watch with glee.

'Let's join in,' says Lewis.

'What, no way!' I exclaim pulling back.

Lewis juts out his lip. 'Please.' It depresses me when someone says please.

Do I have the guts to live? I let myself be pulled.

'Just copy,' he says, 'that's what they want.' Lewis starts to replicate their actions. I follow. 'Just let loose, pretend you're drunk.'

I loosen my shoulders and close my eyes. I feel the beat and dance like the little old goddam Governor's son. The children mutter to each other in their posh accents, asking what the hell we are doing. Do their parents know they are dancing to music which originated from the ghetto – passionate beats filled with powerful lyrics about poverty, abuse and crime? I wonder how much flush-fathered Freddy knows about cultural diversity? What does financially comfortable Connie know about knife crime? Why little Marcus has even taken to wearing a cap, which is acceptable fashion for the white sands of Bermuda, but not for Sunday lunch with the grandparents at the private golf club. Their bodies cannot not dance because their souls cannot dance.

The music stops. Before me is a young boy of about ten, doing a head stand, his blonde curl frizz brushes the pavement. The crowd's clap at various paces and strengths. People always clap for the wrong things. They are trying to ignore us, if they do then we will hopefully disappear – isn't that the British thing to do with one's problems. Surely, we are drunk tourists – unaware of British customs and the country's general abhorrence and avoid-ness of joining in. The British like to watch and judge – this is the polite thing to do.

Their (I'm guessing teacher) comes up to us. She has bouncing silver curls that hang to her shoulders, a dumpling-like frame, and sweat clings to her head as if she has recently rolled in a pool of brine. Lilac leggings and a lightweight camel raincoat. The raincoat is unnecessary given the weather.

'Can you let the children dance please, they've been practising for months and you're putting them off' she asks poshly, 'I adore the fact you're having fun, but it's a no-no for health and safety reasons, you guys can dance elsewhere.'

'Really, Margo (let's call her Margo) …where shall we dance? In deepest space? In Einstein's brain? In your dad's sperm-filled balls? Do you want to shut us in a sleeping bag and zipper us away from life?'

Lewis grabs my hand before I pull Margo's curls or surreally say any of the above. 'Come on Amber darling, let's get back to our 'home'…its nearly time for afternoon tea and our delicious assortment of required and much needed meds.'

I giggle and allow Lewis to lead me away. We watch from the periphery. The youths start to dance to a song by RunDMC. Lewis stands behind me, hugging me tightly, as if trapping me in a little cocoon.

'If a sheep ran away from the herd, would it die?' he asks.

I close my eyes. There is a river inside my bones. I hold on to his arm tightly. It's a question I don't have to answer. I open my eyes and continue to watch the ungenuine bairns. They are as dull as an unattended party.

'What do you want to do now?' Lewis asks.

'I don't mind.'

Lewis removes his arms and stands in front of me. 'Well, what would you be doing if I wasn't here?'

'Erm...getting drunk...taking drugs...and trying to score more drugs.'

Lewis stares at me. 'Will that make you happy?' he asks and looks disappointed.

Tears well in my eyes. I hate myself for needing someone to save me. For not having the strength to save myself and not being able to love myself enough to want to save myself. I am a victim when I want to be a survivor. I am the girl I grew up hating. The princess in the tower who will never be happy until 'the one' saves them.

Interlude about pointless dark daffodils

Once I went on a coach trip to the Lake District. I wanted to be all Wordsworth and that. The perfect spot to think about and reassess life and perhaps gain some inspiration to write poetry. I was just coming out of a dark depression and believed the solitude and breath-taking views would do me good. Well of course there were lots of old dears on the trip, but I tried to ignore and avoid them as much as possible. They assumed I was deaf.

I sat there all week looking at the mountains and lakes. Daffodils did not dance sprightly in my eyes. My black heart trampled on the yellow fuckers. A first the magnificent views did fill me with awe, but I had no one to share it with. I would see couples strolling hand in hand through the greenery and I would think – why not me, why can't I. Then the destructive thoughts would ignite – the ones that had brought me to the Lake District in the first place. I couldn't run from them. The distant stars could not kiss me, the trees could not hug me, the cheap wine could not soothe me.

Going to the Lake District was pointless. Everything was completely pointless. The answers weren't there. The answers weren't anywhere. There weren't any answers.

The answers had disappeared in the rye.

'Don't get upset,' Lewis says and puts his hands on my shoulders.

'I feel overwhelmed,' I say 'everything is happening all at once. I don't want to get hurt again: I can't handle any more...' I can't finish the sentence. Some things can't be explained. I gulp down my sadness.

'I can't promise you anything Amber,' Lewis sighs, 'I could cross the street tomorrow and get run over. However, what I can promise you is that what I say at this moment is true: I think you're an amazing person; unique, full of love and passion, fearless. You have been open with me about your past and the troubles you have faced. All I can see is someone I admire... you're strong and beautiful and strange and wise. I've never met anyone quite like you.'

I snigger, 'I bet.'

'You think I'm talking shit,' Lewis continues, 'but it's true, you'll find that out. If you feel pain, it will be beautiful because we'll feel it together. Let's believe in magic.'

Magic. If love isn't magic, what is. I smile.

'Come on let's get some nice food and then we can go nap and snuggle the shit out of each other,' Lewis says and pulls me away.

We eat at a small Italian restaurant. As I finish my meal with a large dish of Tiramisu – which is always white and gooey like truth- I ask Lewis about his friends and the hotel he was staying at. We decide to find it before heading back. Lewis remembers stone steps that are 'alcohol damp' and lead to a gold framed swinging door. The hotel is next to an Indian restaurant which has garish cerise curtains and a chalkboard outside in the shape of the Taj Mahal with the day's speciality curry written in an elaborate font. This made it easy to find- there aren't any hotels in the city centre with an Indian restaurant adjoined to it.

The hotel is a ten-minute walk. On arrival I notice that the restaurant curtains are more puce than cerise. Most men aren't very good with shades: brown is brown, yellow is yellow, and all other shades and tones are lost.

Lewis explains the situation to the concierge and the concierge explains the situation to Lewis. His friends had put his bag in the luggage cupboard when they left that morning. Lewis laughs and reads aloud the note they had stuck to it.

'Where the fuck are you? Ring us on this number below before we ring every hospital and police station in the area, you ....'

And then there is a large picture of a penis – hairs sprouting from the bollocks and everything ...even a little spurt of semen flying in the air like unnatural rain drops. Silly- they could fall and smear the mobile number. Quick ring Dave. Ring Dave quick. Before the semen destroys all.

Lewis uses my mobile to ring Dave. He speaks to him in that horrid blokey way that men use to speak to other males. The obligatory 'ow mate' and then lots of laughter followed by numerous 'fucking hells' and all in an octave lower than their usual voice. He laughs, looks over at me and then lowers the volume of his voice.

'I don't know when I'll be back mate,' he says to Dave.

Don't go, my mind chants. Don't leave. Don't bail. Not now. I shift onto my other foot uncomfortably – I am on my left foot and shift to the right, for your information.

As if analysing my body language, Lewis says, 'I'm not sure mate. I'm not rushing back. I'm having a great time here. I've met a very special girl.' Laughter. 'No, it's not like that mate, she's different.' More laughter. 'Fuck off you wanker. I'll ring you when I'm back. Just ring my mam and make up some story, say I'm at a last-minute work conference or something.' More laughter.

'You're such a dick sniff, fuck off.' More laughter, 'Later mate.'

Lewis hands back my mobile. 'They were fuming because they waited for ages and had to pay extra for the minibus…but they'll live. I'll buy them a pint to make up for it.' Lewis laughs. 'Shall we go back to the hotel room? I really want to have sex with you. I can't control myself any longer. That's if you want to?'

There's nothing I find more attractive than when a guy says exactly what he wants. Life's too short for messing around.

'Yes,' I reply.

Lewis grabs his bag in one hand and mine in the other and we walk out of the hotel.

'Shall we get a bottle of prosecco to take back?' I ask.

'Let's not,' he replies.

I am completely gutted. I can't remember the last time I had sex sober. What if I can't perform…as in, have no confidence. Will I take off my clothes and run under the covers? Will I lay there like a dead fish? Will I be able to get wet? If I can't, I can't blame the alcohol. A few drinks will loosen me up. I try to think of a way to escape for a short while, to maybe find camper van Morris and get some more stuff. But I can't think of a reason to go off by myself for say thirty minutes. How about: 'I'm gasping for a solitary visit to York Dungeon, see ya later.'

'Penny for them?' Lewis asks.

'It's nothing,' I reply.

'Are you sulking cos I don't want prosecco?'

'No.'

'You can get some Amber,' he says, 'I'm not stopping you. I just think you're better than this. I know you've had a bad time, but none of the stuff you put into your body helps. If you really want to change then you need to at least try.'

I begin to feel defensive. 'I do try, all the time, but it's difficult' I spit out. 'And you were wrecked last night, it wasn't just me.'

'Amber I was on a stag do,' Lewis squeezes my hand, 'you said you get wrecked all the time. Letting your hair down now and again and even doing recreational drugs occasionally is fine. Before last night I hadn't had anything to drink in about three weeks, and even then, it was just a few with a meal one weekend. Wouldn't you rather enjoy life through a sober lens? Think of all the things you could do, all the money you'd save, all the bad decisions you wouldn't make...not that I'm saying I'm a bad decision' Lewis laughs. 'Why don't you put the money aside each week, that you'd usually spend on alcohol and drugs, and in a few months, you'll be able to afford to go on a beautiful luxurious holiday. I'll do it with you, we can go together.' Lewis looks at me. 'Where would you like to go, anywhere you want?'

I've never met a guy who wanted to make plans with me. But how can I possibly save up enough money. Lewis is being unrealistic. I can't just give up who I am. Give up my lifestyle. If it's so easy I would have done it years ago. He is expecting too much.

'I don't know how to stop...everything,' I reply, and a tear falls down my cheek.

'You just stop,' Lewis replies.

'I can't.'

'So, you're an addict?' Lewis asks.

That word.

'I'm NOT an addict,' I reply abruptly.

Is he being patronising? Judging? Is he right?

'I don't want to upset you, some people are addicts and that's fine, the first step to recovery is admitting it,' Lewis puts his arm around me. 'I'm not being an arsehole. I just think you can do it.'

I begin to sob, not caring that we are in the middle of a street. Why are men always making me cry on streets? Lewis hugs me close to him. My wet face clings to his chest. He kisses the top of my head.

'This is a new day,' Lewis says softly, 'It isn't yesterday. It's not tomorrow. You start one day at a time. Try being sober today, well despite that half pint of lager we had earlier. See how it goes. I'm here and I'm not going anywhere. I'll help you, Amber. You're not broken, you just need to heal.'

Lewis wipes the tears from my face. 'Come on, I'll make you a nice cup of coffee when we get back...the sex can wait for another time. I just want to hold you until you feel a bit better.'

He holds my hand, and we walk back to the hotel. I think I am smiling.

Smiling in the rye.

CHAPTER TEN

Lewis makes me a strong coffee. He tells me to put on something comfy and get into bed. He takes off his jeans and lays next to me wearing his t-shirt and boxers. He asks why I think I can't be fixed. Usually, I don't tell anybody anything. If you do, you start missing everybody. But I don't care.

I tell Lewis about my obsession with Holden and how it all started- after my relationship with Josh ended. How Holden became the only person I could depend on, he could never hurt me, he made me feel safe. That I desperately want to catch children as they run out of the rye, before they fall over the cliff into adulthood. But I can't save them because I'm stuck in the rye – lost – and no matter what I do I can't find my way out. The rye's sour smelling reeds hold onto me tight. I've tried to cry for help, but the rye's swishing lullabies overpower my pitiful attempts. In the distance I can hear the children's laughter turn to screams as they fall off the cliff. I'm not strong enough to save them because I'm not strong enough to save myself. I've given up. I've let the rye consume me.

Lewis doesn't say anything. Have I lost him when he realised the magnitude of the mission?

'You know in the film *Hannibal*,' I continue, 'when Hannibal says to Clarice 'Tell me Clarice, would you ever say to me "stop. If you loved me, you'd stop'. That line makes me so sad. If Clarice had said those words, would Hannibal have stopped? Or is being a cannibal just who he is and what he was always meant to be: his destiny. Say Hannibal did stop, could stop, then what would their lives be like? He and Clarice constantly running away from the authorities and his incarceration. Never happy. Never still.

Never trusting. Poor Clarice, every time Hannibal popped out for milk, she'd be paranoid he'd really be nipping out for a bit of the old intestine. Checking his mouth when he returned for traces of blood and meaty bits. What life could they have? It's best she left him to his own destruction. That she didn't ruin her own life. That Clarice never asked him to stop.'

'They'd have each other,' Lewis replies, 'maybe Hannibal could change for Clarice, for love. Change your behaviours - the outcome, the future.'

I don't know what to say, so I awkwardly reply, 'you should be a therapist, I know I said this on page 170 but it's true.'

'Maybe,' he answers. There is a pause. A long pause.

'Will you try and stop for me,' Lewis asks and looks at me with sad eyes.

'I'll try my hardest,' I say and really mean it. 'I'll go back to counselling. I'll go to rehab if need be. I will clean up my act. I'll get a job I actually like, or re-train or something. I'll try to build bridges with the people in my life. Sometimes I am the problem and I need to acknowledge that.'

Lewis holds my hand.

'I'd like a job where I help others,' I continue, 'teenagers, because it's such an awful time. So, they don't run out of the rye and fall off the cliff, so they know how to climb down slowly and cautiously. If that makes sense. I just want them to feel safe.'

Lewis puts his head on my shoulder. We are both smiling. The world swims. We kiss. I pull off his t-shirt, wanting to consume him, to feel his skin. Soon my night shirt is on the floor and then … it's a little bit of this… and it's a little bit of that….we sing *The Birdie Song* and then have sex. Jokes – we just skip to the sex. Our bums did wiggle though.

I have read that sex can feel like an out of body experience, that you can completely lose yourself in the act, and that time can stand still. I always thought this was a load of crap. Until it happened. There wasn't a part of each other's body's that we didn't explore. Everything felt like it had experienced love. I don't want to talk about it, because it's private and why would you want to read a detailed account about us having sex. There's the internet for that, or some books like to go into it. This isn't that kind of book.

After the sex, we cuddle.

'Shall we have a bath together?' Lewis asks.

To get rid of all the sweat and excretion in the most romantic way possible. A bath. A shared bath like you see on TV. Whatever next …rose petals and sunsets. Croissants and dusky pink dreams.

'That will be lovely,' I reply.

Lewis stands up. Naked. Brazen as brass. There is no grabbing clothes or covers, no concealment. Men are like that. Proud of it all, whatever it is. He walks into the bathroom and turns on the taps. I climb out of bed. My groin glistens like diamonds. Liquid dribbles down my leg and for the first time in my life I don't care. I don't feel dirty and soiled. In fact, I want to scope it up, shove it back inside, stick a cork in it, which I can then unplug whenever I want a reminder of this moment. Rub a little Eau de Spermatozoa on my pulse points. A delicious earthy sent – the swimming baths mixed with a freshly opened pack of wafer-thin ham. J'adore.

I walk slowly into the bathroom. Sleep tight ya morons. Lewis is urinating. In his own world, unaware of my presence. He clears his throat, playing with the phlegm, savouring it like a poor man's oyster. I try to be invisible. As quiet as snow. But even snow creaks.

Lewis looks up. 'Hey.'

'Hey,' I smile.

Lewis finishes off his dribble. What a thrill dear Sylvia- a cock instead of a kettle! He starts to pour bubble bath into the running hot water and then sits on the edge of the tub.

'If you don't mind me asking, how did you get those scars on your back?' he asks.

I had forgotten about them. 'I was in an accident when I was younger,' I lie.

Interlude about breakfast and the avengeful bush

The 'accident' happened when I was eighteen. I woke up one day and felt dead inside. I couldn't think straight. I immediately started on a breakfast of wine and cocaine. Mother was away, you see. My 'breakfast' didn't fix me. I couldn't live.

I was on my way to the local shop to buy a bottle of vodka - when one is so down, one might as well drink until one passes out and escapes to dreamland. En-route I scratched my arm on a bush: a wild and cruel piece of nature, ravaged by Autumn and wanting revenge. It had reached out to me, to purposefully cause mischief. I wanted to hurt it. I don't know why. I turned around (to avoid blindness) and threw my body against the bush trying to snap its little limbs. The branches played with and teased my back like a crazed cat. Underneath my feet, the crisp dead leaves crunched loudly like tormented Frosties – orchestrating the event.

It was one of those awful joggers who found me. She told the ambulance staff that I was throwing myself onto the bush like a woman possessed, 'like Regan convulsing on the bed in *The Exorcist*'...she used that very terminology in the police statement. Oh, jog on Susan!

With Mother away, I told the police to contact Dad as my next of kin. I then blackmailed Dad to not tell Mother. I cried saying he had promised to keep an eye on me whilst she was away and she would be furious with him, probably ban me from seeing him ever again. In fairness he had rang a few hours before Bushgate and I said I was fine and snuggled up watching a Doris Day/ Rock Hudson film with a huge bag of Doritos. In reality, I had just opened a bottle of red and text my dealer to bring three bags of his finest Columbian medicine.

My back was cut to ribbons: a Jackson Pollack blood original. My back had never looked so wanted. The doctors said I was lucky to only have surface damage and a few stitches – any deeper and there could have been serious and permanent damage. For all eternity I must now wear a top in front of Mother, so she never knows about my 'accident.' Not that she has any reason to see me topless…topless Sunday Lunch, topless trip to M&S, topless bitch over coffee. To this day I still don't know how, with all the substances in my body, I didn't just fall into the bush and pass out. How did I move back and forth like that–maybe I had been possessed by a demon? Susan was right.

Dad was upset about the incident. A film of moisture brightened his dead eyes when the doctors explained what had happened. Despite evidence to imply the contrary - it was the first time he realised how psychologically disturbed his daughter was. The next day he gave me money so I could go on a nice spa day to clear my head. Which I of course spent on a crate of wine, pizza and bags of whitey.

'An accident?' Lewis asks.

'I can't really remember it to be honest…I fell off my bike into a thorny bush,' I lie.

Lewis nods in a sympathetic fashion.

'That's why I don't wear bikinis,' I laugh.

'The moon is beautiful and that has scars,' he says and gently traces the scars on my back with his finger.

Once we are both in the tub and sitting opposite each other, I realise that sharing a bath is not romantic, just uncomfortable. You can't lie down, so you just sit there, all arms and legs, staring at each other, asking and ensuring repeatedly in a very British manner if the other person has enough room. It's as if we are waiting for something to happen.

'This is heavenly,' Lewis closes his eyes and lets out a long sigh. 'You sure you've got enough room?'

'Yes,' I reply.

Lewis opens his eyes and shifts his legs to make more room. 'Are you sure?'

I can't decide if he is everything or nothing. I just nod.

'How about after this bath,' Lewis continues, 'we get on our glad rags, go for a nice meal, wherever you fancy, and see if there's a band playing nearby or a film at the cinema or something.'

'When are you going home?' I ask.

'Are you sick of me already,' he laughs, but I detect sadness.

'No of course not,' I reply, 'I just don't want you to feel that you have to be here. I'm not a charity case.'

'I chose to be here,' Lewis replies, 'I want to stay with you until you go home.'

'I don't want to go home,' I say, 'there's nothing for me there.'

That's the problems with holidays: they always end, and you must return to reality. Sometimes I think it would be better to never go on holiday then you have nothing to pine about or compare to.

Lewis strokes my legs under the water. 'I don't either, but let's not think about it now. Why spoil this, let's enjoy it.'

'But now becomes then...and I don't want this to be over,' I reply.

'We'll discuss it later,' Lewis says. 'The important question is, what do you want to eat?'

'Somewhere that gives me meat sweats.'

He laughs, 'see that's why I love you.'

Love? Love. Does he love me? Do I love him? Love in the rye. Lewis must have seen me flinch at the 'L' word because he continues quickly -

'Do you mean like a good Chinese buffet with lots of ribs and wings and fatty chicken balls?' he asks.

It's exactly what I want. This is perfect. He is perfect. Isn't he? This moment. The now.

Suddenly, there is a ripple in the water. A stirring from beneath the surface. Freddy's clawed hand appears from between our thighs and slits us both from rectum to sternum.

The End.

We find a Chinese buffet. Twenty quid each to eat as much as we can, including dessert. We gorge until we feel sick. We drink coke zeros and discuss books. Around us are pictures of glaring

Chinese dragons -all smiles, persuasive in their greed, fat and bright- oriental Santa's, lantern lit with claws like sun beams. My pumping heart slowing, blocking. Food coma and happiness warm. We both are. How can I tell he is warm with happiness I hear you yell? His eyes- his eyes are as warm as the treetops in July.

After the meal we decide to wander the streets of York until we find something to do. It is just after nine. A sign outside a bar says there is a drag act on that night called Lana Con Carne – a Lana Del Rey drag act. Perfect. We go into the bar and have non-alcoholic cocktails until the show starts at ten.

I ask Lewis about his childhood. He has had an average upbringing. His father left when he found out his mother was pregnant. They were both eighteen. His father then moved to America where he now lives happily, rich and with a young blonde botoxed wife and two small daughters. Lewis wouldn't ask his father for a penny and never wants to meet him because he is 'the biggest prick in prickland.' His words not mine. His mother re-married an 'ok guy' and had another baby. Lewis' half-brother is twenty-eight and lives with his girlfriend, they have a two-year-old son. Lewis' brother works in Aldi. His mam is a hairdresser. His stepdad is a car mechanic. All very working class and lovely. His relationship with his family is 'fine but nothing to write home about.'

Lewis has always felt different. He pretends to be normal. He has played guitar since he was eight when he bought an old acoustic guitar from a car boot sale. His dream has always been to be a musician; to write his own songs and tour the world. He has depressive episodes knowing this will never happen. He has anxiety from thinking about life passing him by and spending it doing something he hates. That there must be more to life than pretending, for all the thirty-eight years he has been on the planet, to like football and banter and cheap sex and boring jobs and people.

Lana Con Carne comes on stage. She has a massive auburn beehive, lots of black eyeliner and lips too huge to be human.

Copulating slugs. She wears a very simple black sixties style shift dress and heels so big they are senseless. She walks like a film noir extra and has a I-don't-really-want-to-be-alive-in-this-era gaze, the deep drawl and hypnotic pout. Moody– like living in a world of grey smoke. Disco lights dance around the room. Lewis' face is lit up in flickers of green, purple, blue…and then white. White flickers all over his face like the confetti of an invisible bride. I have nothing to give him. I do not take thee. In sickness. No bouquet. For worse. Never better. No finger-buffet. Til death. Just something borrowed and blue. Never new.

Lana Con Carne looks straight at me. I feel breathless as if this beautiful and intoxicating flower is slowly eating away my oxygen. I am dizzy and overwhelmed. Lewis deserves another. A woman dependable and strong. A woman in health. Not someone half in and out of a body bag. A thrown away weed. Someone he can hold. From this day forward. Cherish. Love. Troth. (Troth lol).

Lewis' hands are hidden in the cuffs of his jacket. What are his hands thinking? Of space and time. Love and wine. Angels and crime. You get the picture. My thoughts are chaotic. Absurd. I am falling. I said I would never do this again. I can't play checkers with Jane. My heart, my head, they aren't rentable space – to be used and filled and then abandoned once something better comes along. There is always someone better. How can I be sure? What is truth anymore. Can I do this? A breakdown is brewing. Is that the kettle whistling? If my sighs turn to shrieks, will he meekly applaud the titillating breakdown? Does he have the patience of a true devotee? I wish you could turn feelings off the way you do a car engine. Hot energy vibrations to nothingness – cooling in seconds as if the journey has never happened.

Lewis reaches over and squeezes my hand. 'This is my favourite Lana song will you dance with me?' he asks.

It is *Born to Die.*

He holds my hand, and we walk to the small dance floor in front of the stage. People stand swaying to the music. We dance slowly facing each other the way I have seen it in the movies: my arms around his neck, his hands around my waist. Touching. Melting. Do we look in love - to the people watching, to the passers-by, to the bar staff, to Lana? Is there a lonely girl in the corner, usually me, sat in sadness and envy, drinking and gorging to forgetfulness? She will hate everything, but deep inside she is full of hope that one day she will be in my position. That she will feel as I do. But for now, she will drink. She will pass out either alone or in the bed of a stranger. She will hate tomorrow. And the next day. But then the following day that twinge of hope will return. She will go to a bar and sit there in the corner, full of sadness and envy, drinking and gorging to forget, hating everything, but hopeful that one day she will be that woman on the dancefloor, swaying slowly with the man she loves. She prays that one day she will feel as I do now.

There is a shaking distress in Lewis' hand. I look up. 'I need to say something? he says his eyes widening.

Girlfriend? Wife? Children? Gay? Addict? Criminal? Aids? Harry Potter fan? Torie? My mind reels.

'Yes,' I reply and wait for happiness to end.

'I know we've just met,' Lewis says, 'but I really want us to work. I want to see you again. That is if you'd like to?'

Field of rye. Field of rye.

'Of course, I do,' I say, trying to act cool. No biggie. Nothing to see here people. Just true fucking love. Move on.

'We can help each other you know, create happiness, just us two against the world,' he continues.

'A cabin in the woods?' I ask.

'Perfect,' he replies. He doesn't get my reference. Does he. I don't care. 'Or by the sea,' he continues, 'or...whatever we fancy. Isn't our future exciting?'

'Think of all the places we can visit together,' I join in.

He kisses me excitedly. The song finishes. We applaud.

'I need the toilet,' I say to him, because I need the toilet.

'I'm going to get us a glass of champagne, just one, to celebrate us,' says Lewis.

'Perfect,' I reply.

I go to the toilet. There is no light in the cubicle: just a black hole above where a light fitting should be. An open screaming mouth. Is this a sign? That I shouldn't fall like this. I shouldn't step off the kerb. That rush. That nausea. Like the first time I read the book. The first time I felt understood. When I needed someone to help me, and he did -my Holden. How can I forget about him, the only person who makes me feel safe? Could Lewis be my Holden?

I check my phone. I haven't looked at it for hours. There are twenty missed calls from Mother and a few texts from Erin. I send them both the same text.

'Sorry for not replying sooner – I'd ran out of data and couldn't find Wi-Fi. Having the time of my life, for the first time ever I am truly happy, I feel alive, see you soon, love you xxx'

Is Michael Ball right: does love change everything? Live or perish in its flame. To be alive or to be an olive. Squidgy green veil. Is my mind a poet because I am in love? Talking shit as the hysteria rises. I am crawling on satin in a room filled with the ghosts of lover's past. What does that even mean? Breathing in the rye. Making love in the rye. Hours will pass as we explore each other's bodies - exhausted and hungry, we finally make our way out of the reeds. As we reach the clearing there are hundreds of children waiting for us: the ones we have saved from falling off the cliff. They applaud us so loudly that the sky ripples and the rye sways with excitement. Cherubs asphyxiating in paradise. Big fat tongues licking petals. Sheets heavy under candlelight sin. Oh love! Love you are the devil within.

I leave the toilet having washed my hands in an extremely thorough fashion. I worry that if Lewis holds my hand and it bears traces of urine, it will transmit to his hand, and then if the rousing dust from a warm summer's night breeze annoys his eye, and he gives it a gentle rub, then he may get pink eye, or some kind of eye infection and I will know I have caused it by not washing my hands thoroughly and hate myself a little. Or what if I came out of the toilet and Lewis, overcome with lust at my sudden entrance, takes my hand and licks my fingers seductively, then he will taste urine and pull a face of utter disgust and start vomiting and disrupt Lana's encore in the worst possible way. So, this is why I washed my hands in an extremely thorough fashion.

There are two delicate flutes of champagne in the middle of the table. Honey bubbles rise ready to be consumed. Lana Con Carne finishes her last song, *Videogame*. There is a standing ovation. Heaven is a place on earth with you.

Sorry to interrupt, but I am one of the champagne bubbles in the glass. Ambers glass to be pedantic. I see these two and know they are in love. I have seen other lovers – married for eternity – they do not look at each other as they do. Their eyes waltz together. The only thing before them is air. Isn't that strange - an invisibility getting in the way. Their smiles try to disguise sorrow and unmet expectations. Their souls try to avoid disappointment. I hope they lose themselves and find themselves in this love: in this unspoken beauty between them. But now I must rise and pop. Oh wait. I am in Amber's mouth. Let me know how things work out when I reappear as urine in an hour or so, unless I am of course absorbed by the body, if so, ciao, nice knowing you, see you in the next life.

'That was so good,' Lewis says, applauding Lana loudly.

'The best,' I reply.

'It's been the perfect night hasn't it?' Lewis continues, 'let's finish this champagne and then go back to the hotel and snuggle in bed.'

I'm not sure if I am feeling slightly tiddly from the champagne, or I am just happy – because I literally want to dance and drink the night away.

'Don't you fancy going out?' I ask, 'you know dancing and stuff.'

'Surrounded by strangers?' Lewis asks, looking unimpressed, 'when we could go back after this, have a lovely night and wake up tomorrow feeling fresh. Do you enjoy living life through a hangover Amber?'

'No,' I reply. I feel sad. And a hunger. More alcohol. More drugs.

'Then why do you want to continue and get wrecked?' Lewis asks.

'For fun,' I reply and shrug.

'I lived your life for years,' Lewis says, 'I'm no saint. The wild weekends, the beginning to recover around Wednesday, to do it all again come Friday. The constant 'never again.' The constant - 'I can change I'm just going through a bad patch right now.' The constant 'yolo.' But then the bad patch doesn't end. No one comes to save you and you can't save yourself because you feel you're not worthy. The gun's against your skull. Do you know what I mean?' Lewis grabs my hand from across the table and tightly squeezes it. 'Do you believe in fate? That of all the bars in town, I went into that one, at that time and met you. I just knew, knew who you were instantly. Do you feel it...or am I talking shit?' He laughs.

'Of course, I feel it,' I reply, 'I just find all this difficult, like is it real, pinch me. I feel it's all too much, too quick.'

Lewis spreads his fingers through mine like a river and says, 'let's just completely go for it, completely fall and if things go wrong then it's a lesson learnt. Promise we'll try.'

We pinkie promise. Lewis screws up his face. 'Gosh I cringe at how romantic I am, I've always been like this, an idealist I guess.'

To think he could have been like this with anyone else makes me feel sick. Is this my chance to ask about exes? What does it matter. It will only feed my insecurities. The past is the past. I have a past. He has a past. I've been in love. Once with a real person, the second time with a fictional character. The future is what's important. Then why does it matter so much to me? That I have to be special. The one. The only.

Lewis finishes off his champagne. 'Let's have a slow walk back to the hotel.'

I finish my drink and we walk outside. It is a still night. Eerie and full of shadows. The streets are practically empty. Lewis holds my hand.

A page from a discarded newspaper flies towards us. There is barely a breeze, yet it seems to have a life of its own. A black and white flower, nay a lightweight monster, confronting and scaring us and then continuing its journey. As it goes past, I notice the headline before it rushes away: Holden. Is this a sign?

I break free of Lewis' hand, 'I need to follow that newspaper.'

'What?' Lewis exclaims.

'I need to follow it. I need to read the story.'

'Are you joking?' he looks at me as if I am insane, 'for a start, it's going in the opposite direction.'

'I need to see what it says,' I reply, 'I have a feeling.'

Lewis sighs. I run after the newspaper, not knowing when, or if, it will stop. Not caring if Lewis follows me. I run over the cobbles, in heels, not slipping once, so set on the object I must capture. I can feel Lewis behind me, begrudging the detour. Luckily a street down, the newspaper gets trapped in the doorway of a bar. I quickly grab it before it escapes.

'Pensioner Beholden to Stranger' – the story goes on to say how an old woman fell on a road, but was helped by a young man going past on his bicycle, who took her to hospital. Not Holden...

'Beholden.' An absolute bore of a story. Lewis reads it over my shoulder.

'Does the story speak to you?' Lewis asks, 'were you the said old lady?' He laughs.

'I feel silly now,' I say, 'I thought I saw something, but I was wrong, I thought I needed something else, but I don't. I have what I need right here, with you, right now.'

Lewis laughs again, 'that's life.' He puts his arm around me and squeezes. 'I think it's cute that you get sudden urges to run after newspapers.'

The door to the bar opens. Amidst waves of hops, disinfectant, aftershave and fun... out walks Shona. A mouth of O when she sees me.

'Whatever I say just agree with it,' I whisper to Lewis.

'Oh my gosh Shona!' I exclaim, 'twice in a week, what are the odds.'

'I've just been for a drink,' says Shona, she looks around

nervously. No one follows her out of the bar. I wondered if she is alone. She doesn't seem her usual annoying, confident, twee self. She seems shaken, distracted, sad, her bob less bouncy.

I gesture to Lewis, 'Shona this is Spencer.'

Shona looks genuinely put out, 'Spencer,' she says barely above a whisper.

'Spencer, Shona and I used to go to uni together, back in the day.'

'Nice to meet you,' Lewis says.

'You too,' Shona replies and looks behind her as if expecting friends to appear.

'Spencer's business trip to Prague finished earlier than he thought,' I lie 'and my mate had to go home suddenly, so he came and surprised me. He's such a darling.'

Lewis kisses me on the cheek. Shona gives a wry smile.

'Congratulations on your wedding,' she says to us both.

I am about to speak but Lewis cuts in, 'it was the best day of my life, well the second,' he laughs, 'the first was meeting this absolute treasure.'

Lewis is excellent at playing along. What a liar! Shona's face is priceless – if only I could take a photo of her expression- I would get it printed on t-shirts in a variety of colours and wear them every day. Shona is struggling for words.

The door to the bar swings open and out walks a rough looking man: more stubble than sense, wearing a checked shirt and falling over his feet with intoxication. He stops abruptly when he sees Shona.

'What the fuck are you still doing here?' he shouts.

Shona goes to reply but he cuts in.

'I told you to get out of my fucking sight, you're nothing but a drunken slut.'

Shona looks at us and then at him. 'You have it all wrong,' she pleads, tears in her eyes.

'Wrong,' he bellows, 'Wrong! My mate told me, he's no liar. He saw a bloke coming out of your place the other morning.'

'It's not true,' Shona shouts.

I need to stick up for her, that despite whatever she's done

(I've probably done far worse) she doesn't deserve to be spoken to in that way, especially in public and in front of the likes of me. Shona looks like she wants the ground to swallow her up.

'If Shona says it's not true, then it's not true,' I but in.

That riles him even more: 'Not true! I have proof. I went through her phone when she went for a piss, probably shagging some guy in there too. There were at least four guys names in her phone.'

'It's not a crime to be friends with the opposite sex' I interrupt.

'Friends!' he scoffs, 'I read some of her messages. The things they say to each other should only be in a porn film. Filthy bitch.'

Shona begins to cry.

'Leave her, she's upset,' I say.

'She's not worth my fucking time, she's a waste of space,' he spits on the floor as if sealing the end of their whatever-it-was. He aggressively nudges her as he goes back into the bar. Shona cries harder.

'Shona it doesn't matter,' I say. I leave Lewis and put my arm around her, 'let's get you a taxi home.'

Shona doesn't say anything. She lets herself be guided by my arm as her tears flow.

We go to the end of the street where taxis are lined up. I want to do a girl power speech about double standards and how men are always doing the dirty on women. But I can tell that Shona needs silence.

'Here's money for a taxi,' Lewis says, handing her a twenty.

'Do you remember where you live?' I ask, realising that not everyone has my genius house remembering skills when they're drunk.

Shona nods. She is about to get in a taxi when she turns to me and says: 'thank you Amber. I know your life is perfect, but mine obviously isn't.'

'Listen, there's nothing that you're doing that I haven't done before,' I reply, 'we all go through difficult times. Look after yourself.'

I hug Shona and kiss her on the cheek.

'You must think I'm a disgrace,' she says, 'please don't tell anybody.'

'Of course, I won't,' I reply, 'as long as you don't tell anyone about what I asked for the other night.'

Shona nods, 'it was for you, wasn't it?'

'Yes,' I say, then lie some more, 'Spencer and I had a huge argument about the sauna, and I just wanted to feel better.'

Shona smiles, 'sometimes we do things we shouldn't do to feel better for a little while.'

I nod. I mean, really, preach honey.

'So that's really why he's come here to see you, to make up?' she asks.

'Yes,' I lie.

'Nothing's as perfect as it looks, is it?' she says.

'Very rarely,' I reply.

Shona gives me a huge hug, 'thanks Amber, you take care. And next time you come to York please don't stay in a hotel, stay at mine.'

I smile: 'I will do.' I pull the red hunting hat out of my bag and give it to her. 'This will bring you luck. I don't need it anymore.'

Shona looks confused but takes the hat and clutches it to her breast. When you're down you'll do anything to feel better, you'll accept some token of luck, even if it is a red hunting hat whose reference you don't understand.

'Thanks,' Shona says and gets into the taxi. She waves goodbye as the taxi pulls away.

It's closing time.

But now I am not alone in the night with an empty bottle in my hand. I have Lewis' hand in mine.

'So, what was all that about?' he asks.

'Sorry I lied,' I reply, 'sometimes one lie leads to another until you can't stop.'

We start to walk back in the direction of the hotel.

'No more lies,' I say and squeeze his hand.

Shona's life seems so clean cut and perfect, but everyone has demons. She looked for love the only way she knew how. We've all been there. Everyone is fighting something we know nothing about: be kind always. I will visit Shona soon and we will talk. I will reveal my lies and she can reveal hers. Perhaps over tapas… and a few lines…jokes.

In the distance I see camper-van Morris, finished for the day and heading home. He holds up his thumb and climbs into a blue Volvo. Free - in his own unique way. Happy with his life – and that's all that matters.

Lewis and I walk back to the hotel via the river. The streetlights glimmer on the water, like multi-coloured flames trying to pierce the surface.

My phone vibrates: it's Mother. I would usually ignore it, but I want to hear her voice.

'Hello,' I answer.

'Amber,' she sounds cross, 'I've been worried sick about you.'

'Sorry I've been busy.'

'What have you been doing?' she asks.

'I have had the best time of my life.'

'Good,' she replies, clearly taken aback by my reply, assuming that the reason I hadn't answered was because I was intoxicated, wanting to die, or fucking up my life in some way.

'When I get back, I'll come round,' I say, 'We can order pizza and watch a chick flick.'

'But you don't like chick flicks,' Mother replies, 'you always say they are corny unimaginative pieces of…'

'Well, I'm going to try and like them for you,' I reply cutting in. 'We need to talk about a few things. I haven't been the easiest daughter to get on with, but I'm trying to change. Thank you for everything you've done for me.'

'Well I hope you mean it this time,' Mother replies.

'I really do,' I reply, I look over at Lewis, 'I've got someone to help me now. I won't be such a burden, I promise.'

'You've never been a burden Amber,' Mother sniggers, 'you've just been difficult. But what have I always said to you, nothing worthwhile is ever simple.'

'I'm going to go back to therapy and get better. I know I can be happy,' I say.

'I'm glad to hear it. You know you always have my love and support' she replies.

'Will you let Dad know I'm safe and thank him for everything too?' I ask.

Mother hesitates, 'I'll text him.'

'No ring him,' I demand, 'you two need to sort things out or you will live with bitterness and anger your whole life.'

Mother tuts. 'Okay.'

'I'll check with Dad,' I say.

'Okay I will,' she replies meekly, shocked by my adamance.

'Okay goodbye mum, love you.'

'Bye Amber darling.'

We hang up.

Lewis hugs me.

'There are a few people I need to contact,' I say pulling away, 'is that ok, I'll only be a few minutes?'

Lewis smiles and we sit on a bench overlooking the river.

I email my dad: he is the kind of person who doesn't say much. He is better at writing stuff down, so emails are better than phone calls.

'Hey Dad

Just to let you know that I'm safe and having a truly amazing time. Thank you for the money, it really helped.

I want to say sorry for what I said before, about how you never got to know me. I've realised that this works both ways. I never got to know you. I also never let you see the real me. I felt abandoned when you left. You never came around much, or phoned, and I guess that hurt. It seems as if I've never gotten over the hate-and-blame teenager phase. I need to. You and mum have done a good job. You have your own issues, and I should consider this.

I'm going to go back to counselling to work through my problems and I'm going to retrain and get a proper job. I'd like to help teenagers.

I want us to be friends. Let's not waste another thirty-odd
years as strangers.
Love you always
Amber.'

I'm not sure what dad's response will be. I have two streams
of thought about our relationship. Either he really doesn't give
a shit. If so, that's fine and I will have to get through that with
counselling and support, support which doesn't include scoffing
alcohol and drugs. Or Dad does care but finds the situation
difficult, so avoids rather than confronts his discomfort i.e., me.
Mother said that spending time with me causes him too much
pain: to think how things could have been if he'd stayed and that
he is to blame for my poor mental health. Dad shouldn't feel
guilty about my issues. There's a good chance I would have been
fucked up anyway. Who knows? I guess every single one of us is
fucked up in our own way. Maybe it is our parent's fault, maybe
not. Cheers Larkin.

I text Erin:

'Sorry for everything. All the booze of yours that I drink, for
taking you for granted and not appreciating you for you. For
making you live with a fuck up. It's like at the end of the film,
Whatever Happened to Baby Jane when Baby Jane says to her
long-suffering sister 'you mean all this time we could've been
friends.' You'll have no idea what I'm on about. But basically,
I'm so grateful for you. When I'm back let's have a girly night
and a good chat xxx.'

I look at Lewis and sit closer. I hold his hand.

'All done?' he asks.

'Yeah,' I let out a great exhale, 'I feel lighter already.'

I feel calm and still. That this is the start of something.

We both look at the river. It is empty apart from a few ducks
sleeping near the bank.

'By any chance,' I ask Lewis, 'do you happen to know where they go, the ducks, when the river gets frozen over?'

Holden assumed that someone came round in a truck and took the ducks away, or they flew away by themselves. Holden never found the answer.

I didn't think Lewis would reply: that he would shrug, or chose to ignore the question, or reply with a simple 'No.'

'Ducks are like humans,' Lewis replies, 'when things get too much, or they need to escape or rest.' He gives my hand a reassuring squeeze, 'they just find somewhere they feel safe.'

'Or they find someone who makes them feel safe,' I add.

I rest my head on his chest and we both look at the river.

I hope.

ABOUT THE AUTHOR

G.j. Quinn

G.J. Quinn lives in Middlesbrough, UK. This is their debut novel.

Printed in Great Britain
by Amazon

40641626R00129